Do not go to school tomorrow.

How come? Are you ditching?
Ditching is bad for you, you know ☺

Just don't.

What are you talking about?

Hey man, what are you talking about?

What's up?

Dude come on

Text me back

# Mercy Rule

# Mercy Rule

WITHDRAWN

# TOM LEVEEN

Sky Pony Press
New York

Sky Pony Press books may be purchased in bulk at special discounts for sales promotion, corporate gifts, fund-raising, or educational purposes. Special editions can also be created to specifications. For details, contact the Special Sales Department, Sky Pony Press, 307 West 36th Street, 11th Floor, New York, NY 10018 or info@skyhorsepublishing.com.

Sky Pony® is a registered trademark of Skyhorse Publishing, Inc.®, a Delaware corporation.

Visit our website at www.skyponypress.com.

10 9 8 7 6 5 4 3 2 1

Library of Congress Cataloging-in-Publication Data is available on file.

Cover design by Sammy Yuen
Cover image credit iStockphoto

Print ISBN: 978-1-5107-2698-7
E-book ISBN: 978-1-5107-2701-4

Printed in the United States of America

# Mercy
# Rule

*Rock 'N' Roll High School*

# DANNY

Dad starts in before my ass even touches the kitchen chair.

"You're going to school like that?" he says, shoveling four metric tons of waffles and sausages into his big cheesehead mouth.

Mom lends her agreement. "Oh, Danny."

"What," I say, and sit.

My sister pleads with the yellow ceiling, like maybe that's where God lives.

He doesn't. I've checked.

She whines, "Can't you make him change out of that shit?"

Mom's eyebrows indicate, *It's out of my hands.*

"Shitty McShitshit," I say, as an experiment.

"Watch your mouth," Mom says.

"Just testing," I say. I wasn't hungry before this, and now I'm super not-hungry.

"You need to eat something," she says.

Dad stabs a piece of meat. Wishing it was me. He scarfs it, and the four waffles on his plate vanish next. He vaults out of his chair in his haste to get more from the stack on the stove and agrees with Mom. "Wouldn't kill you to put on a pound or two."

"Speaking of putting on a pound or two," I say, turning to my sister.

"Hey!" Dad snaps, and Mom says, "Danny!" and my sister

says, "Fuck you!" She says it in this wounded singsong that turns it into four syllables: *fu-UCK yoo-UH*.

She does not get told to watch her mouth.

"I see my work here is done," I say. My sister is not fat. She is opposite of fat. Like me, I guess. I just know what buttons to push. It's a gift.

"Damn it, Danny," Dad says, lancing more waffles with javelin precision. "You go to school like that, you're liable to get your ass handed to you."

"Really?" I say. "By whom, Father?"

He doesn't answer. Mom dares to make contact, putting one hand over mine.

"Please," she says. "Dad's right. You don't want to start your first day of high school like this."

"First day at *this* high school," I say. "*This* one. I'm a sophomore. I didn't want to go to this school at all, if you'll recall. I made a very convincing argument for staying at—"

"Stop," Dad says. "You had your shot, you blew it. Now you deal."

I shut up for a second, then ask, "So how do you all recommend I start my first day at *this* school? Being that it's such a fine institution of learning and, no doubt—" I gesture to Big Sis. "Civility?"

"Start by staying way-far away from me," Big Sis declares. It's the first day of her senior year, and I pose a threat to her social standing. "I'm out of here."

"See you at lunch," I say. "Shall we dine together in the quad?"

"Listen, you little geek," she says. "I'm not kidding. You stay away from me, all day, every day, until and unless you stop wearing dresses around. All right? I've got enough shit to deal with without you being a pain in my ass."

No one says anything. I lean over the table and raise my index fingers. "So, she can swear, right?" I ask my parents. "Just for clarification. She can cuss, and it's okay?"

Dad doesn't sit back down to finish off his waffles. Just stays standing by the stove, letting his height dominate us as he says, "You've got bigger things to worry about than your sister."

"Well," I say, unable to resist the obvious bump-set Dad just gave me. "She *is* a big thing."

"*Bye*," my sister hurls in our general direction. She heads out the kitchen door when one of her meathead boyfriends honks his horn outside.

"Thank you for a lovely breakfast," I say, getting up.

"You need to eat," Mom says.

"No, I just need a ride."

Dad wipes his mouth with a dish towel. "Good luck with that."

"I can't take him," Mom says. "I've got a meeting at eight."

"He can walk, then. Do him some good."

"You want wind sprints too?" I ask. I can't believe he's actually going to make me walk.

Dad says nothing. He hefts his bag, gives Mom a rough kiss on top of her hair, and goes to the door leading into the garage.

All the garages lining our street are decorated like modern art museums that cater to the owners' tastes. For example, one is dedicated to aircraft, another to billiards, another like a 1950s soda shop.

Dad's? The Green Bay Packers.

We don't live anywhere near Green Bay.

Or Wisconsin.

"You decide to start dressing like a normal human being, I'll drive you anywhere you want to go," Dad says from the doorway. "Till then, you walk."

He shuts the door. A second later, his enormous silver F-150 guns, and I hear it move out to the street.

"Is this for real?" I say to Mom.

She carries her plate to the sink. "You're wearing a skirt, Danny."

"It's a kilt. The MacDougall Clan wears them all the time. It's a statement." The MacDougall Clan is a Scottish-pub/industrial band I love. No one's heard of them.

"I don't care what it is, you know better," Mom says. "You're asking for trouble."

"Not if I was at my *real* school."

"You should have thought about that before you forced us to take you out of your 'real school,'" Mom says. "Danny, you've got to learn to control your temper."

"I was controlling it."

"Some way other than drugs."

"Drugs *I* procure, you mean. If I get them from our lovely family doctor, then it's okay. Right? Even if they're the same drugs? Explain that to me."

"You're not a doctor. The end."

So that's where I get my sarcasm from. It's sure not from Dad.

"Fine," I say. "It's still got nothing to do with my clothes. Why can't I wear what I want?"

"You can. Just be prepared for the consequences."

And with that sound motherly advice, she walks out of the kitchen.

I change into black jeans, and take my time walking to my first day of classes as Karate High School jams in my ears. About a block from school someone honks and shouts something at me. Fortunately, the music cancels out most of it.

Most of it.

# CADENCE

*That kid is going to die!*

That's the very first thought that passes through my wee little freshman head the very first instant my foot crosses from the sidewalk to the parking lot on the very first day of school.

For starters, if he'd read the student handbook, which I did, because Dad made me, he'd know trench coats and dusters were banned years ago. I'd rather be wearing one of my tank tops today, but those are outlawed too, so I'm making due with a Ramones T-shirt like everyone else. Not that everyone else is wearing a Ramones T-shirt, I just mean a T-shirt in general.

Second, it's hot. Hot like, stupid-humid hot. Hot like, why-am-I-wearing-makeup-today-it-will-only-melt-off, hot. That makes his coat a "statement." A big loud statement that will *definitely* get him noticed, and not in a good way!

Third, if he was looking to accessorize with a studded belt or something, he could probably get away with it. But he has about five too many buckles, studs, and spikes sticking out from various pieces of clothing and he doesn't have the body to support any of it. He looks like the firstborn of Hot Topic and KISS, or maybe Slipknot and Carpathian Forest. That's fine with me, as it should be, considering I've got a bright-pink Jolly Roger pirate flag on the back of my black shorts, but I am pretty sure it's not the first impression he should be giving.

I try to push through all the other students, cars, bikes, and boards to get to him, tell him to go home, take the absence, change your clothes. A friend of mine tried that look last year in junior high and paid for it every day till we graduated. No one deserves that, not for something as stupid as clothes. He ended up going to a private school this year. *Sad face*! Maybe I can help this kid the way I should've helped him.

But the trench coat kid disappears inside the school before I can get to him. Well, I'll run into him sooner or later. Three junior highs feed into this place, but no matter how big a school is, it's small. Word'll get around fast about him, I'm sure!

As for my wee self, my first actual encounter with high school kids starts with a girl passing me in the breezeway, glancing down, and saying, "Nice *shoes*," in that way that makes it pretty clear she does not think they are nice at all.

I freeze and look down at my Kermit the Frog Converse, because it's better to let the girl and her friends move along. A person who acts and talks like that? Her vision is based on movement. She can't see you if you don't move. *Rawr.*

I *knew* my Kermie shoes from last year were a bad idea, but did I take my own advice? Nooooo. Mom and Dad and Johnny have given up trying to stop me from making decisions like that, for which I bless them. Still, I wish someone had given me a heads-up.

One of my friends would have, I'm sure, but they're all gone. I ended up here while all of them went to another school. Plus, Faith moved in June, Gloria got *pregnant* for God's sake, and Liza hasn't been let out of rehab yet. What a summer! Sad face!

The girls pass. The combination of hair flips, hip tilts, and trendy bags makes it pretty clear they're probably sophomores. Or juniors even. Seniors wouldn't have bothered with me, I don't think. Seniors have Big-Kid-College-Prom-SAT Plans, like Johnny did last year. And yet he still lives with us! I guess some plans just don't go according to . . . um. Plan.

Since I have already ceased to exist to them, I follow the crowd inside and try to head for my locker, except when I turn to look for it, I plow into a wall. Awesome!

Wait, nope. Not a wall, a guy.

"Whoa, sorry," he says.

He's stopped beside me. I look up at him. I keep looking up. And up, and up, and up.

"*Wow* you're tall," I say.

"Thanks," the guy says, not quite smiling, but not quite *not*.

"And really cute," I add, because if there's one thing I cannot do, it is keep my mouth from running.

"Thanks," he repeats, but he doesn't sound too sure he should be saying it.

"I'm Cadence."

"Zach," he says.

"Cool! Do you play basketball? I like the Suns."

"I do not play basketball, no."

"How come?"

"I avoid sweating as a matter of course. That's hard to do playing sports."

"Are you smart?" I say. "I bet you're smart, you sound smart."

"I'm pretty bright, yes."

Now Zach is smiling for sure. "Awesome!" I say. "Are you a freshman? I kind of doubt it. You're too tall."

"Junior. And I'm only six one."

"Ah," I say. "So I won't see you in English. Or the short-girls-only class. Or any other class, I take it."

"No," Zach says. "I did try to get into that short-girl one, but it was full. Maybe next semester."

I laugh out loud. He's fun! I like it when people are willing to play a little bit.

"Since I've got you here, can you tell me where English is?" Then I sing a line from the Ramones song "Pinhead." Zach adjusts his backpack like my voice is making it dig into his spine or something.

"That's me," I say. "D-U-M-B. For, dumb. It's the Ramones." I point to my shirt as evidence. "It's a song. 'Pinhead'?"

"You are fascinating."

I can't tell if he says that because he likes the Ramones or just because I'm a nerd. I decide he likes the Ramones, because that thought makes me happy.

"Sweet!" I say. "Fascinating is good, I'll take fascinating."

"The English department is that way," Zach says, like he's amused.

"Awesome! Thanks, Zach. See ya 'round!"

He laughs as I move down the hallway, which I choose to take as a good sign. I decide that next time I run into him (literally), like just now, I'll have something *fascinating* to say.

Which reminds me, I still have a life to save! I get distracted too easily, Dad always says, and he's right, because I'm always like, blah blah blah *squirrel*!

I run farther down the hall to where it splits in three and look all around, searching for the trench-coat-buckles-n-studs kid, but I don't see him anywhere.

Dang it! Maybe he's already been eaten by seniors.

Sad face!

# DONTE

I got the car yesterday, just in time for school. It's older than I am, but to me it's new. Spent this summer working two jobs, with short breaks for a free football combine in Los Angeles, then an NFTC in Oakland. Saved up money from the bit Mom's able to dole out from her three jobs from time to time, and I finally got it.

Red 1995 Honda Accord, 198,476 miles—about the most boring car ever produced on planet Earth, but it came with a Pioneer CD receiver and twin twelve-inch subwoofers. The system is only 150 watts RMS, and there's no way to jack in my old phone, but it thumps good. It thumps great, for the price.

And it's mine.

I drive it to pick up Amy, because I promised her I would when I got a car. But I turn my music down when I pull into the driveway because Amy's parents probably wouldn't care for the noise. Or rather, their neighbors wouldn't, and I'm not about to get anyone in this neighborhood mad at me. Coaches and coordinators have seen me now. Things are going to start happening. Just need to find a college that'll give me a full ride and I'm out. Maybe Amy will even come with me.

"Damn," I whisper. Got to stop dreaming. Keep my head in the game.

Amy dashes out of the house and leaps in, squealing. That makes me smile big.

"This is it!" she says. "You really got it!"

"Hell yeah, I did."

"Nice. Happy senior year." She swings her hair into place, and I smell coconut. "Now turn your music up!"

I crank the volume.

"You're so lucky!" Amy shouts over the bass.

"No way, it's more than luck." I worked hard for this car. Though finding a vehicle with a decent system, at the price I paid—that might've been luck, sure.

This is going to be a great year.

"We meeting up with Brady at school?" Amy shouts.

Damn. Not what I want to hear. She should be focused on being in the car with *me*, not worried about Brady Culliver. B is my best friend, but he's not what I want to be talking about right now. Damn.

"Probably. Don't know for sure. Never heard from him."

"Is he okay?"

"Yeah. Most likely."

I decide to go all in now, man up, get it over with. I turn down the stereo. "So, hey, do you like . . . you got a thing for him? For Brady?"

Amy laughs. I love how it sounds, even in this context. "Why, you jealous?"

I wave it off, like I'm just messing around. I hope she'll see through it. See that I'm not messing around at all.

But it doesn't matter. If I can't have her—and I can't—Brady sure can't either. No way. Amy even confirms it when she says, "I can't go out with *any* of you guys."

# BRADY

Wake up thinking that I'm lucky it's warm out at least. Won't be able to sleep out here by Halloween. Be too cold.

Check my phone before sitting up. How much sleep did I even get? Three hours. Maybe four. It'll do. At least no cops pushed me out. Good start.

Roll off the picnic table. Stretch out a bit. Tight. Not too bad. It'll ease up. Pick up my bag. Slept with it looped around my foot. Head for the park bathrooms. Somehow they're cold even though it's warm outside. I go in. Glare at my reflection in the warped mirror.

"Hoo," I grunt. Make my abs clench hard. Like concrete. "Hoo, hoo, *hoo*. This a man's game."

Roll my head on my neck. Stay loose.

"This a *man's* game now. Hoo. *Hoo*."

That helps. Keeps my head in the game. Clean up best I can using a sink and the deodorant in my bag.

Change clothes. I should text Donte. But I don't. I'll see him at school. I know he's got a car now. Could give me a ride. But I don't know. Can't do it. Feels like charity. Screw charity. I'm not a pussy.

Get done getting ready. Take a long drink from the fountain outside. Tastes like metal. But cold. Then I start hoofing it to school. Shit I'm hungry.

First day of senior year.

"Yeah, I've heard something like that," I say, squeezing the wheel tight for just a second.

There'll be other girls. Lots. None of them will be Amy, but. Me and Brady will have our pick this year.

Except I don't want lots of girls. I want Amy.

But the pause in conversation makes me wonder: where is B, anyway? Haven't heard from him since a couple days ago. Damn. I should check up on him. I turn right when I should go straight.

"Where're we going?" Amy says. "Oh my god, are you kidnapping me? Is this some senior prank thing?"

"Just want to swing by his place," I say.

Amy shrinks a little in her seat. "Brady's house? Is that safe?"

I give her a confident smirk and set my bicep on the open window, flexing. "Who's gonna mess with *this*?"

Amy swoons all fake-dramatic. She's joking around, but I still like it.

But when we get closer to Brady's neighborhood, I turn off the music and roll up the windows. No one is supposed to know where Brady lives, but some people do. They don't talk about it. Brady always says he's just waiting for some money from his dad so he and his mom can move into another place. Maybe someplace near Coach. Everyone accepts that. They'd better. Otherwise they'll answer to me.

But Brady's apartment building looks dead. Vacant. I keep driving but I ask Amy to text B. Check in. Just to be on the safe side.

Start the clock, Mom. You hear me? Wherever you are. Start the clock. 'Cause this shit's gonna end.

Get a text from Amy. Asking where I am. Tell her I'm on my way. She sends a smiley back.

# VIVI

I don't want to be here.

Keep your head down.

*Down.*

Don't look up.

They'll see you.

Down!

Hold your books. Tight.

Don't look up.

Dodge!

Okay. Good. Safe.

I pass a tall, athletic girl hugging an enormous guy. He grins as she pulls away and promenades down the hall. Three younger girls scurry toward him like ants to sugar. Each is more beautiful than the last. I want to be one of them.

But they see me.

"What are you looking at, bitch?" a girl says.

Oh, no. I'm visible. The guy notes me, but his eyes flick toward the athletic girl walking down the hall. That's where he wants to be. With her. The three girls surrounding him don't seem to know it yet.

All three of them bare fangs and raise quills at me.

Head down.

*Down.*

Don't look up.

Just move.

"Yeah, you *better* keep walking," the girl says.

Don't look up.

Two more years.

Just two more years.

I miss South. I miss the Dez. I wish Daddy had never been hurt. I hate this place.

# DANNY

I can't make this stuff up: the gym is in the center of the school building. Like a gladiatorial arena. When you walk in the main entrance, the halls go left, right, and straight ahead. To the right, the hall continues on to more classrooms. If you go left or straight, though, you'll follow the hallway around in a big rectangle. Huge windows look down into the gymnasium, which is sunk into the ground like a strip mine. It's like the hall on this level is one big skybox surrounding the gym.

Unreal.

All you have to do is walk into the school building through one of three sets of double doors and *blam*: you can't *not* see the

GYMNASIUM

in the

CENTER OF THE SCHOOL.

Bet I can't find the library without consulting three maps and a GPS.

*Ooo, education is broken in this country! Ooo, how do we keep up with Chinese? Ooo ooo ooo, my pussy hurts!*

Jesus. This reminds me of the time I saw the football players' bus being escorted to the game by cops. Two motorcycle cops riding in front, clearing the way. Again, I cannot make this stuff up. Like the football players were the god damn president.

I should take a picture of the gym and send it to the actual president and say

HERE! THIS! THIS IS WHAT IS WRONG WITH OUR EDUCATIONAL SYSTEM, DUMBASS!

But they probably throw you in jail for that.

At first, things seem okay. Roving the hallway looking for my first class, I get some looks, but that's nothing new. Everyone here, unsurprisingly, comes off as pretty vanilla. I pass a few degenerates, malcontents, punks, and assorted high school flotsam among the facial-hair seniors, varsity date rapists, and professional teen alcoholics. A mixed bag.

I decide to take a picture of the gym and send it to a friend, who is at this moment probably sitting down to a visual art class at my school—the school I should be at, the school that doesn't have a gym in the middle of the god damn building.

Except my phone is not in my bag. I pull out of foot traffic and rummage through the entire thing. Nowhere.

"God damn it," I say out loud.

As if my profanity has upset the student body, someone twice my height pushes past me and whispers, "Skinny little faggot."

I simply cannot make this stuff up. People still say shit like that. At least he's bright enough to not say it loud enough for people to hear. Just me. He's wearing a football jersey in our school colors. The back reads CULLIVER.

I shoot back, loudly enough to be heard over the hallway's ruckus, "Your mom called. She said to go fuck yourself, 'cause she had plans already."

Three seconds ago, no one would have heard me scream for help if I was on fire. They wouldn't even have noticed the "I am on fire" part. Now, suddenly, the entire hallway is listening in—and they all shout "Ooooo!" in unison like third graders.

Culliver stops in his tracks. I see I've made my first enemy of the day. Of the year. Of the next *three*.

His eyes zero in on me, and I figure I'm about to get tossed through these skybox windows and down onto the court below. But a teacher in a rumpled pink button-up and blue tie steps between us and leans in front of Culliver, saying something I can't hear. Culliver listens, still glaring at me over the teacher's shoulder. Finally, he turns and continues down the hall.

Interesting. Looks like I got a "Get out of ass kicking free" card. Or, *had* one. Maybe I just played it. The pink-shirted teacher glances at me like I irritate him. Like I'm the one who did something wrong.

Whatever. My phone is gone, and I'm going to be late for my first class. According to my dandy new schedule, it's Mrs. Garcia, for English.

Who teaches Spanish, I wonder—Mrs. Smith?

# BRADY

I want to kick that kid's ass. Would have if Mr. Butler hadn't stopped me. Kid's lucky. Real lucky.

I see Donte leaning against my locker. That helps. Me and Donte slap hands soon as I get there. We bump chests. Growl, howl, and laugh. Camp went great. Two-a-days went good this summer. Except for being so hungry. Last two-a-day was three days ago. Only have them once a week now that school's back.

D chews on his lip like he's gearing up for a fight. Sticks his face in mine. "You got my lunch money, bitch?"

"Girlfriend, you look like you already ate a whole cow!" Grind my pecs into his.

We both laugh again. It echoes up and down the hall. Some people grin. They want to be a part of it. Some people walk faster. They want to get away from it. Either way's fine with me.

D leans against the blue lockers. "I went by to pick you up this morning."

Slam my locker door shut. Don't like people going to my place. But it's D. Can't get too pissed. "Sorry, man. I was already up and out, you know."

"Cool," D says. "You want me to pick you up tomorrow?"

"Yeah sure, maybe at Starbucks, something."

"Right on."

We start heading for English. Warning bell rings. Everyone runs. We walk.

"So hey, man," Donte says. "My mom packed the biggest lunch today, like a grocery bag. It's Chinese. You gonna eat some of that? It's in Coach's fridge."

I bite down hard. Grind my teeth. Try not to wait too long before saying, "Sure, if you're too pussy to eat it all."

Donte hoots again. Punches my arm. Then we walk into English together. We have seats in the back. Like last year.

"State?" Mr. Butler says to me as we walk past him into the classroom.

"Hell yeah," I say.

He says it again to Donte. Donte also says, "Hell yeah."

Mr. Butler grins and says, "That's right, that's what I'm talking about. Welcome back."

Butler loves Shakespeare and the Niners. I don't know how. Don't care. Pretty much our whole team's in his class. Nobody ever flunks Butler.

None of *us* ever flunk Butler.

Butler does some texting before the last bell rings. So does half the class. He doesn't care if we text right up to the bell. We put our phones away when it goes off.

Butler goes to the whiteboard. Writes down the word HAMLET.

"Anybody know who wrote this play?"

"Jesus!" my wide receiver shouts.

"Mr. Butler!" says my fullback.

"Shakespeare, you lumpish puttocks," Butler says. Writes SHAKESPEARE on the board under HAMLET. "Turns out the drama department's putting it on this semester, so that's where we're going to start."

We all groan at the same time.

"Oh, really," Butler says. He rolls up the sleeves on his pink button-up shirt. Getting down to business or something. "Anybody know what this play is about?"

No one answers.

"Who in here ever wanted to get even with someone?"

I almost raise my hand. There's lots of mumbling and grunting. Dudes shuffling in their chairs.

"Like who?" he says. "Who have you wanted to get back at?"

"The Titans!" one of our boys shouts. Others shout, too.

"Matadors!"

"Bulldogs!"

Other high school rivals get called. It's like a pep rally in here for a couple minutes. We start our *hoo-hoo-hoo-hoo!* chant. It vibrates the windows.

Butler lets us go for a while. It's one reason we all like him so much. Then he raises his hands. We shut up. It's respect.

"Well then," he says. "You're going to like this one."

We start nodding. Lean forward in our desks. Most of them're too small for us.

"They any sports in it?" says one of my guys.

We laugh at him. Give him shit. But Butler says, "Actually, yes. Hamlet uses sports to get revenge. Well, in a sense."

He's got our attention. Butler claps once and points at Donte.

"Heavy D," he says. He's prolly the only teacher who can get away with the name. "There's a stack of books on the back counter. Pass them out, please."

D does what Butler says. We each get an old paperback of *Hamlet*. The cover shows a dude dressed in black, holding a skull up to his face. Like two football helmets about to clash on the opening credits of a game. Usually I watch at Donte's. Mom sold our TV.

I flip through the book. This might be kind of cool. Revenge. Skulls. Sports.

Gotta love Butler's class.

# DREA

My full name is Andrea Stephanie Townsend. I want people to call me Drea, or Dre, because I figure it sounds sophisticated and mature, you know? I've been growing out my hair for a year now so that it's long and shows off the dark red better, not like the pixie cuts I used to get all the time, so hopefully I'll look older. I've decided this year I will at least get people to call me AHN-drea instead of ANN-drea. But probably they'll just call me Andi. With an *I*. Everyone calls me that. No matter how often I try to change it, it keeps coming back to that *I*.

A brown-haired girl reading a paperback copy of *Hamlet* notices me wandering around the cafeteria for ten minutes with my blue plastic tray. For no good reason that I can see, she waves me over to her table. Not many people are sitting there. It might be *That* table, where *Those* kids sit. There must be one of *Those* tables in every cafeteria in the world.

But I go stand across from her, because at least she waved. She stares up at me for a second, then blinks quickly like she's trying to stop thinking about something.

"You need someplace to sit?" the girl says. "I remember freshman year."

"Yes," I say.

"Cool. Have a seat then. If you don't mind sitting with a senior."

I sit down, several seats away from the rest of Those kids, who all have earbuds in.

"What's your name?" she asks.

And I get to say "Drea, or Dre," and not Andi.

The senior says, "That's cool. I think I'll go with Drea. I mean, if I get to choose. I'm Kelly."

I sort of smile, because maybe high school is off to a pretty great start after all.

Maybe I won't need to cut anymore.

Because I still do it. Sometimes every day. It's been every day more often over the summer.

No one knows. Not my mother and not my father. Not my friends from last year who promised we'd always be friends and we'd text and chat and talk but somehow haven't.

It's a release, that's all, a way to deal. I'd never, like, *go through* with anything, you know? It's wrong to cut, and I know it. I feel guilty every time I slide a box cutter or razor or knife or paperclip across my upper and lower arms. But for that moment, the world is silent.

These are all things running through my head when Kelly, who's wearing a yellow T-shirt that says Beetlejuice Beetlejuice Beetlejuice, asks why I'm wearing long sleeves and jeans when it's so hot out.

And I say, "To hide my scars."

Why'd I say it? Because I have to keep so quiet at home that I just wanted to hear myself say it, you know? I think that's why.

It's as if the entire cafeteria hits an enormous mute button. I hear nothing, not a single sound, though I'm aware of life cruising along as usual around me, first-day hoots and hollers echoing through the room. This silence is spongy, airplane-landing stuffy, beginning in my nose and moving up to my brain.

Kelly looks at me like she can't tell if I'm joking or not.

Then she says, in a reasonable tone, "Can I see?"

I roll up one blue sleeve and display the scab hatching there. Hatching is an art term for drawing parallel lines close together, I just learned. It's used for shading. I did some last period in art class. The guy at the table beside mine, who must have weighed as much as three of me, was already amazing at it.

But his were done with pencil. Mine are done with a razor.

Kelly takes my forearm in her hands. Her fingers are cool, her touch soft.

"Wow," Kelly says. "That's intense."

She lets a thumb drift across one series of lines. I can't feel it over the scabs. But I imagine it must feel like braille to her. What do the raised bumps say?

"You won't tell?" I ask.

"I won't tell," Kelly says.

"You don't think it's gross?"

"I think it's too bad that you feel like you need to do it. That's all."

I start crying and reach for the paperclip in my pocket, but then Kelly puts an arm around me and says something like, "It's cool, I got your back," and I, Andrea-Andi-Drea-Dre, decide I can wait till after lunch to use the paperclip.

Just as I get myself back together, a group of huge guys

passes by our table and one of them tells his huge-guy buddies, "Hey, Mister Kelly's back this year. How's it going, chickdude?" He doesn't stop to listen for an answer.

Kelly acts like she didn't hear them, but it's obvious she did.

"Why do they call you that?" I ask.

Kelly snarls. "Because they're Brady Culliver and Donte Walker, and that's what they do."

When I blink at her, Kelly explains: "They're football players. They've been using me to cover up their own gender identity issues for the past three years." She says it like it doesn't bother her except I can see that it does.

Kelly's snarl does not change as she says, "What I want to know is how the hell they get off campus and to a Pei Wei so fast. Maybe the coach has it delivered. It wouldn't surprise me." She crunches down on a celery stick. "Blegh, who cares? I'll be out of this place in nine months, and in ten years they won't have the social heft to start a Twitter account."

A laugh pops out of me. It's not much more than a squeak, but I decide to count it as a laugh, anyway.

"On the other hand," Kelly says, glancing at me sidelong as if to see if she can make me laugh again, "where will *I* be ten years from now, Drea? One of the five most influential businesswomen in the world! Yeah, no."

She called me Drea like it was my real name. I smile.

Kelly sighs and moves on to a bag of Cool Ranch Doritos. "I mean, senior year is freaking me out. What's out there for me? I'm not good at anything. I've failed at band, I've hurt myself and others in just about every sport, my grades are all Ds and Cs. I haven't so much as Googled the word 'college.' Mom needs help with the twins. And my sister. And maybe even my brother even though he's in sixth grade this year . . ."

"I'm making you nervous," I say, interrupting. It's why she's talking so much.

Kelly shuts her mouth. I almost can hear her teeth clack together. Then she smiles. "It's that obvious?"

"I'm sorry, I shouldn't have—"

"Hey, never apologize!" Kelly declares. "We do that too much. No apologies."

I don't know if she means she and I apologize too much or if she means women, like a feminist sort of thing, or if she means something completely different, so I just nod and don't say anything and point to her book. "You like Shakespeare?"

"Not particularly, but auditions for the fall play are on September ninth and tenth. I'm taking Drama Four, so Mrs. Tanner has to give me a shot. I mean, it's senior year! What're you doing after school, do you know yet? You have to do something. Or maybe not. I just have to because if I don't then I'll end up at home and I am so beyond done with *that.*"

She's still nervous around me, me and my scars, but I don't bring it up. I also don't tell her how much I already know about theater because that just reminds me of Mom and Dad and when I get reminded of Mom and Dad I want to use my paperclip.

"So?" Kelly says, staring me while she eats her chips.

"So?"

"So are you going to be in any clubs this year? Obviously, *I* am kind of a drama kid."

I point to the loudest group in the cafeteria, the one singing songs from *Hamilton*. They are definitely drama kids, and they are not throwin' away their . . . shot! "Aren't *those* the drama kids?"

Kelly glances at them, then away, shrugging. "Okay, so I'm not technically one of them, yet."

"Well, maybe I can come with you? To the auditions? Just to check it out, you know?"

There's no way I'll audition, but the bell is about to ring and Kelly is nice and I want to make sure she'll talk to me again.

Kelly looks like I just made her day, which I don't understand. She puts a hand on my arm like she's known me forever and says, "Absolutely!"

She doesn't even wipe her hand on her shorts after touching my scars.

# CADENCE

At lunch I find a table of girls who are giggling and talking and doing all sorts of things with their phones and I zero in on them. Maybe next week I'll find some boys to hang out with, too, but I think for my first day, girls are probably safer.

I go to their table and sit down at one end. "Hi! What's up?"

The girls, there are four of them, all stop talking and look at me. One of them says, "Uh, hi?" With a question mark. She's wearing a shirt that says ADMIT IT, YOU'D GO TO JAIL FOR THIS, which takes way too long for me to figure out is a joke. But it's not really funny, anyway.

"I'm Cadence," I say.

". . . Okay?"

Hmm. I feel like this isn't going well. "Are you guys freshmen?"

". . . No?"

Those question marks are really weird. "Oh. So, who do you have for English? Maybe we have the same teacher at some point!"

". . . Mr. Case?" the spokeswoman says.

"Oh. I have Mrs. Christiansen."

She doesn't say anything this time. They just keep *staring*. Jeez, do I have tentacles?

"Do you like the Ramones?"

". . . No?"

Sad face. Definitely not going good here. Maybe girls were the wrong choice.

"Okay, well, is it okay if I sit here? There weren't a lot of places to sit, and I thought—"

"Uh, okay?" she says.

I start to say thanks, except they all get up at literally the exact same time, carrying their trays, and walk away so it's just me.

Dang it. And I don't see Zach anywhere. I bet he'd let me eat with him. I put in my earbuds and let Joey try to convince me that this is a rock 'n' roll high school. Fun fun! But honestly, I'm kinda doubting Joey right now.

# COACH

His office smells of old shoes and grass clippings. Locker rooms, gymnasiums, coach's offices the world over—they all smell exactly the same. This office smells just like all of the offices of his own coaches: high school, Coach Page; college, Coach McMann. Then that all-too-brief stint in the League. He made it as far as practice squad, further than he'd really believed he could. That triggered the dreams of being a backup; maybe starter someday.

Then, during practice: the god damn knee. No starting, no second string, no practice squad. Just back to school to find a way to keep doing what he loved. And what he loved was this game. Coach Page had made an impact on him back in high school. While coaching a Pop Warner team, he discovered that he wanted to do what Coach Page had done for him: help other high school kids. Seemed like a good fit.

In hindsight, he wouldn't change a thing. Yes, even an NFL practice squad would have paid better, but here he can actually mentor. NFL stars can be role models, but they can't be in the day-to-day grind that is high school life.

He drops into his ancient swivel chair for the eighth year of his tenure as head coach. The chair is older than his children, a relic from the 1970s that creaks and whines and clunks. People say football programs get all the money. Where's the money for a new chair?

He rocks back and forth, easy, toes of his Nikes resting lightly on the thin, industrial carpet. This is going to be a good year. Brady Culliver's in pretty good shape, despite all the odds against him. Donte Walker came back from summer camp with a ferocity he can't wait to unleash, and a Sparq score of almost 94. The other boys look good this year, too. A good crop of JV coming in, and the varsity must've put on an extra two hundred pounds between them over summer.

Except for Culliver. That boy's got to get fed more.

A bell rings. Second period is about to start. He doesn't have a first this year. Gets to hit the gym first before coming to work. He doesn't use the school gym. He loves his fellas, but doesn't need to get into a pissing contest about bench presses. Better to let them wonder just what he's pressing these days.

Two-ten, it turns out. Not bad at all.

Coach picks up his class rosters, flipping through them. Time enough to worry about football this afternoon. First, get through the rest of his classes. Maybe start with some laps to get everyone warmed up.

He winces as he recognizes a name on the attendance sheet. There's one every year. One class, and at least one kid, that's a problem.

Well, that's just fine. He'll sweat this little snot until he can't run his mouth anymore. And maybe, just maybe, turn him into a bit of a man by the end of this year. That's what Coach Page would've done.

Coach rubs his thumb across the roster, smearing a little of the ink that spells out JENNINGS, DANIEL.

Just after the bell rings, ending first period, he shoots a

text message to Steve Butler over in English Ed. Steve is his best friend at work, and biggest NFL rival. The vast majority of their conversations are heated debates about Monday Night Football.

*Culliver show up?* he writes.

His phone buzzes right back: *Yes. Seems fine. Tired maybe. State!*

Steve wants the Spartans to take State almost as bad as Coach does. Another reason they get along so well.

Coach puts his phone in his desk and rises at the sound of people shuffling hesitantly into the gymnasium. Freshman and sophomore PE. If he were a traditionalist, he'd start the morning with dodgeball. But that strikes even him as cliché. Laps will have to do. Laps are simple, but they tend to reveal character—or lack thereof.

The bell rings, starting second period. He steps out of the football office and follows the hall to the gym entrance, where dozens of boys are standing in loose clumps or sitting on the floor. One, he sees right away, has elected not to dress out and is seated on the top, furthest bleacher, like he hopes the windows up there will open and he can slip away.

*He looks like a god damn vampire*, Coach thinks.

He blows his whistle, making most of the boys jump. They're nervous. Sweat will help. Sweat heals a number of things. Including nerves and attitudes.

"Hello, boys," Coach says with his biggest smile. "I'm your coach for the period. I say it, you do it, we get along fine. You hear the whistle, you put your eyes on me. Those're the only rules. Got it?"

Some nod. Most look terrified.

"Good," Coach says. "Start running. Around the sideline. If you don't know what that is, you can start doing push-ups instead. I see you cut any corners, you'll do 'em anyway. Go."

He tweets the whistle, and the boys drag themselves in a circle around the court.

Coach eyes the lone deviant at the top of the bleachers. "Mr. Jennings," he calls, "how about you get yourself into your PE uniform and join us?"

"No, thank you," Danny Jennings calls.

"All right. Then you can head on over to Dr. Flores's office. Let's go. *Now*. Hustle."

"I could take health instead," Jennings offers.

"That class is closed. So you either get to work in here, or you go talk to the principal, your choice."

Jennings stands, shoulders his bag—which looks more like a god damn purse—and clomps down the stairs in boots that reduce his already skinny legs to the width of hockey sticks. He heads for the staircase that will take him up to the doors out of the gym.

As he passes Coach, he says, "But it's not my choice, is it? Not really."

Coach inhales, about to give the little snot a piece of his mind, but Jennings is already past him, raising a hand.

"Never mind," he says. "You don't have to answer that. Peace."

He disappears through the double doors.

He'd never say it out loud, not during regular school hours; but in his head, Coach says, *God damn that kid.*

Then he tells the other students to pick it up. Hustle. Put some effort into it.

# BETWEEN CLASSES

It takes only seconds for the phone's built-in flash to pop—

For him to shriek in surprise—

For a fast, athletic thumb to strike the right icons—

And then:

It takes only seconds for a full-frontal, naked shot of The Fat Kid to land online.

It's an instant crime; legally, it's child pornography, and the guy responsible should be brought up on charges. Big ones. *Bad* ones.

Except the phone doesn't belong to the guy who took the pic. It belongs to a skinny sophomore piece of shit, and this guy got the requisite passwords from the sophomore's sister.

And The Fat Kid won't say anything. Because there are worse things than naked pictures of you on the web. And those things happen to people who go to The Authorities. The whole point in taking weight room this year was to work off some of the girth. Sitting at a drafting table or easel doesn't make for a great weight-loss regimen. If he keeps losing weight, maybe they'll leave finally him alone.

But they won't, will they. They'll make it impossible. They won't let him change.

He rushes from the shower, red-faced and burning furiously on the inside while the laughs of zoo animals follow him to the lockers—elephant linebackers, panther receivers, rhinoceros forwards, cheetah pitchers. He tries to get dressed quickly, never mind trying to dry off . . . except his clothes are already wet, why are they wet?

And why do they smell like—

When the laughing gets louder, including hoots and jeers now, that's all he needs to know.

He'll be throwing away his favorite Da Vinci T-shirt, forced to wear someone's leftover PE jersey from the coach's office. The coach who will do nothing, even if he were to say, *Someone pissed on my clothes, and by the way, there's a naked pic of me floating around today, I can tell you exactly who did it, but I won't because you love the prick and you love to win and I'm just—*

The Fat Kid.

*I Wanna Be Sedated*

# DONTE

I don't know the exact temperature, but it's over a hundred. That's without all my pads and helmet. Or running full gassers on the field.

"You can stop anytime," Coach says to us as we line up after the first round of running from sideline to sideline. "Be my guest. Take your gear off, go home, and don't look back. Fine with me. Or you stay here, and you want it. You want it?"

I want it. I make eye contact with Brady—quick, though, because the standard is we watch Coach when he's talking. Brady meets my gaze fiercely. He's dialed in. He wants it, too.

Most of the varsity team wrangles up a "Yeah!" in unison. It's only been one gasser so far, fifty-three yards and back, twice in a row. Our hearts are pumping, our sweat is flowing, the sun's heat pierces our helmets like a laser beam. And it's gonna get worse. But we are the boys who are going to State this year. A few gassers can't take us down.

"One more," Coach orders, and blows his whistle.

The team races for the opposite sideline. We lose a second or two from the last time, I'm pretty sure. *Damn.*

"You think this is for time?" Coach shouts as we re-form the line. Lots of the team have their hands on their hips as we watch him pace. Somebody on the line dry heaves. I don't look to see who. "You think I got stopwatches on all you boys? 'Cause I don't. This is not for time! This is for heart!"

The whistle blasts and we go again.

Some workouts *are* for time. Some are for strength, some for agility, some for cardio. That doesn't include practice, which is all about sharpening skill. Today's the first full day back at school and a Long Day practice. This one is about guts—and man, I got more of those than ever before. I cross the final sideline first in that round, and it feels great.

"You want to win?" Coach says.

"*Yeah!*"

"That's a word! I want proof." The whistle blows, and we go again.

On this return trip, one of the linemen stumbles past the sideline and pukes through his face mask. Coach blows the whistle and calls for a knee. The team surrounds him. Me and my teammates breathe hard, panting, as we take off our helmets and gaze up at Coach.

"Now, I can run you till you die," Coach says, as if resuming a conversation we started earlier. "I can run you till you puke, Monty. Right?"

Monty, the lineman, nods once, looking both embarrassed and determined.

"But that's not what I'm here for. That's not what *you're* here for. Anyone can play a game. We can come out here and play Candy Land if you want, it doesn't matter to me. That what you wanna play?"

Me and the others know not to answer.

"You came to play football. You came to play hard and train hard and win hard games. This Friday, that's what we're going to do against the Titans. This is a man's game now. Suck up the tired, suck up the doubts, and man up. You do not have to win, but you *CAN. NOT. STOP*, ever. Because if you do not stop, ever, if you do not stop pushing yourself and your team, then you will win. That's just what happens. Don't be afraid, of anything, ever. Just keep pushing. Hoo?"

The team, having barely caught our breath from the gassers, bursts into our favorite chant of *hoo hoo hoo hoo*, great guttural vocal punches that announce the season is now in full swing.

"All right," Coach says. "Get some water."

The team hops up and heads for the white plastic tables where the water is waiting. Also waiting? The water girls. The best part of practice.

I chug cool water, grateful for the relief. I am pumped, ready for Friday. Three more practices before then; two Shorts and a Long, with a break on Wednesday to recover. I turn my face up to the sun, eyes closed, daring the star to beat me down. Then a cold splash against my face makes me shake.

"Oops! Sorry," says Amy, not sorry at all.

I smile, happy with both the cold splash and her attention. When I catch Coach's glare, I stop smiling and turn for the field instead.

Damn. I hope Amy understands. She probably does.

After some parting instructions from Coach, the team jogs to the locker room to clean up. We run through some locker-room talk, literally—comparing the various water girls at practice— but no one talks that way about Amy. Not me, not anybody.

Me and Brady finish cleaning up at the same time and head out of the locker room together. Brady looks pale to me. And, *damn*, way too skinny.

"Hey man," I say to B as we walk. "I'm gonna get some pizza, want to hang with me?"

Brady hesitates for only a second. "Yeah, sure, that's cool."

"Cool."

We take my new-old car to this hole-in-the-wall place called Chizona's. It's a few blocks from Brady's. The pizza's damn tasty. I order an extra large with sausage, pepperoni, green peppers, olives, and onions. We grab a table near the windows and talk strategy *and* shit about the Titans.

"Mercy rule," I say.

"Mercy rule," Brady says, thumping my fist with his own.

When the pizza arrives, I shake my head and say, "Damn, that is way bigger than I thought. I won't finish this. Jump in, man."

So Brady grabs a slice, and together we take out the entire pie, barely speaking through it, watching ESPN on Chizona's old boxy television hung up high in one corner.

After a series of belches that take about ten pounds off me, I say, "I got to head out. You want a ride?"

Brady gets up from his chair with a wave. "Nah, I'm gonna get another run in before I get home."

No way is he running anywhere. But I don't say it.

"Cool," I say instead. "Tomorrow, pick you up at that Starbucks down there? Seven?"

"Seven's good. Hey."

"S'up?"

Brady squints at me. "You and Amy. That a thing?"

Damn.

"Man," I say, "Amy and *nobody* a thing."

"Yeah, but if you could?"

I consider how to answer. In the time it takes me to make a decision, I realize the pause was answer enough.

"Yeah," I admit, "if I could. You?"

Brady shrugs, but doesn't look pissed. "If I could. But Brianna's been hanging around. I might go that way."

I whistle, screwing my face into a mask of make-believe pain. Brianna's damn hot. Not my type, but hot. "Montaro? Damn, son. You could do worse. You could do worse."

That gets B to grin. "Yeah. I guess. Later."

After he leaves Chizona's, I watch B walk down the sidewalk, not even pretending to start running. Suddenly depressed, I climb into the new-old car and drive home. I've lost twenty or thirty minutes with Mom by going out for the pizza, but that's what Mom would have told me to do. Now I'll only have fifteen, maybe twenty minutes with her.

I park on the street in front of the house, because there's only room in the driveway for my mom's even *older* car—one that's kept running by a guy down the block in exchange for meals from Pei Wei. I find Mom at the same place she always is between shifts: on the couch watching *Judge Judy*.

"Hey, you," Mom says.

"Hey, Mom."

I crash down beside her and throw my big old feet up on the coffee table. I do this every day. And every day, Mom slaps my knee and I move them down. We both smile.

"How was practice?"

"Good. We got this."

"How's Brady doing?"

"Hungry."

"Mmm," Mom says, her smile gone. "I'll bring some extra home tonight. You make sure and take it tomorrow. How's he playing?"

"Good. But I think he lost some weight this summer." I shake my head. "Why doesn't she take care of him?"

"Oh, I don't know. She thinks she's got a good thing going with these guys and their presents, I guess."

"I don't like how he looks."

"How's he look?"

Actually, I've spoken before really completing my own thought. I have to struggle to find the right words. "Like he's being chased."

"Mmm," Mom says again. "I know that feeling, Donte. And he can't be a quarterback on an empty stomach."

She's right about that. And if I'm going to have more than one school to pick from, I need our quarterback's head in the game. Me and B both need those opportunities.

"How about you, you hungry?" Mom says. "Can I make you something before work?"

I'm full to bursting from the pizza, and even if I wasn't, I know by now how to make just about anything from nothing. Since she's usually working two jobs, sometimes even a third, Mom isn't around much to cook. My little brother Ramon won't be home till late; it's his day with his dad. This is the only time me and Mom get. These quick times together, specifically scheduled by her, mean everything. To both of us, I know.

Though the thought of more food makes me queasy, and I hate to make Mom get up, knowing she'll be on her feet for another six hours tonight, I also know this is what she wants more than anything. "Sure, yeah," I say. "I could use a bite."

The way her brown eyes dance, I know I chose the right thing.

# BRADY

Pizza was great. But I feel sick.

Donte knows. 'Course he knows. That's what's making me sick.

Least he's cool about it. And at least I ate. Don't know when that might happen again.

I walk home from the pizza place. No way am I running. That was just a scam for Donte. Prolly didn't need to bother. Still. Makes me feel better to have an excuse.

Some bum in an alley down the block offers to blow me. *Not even if I had the money*, I want to say. But I don't. Doesn't matter.

Door is locked when I get to our unit. Son of a bitch. I climb the back wall into the porch. Back door's locked, too.

My eyes shut. I grind my teeth. Make a pair of fists. Should just break a window. Hell with her.

But I won't. I know I won't.

Pull out my phone and rub my eyes because men don't cry. Pussy.

"Hello," Coach says.

"Hey," I say. "I, um . . . she's not . . ."

"No worries," Coach says. "You head on over any time."

I try to say *Thanks*. I know he can't hear it.

"You know where she is?" Coach asks.

"With that new asshole, or maybe jail again. I don't know. Man, I got to turn in my permission slip still . . ."

"Don't worry about that right now, you just head over whenever. Monica will fix you up something."

"Thanks." Say it louder this time.

"You're gonna get through this, chief."

I don't answer because men don't cry. They don't. After a minute I manage a grunt back.

"See ya," Coach says, like he knows.

"'Kay." Hit the end key. Stare at the locked back door and the window. Could still just break it.

But what's in there? Fridge is empty except for diabetes meds and old Ritz crackers. Maybe some mustard. Rotten eggs or something.

I'll come back in the morning to shower and change. If she's home. Or maybe I'll just stay at the park again.

Climb back over the wall. Walk a few blocks to catch a free trolley. They're not like the ones in San Francisco. Just buses painted to look like it. Take a roundabout path to Coach's house. On the way, I check my phone. Laugh when I see the Fat Kid's pic has made the rounds.

That makes me feel better. In a sick sort of way. Prolly shouldn't have done it.

But hey. Life's not fair. Gotta laugh when you can.

# COACH

Jennings is back in his spot at the top of the bleachers on Friday. Where he's been every day the entire week.

"Gonna join us today?" Coach says, chewing on the rubber tip of his whistle like a cigar, giving his words a mobster lisp.

"No thanks, Coach," Jennings calls. He's reading a book, does not look up. Coach can't see the title.

"You want to go sit in the principal's office again?"

"I'd love nothing more, Coach."

"Well then go ahead march your smart ass right down there."

"I'll need a pass, Coach."

"Deal with it. Get out of my gym."

"Whatever you say, Coach."

Jennings shoves the paperback into his bag and marches down the bleacher steps. The rest of the class pays no attention. They've adjusted to him.

Jennings walks past, saying, "By the way, you know I can take health, right? How about you just give me the old transfer over there? Whaddya say, chum? It'd make life a lot easier for both of us."

"That class is full. How about you dress out and take a lap? I'll even give you a full week's credit if you put in even that much effort."

"You're seriously going to fail me at PE?"

"You're going to fail yourself. You don't have to be some

athlete. You just have to show some effort. Look at those other boys. They strike you as athletes? They're trying to do what I asked. That's it." Coach rubs his forehead as if it pains him. "My god, son, it's an easy A if you'd—"

"*You don't call me that!*" Jennings's face twists as he screams. Both the volume and the pitch are enough to make the runners stop, crashing into each other. Even Coach is momentarily stunned.

"You don't ever, *ever*, call me that," Jennings seethes. Quiet now, but scary quiet; the quiet of the moment before a firing pin pricks the primer of a bullet.

But Coach doesn't sway easily. He recovers in an instant. "March your ass to the principal's office. *Now*. Or I'll happily march it there for you."

Jennings's rage is gone as quickly as it manifested. A calm look spreads over his face as he heads for the stairs. "Whatever you say, Coach."

Coach blows his whistle and reams out the freshmen and sophomores who've stopped running to watch the scene. They scurry back to the laps. He walks the interior of the sidelines, twirling his whistle lanyard and trying to get his heart rate back to normal.

*God damn that kid*, he thinks.

# CADENCE

The cafeteria is like a soundstage in Hollywood where a million dramas happen every day. This cafeteria's food is way better than my junior high's, though, and there's lots of big windows to let in the sun. And the ceiling is high, which lets all the nose-clogging, steamy-food smell rise. Will it form clouds up there and condense, raining mashed potato moisture upon us all? And if so—yum? I'm not sure.

I buy a Dr Pepper to go with my pizza, happy that Friday is always Pizza Day, and stand off to one side, trying to decide where to try to sit this time. The week hasn't gone real well in terms of meeting people. High school's not turning out to be as rock and roll as expected. The other day, this guy told me to screw my sunny disposition. Jeez, relax, right? So I've been eating on the go since then, wandering around with my food and watching people, looking for anyone *fascinating*. I haven't seen Zach again. Sad face! Maybe he has a car and can drive off campus for lunch.

It's hard to get to know someone when they're never around. I listened to music and texted with Gloria the last couple days during lunch, but she's at a doctor's appointment today.

Before I leave the cafeteria with my pizza, I spot the spikes-and-buckles kid from the first day. He's sitting on the floor, his back against the west wall, legs out in front of him and crossed at the ankle. He's got earbuds in.

So he survived his first week! That's good. I wonder what kind of music he likes.

I walk over and sit down next to him, crisscross applesauce. He looks up with an expression of surprise that immediately turns to crankiness.

"What's up?" I say, setting my soda beside me and resting my plate in my lap.

He darts his eyes to one side and the other, then back to me. "Have we met?"

"Nope. I'm Cadence."

"Like the chant that army guys do when they march?"

"Actually, yes, but my dad was in the navy, not the army. I don't know if the navy does cadences or not. Probably they do. I'll ask!"

He pulls one earbud out. "The navy, huh?"

"Yep!"

"He have, like, a bunch of guns and stuff? My dad's a gun guy."

"I don't think so. He worked on a submarine."

"Whoa."

He must honestly be interested, because he takes the other earbud out, too.

"What're you listening to?"

He passes one of the buds over. "MacDougall Clan."

"Is that like German death metal?"

"No, but why do you ask?"

"Because you dress like it."

"You're very forward."

"And you're very dry. I mean, like, chill. You don't make very many expressions, did you know that?"

"It's a skill."

"Your face might freeze like that if you're not careful!"

"Trust me. It already has."

*That's* funny. Maybe he didn't mean it to be, but it is. "What'll you give me if I make you smile?"

Well, that gets his attention. I can tell he's struggling not to show it though. Except—oh, crap. He probably took it in like a sexual way.

So I say, "I didn't mean that in a sexual way."

"Of course not," he says, and twists one of the earbuds back in.

I figure I am dismissed, but he holds up the other bud toward me, but without looking, like he doesn't care if I take it or not.

I take it. MacDougall Clan sings something I can't quite make out. It's got a decent beat, anyway.

"Do you like Rancid?" I ask, tapping out the beat on one leg.

He nods.

"Sweet!" I say. "How about the Ramones?"

He shrugs. His eyes are only half-open. Or is it half-closed?

"You *have* to like them. I'll teach you. What's your name, anyway?"

"Danny."

"Cool. Hi, Danny."

"Hello, Cadence. Why are you talking to me?"

"I'm trying to save your life. My friend Colin wore clothes like yours last year, and everyone made fun of him, even when he stopped."

"So now *you* don't like how I dress, either," he says, like he's pretending to say it to himself, but I can obviously hear him. "What a fine, fine place this is."

"I didn't say I didn't like it, I just said—"

"Everyone made fun of your little buddy. I get it."

"Are you mad at me now? Because the thing is, it's been a week and I've met some people in class and stuff but honestly, there haven't been a lot of people to talk to. It's really hard to make friends here for some reason."

Danny glances at me. "Yeah. I've maybe noticed that. I'm not mad."

"Cool. What other bands do you like?"

Danny shows me. Or is it *hears* me . . . ?

Lets me *listen to* his music. That's better. Lunch goes by pretty fast after that.

# VIVI

Mrs. Garcia hands our writing assignments back—our first grade in her class. In red pen, she has circled an A on my paper. She smiles at me when she puts it on my desk, and touches my shoulder for a moment.

I wonder if she's allowed to do that. To make physical contact, I mean.

"Nice work, Vivian," Mrs. Garcia says before moving on to the next student.

The girl next to me leans over and demands, "What did you get?"

Don't look.

Don't move.

I turn my paper over, so only a blank white page shows.

"Hey!" the girl snaps.

I've already learned her name is Brianna. I've learned she is ridiculously smart, or at least knows to only raise her hand when she has the right answer. She does this several times a day. I know this because we have far too many classes together. Honors and AP classes. I've heard people in the hallway snickering and calling her "THE Brianna Montaro." And it always makes me smile inside.

Only inside. Never outside. Never smile on the outside here. And never when THE Brianna Montaro can see it.

Of course we are in all the same classes. Of course.

"What did you get?" Brianna Montaro says again. She

wears black tights and a brilliant blue shirt, artfully tattered, punctured, and knotted. It says DANCE on the front. And at this school, there are no ugly dancers, flagettes, or cheerleaders.

I am not a dancer, flagette, or cheerleader.

I say nothing. Stare at the blank side of my assignment.

Don't look.

Don't move.

THE Brianna Montaro rolls her eyes and says, "Ugh!" then rips the essay off my desk and flips it over.

I gasp, but do not reach out to stop her. THE Brianna Montaro stares at the A.

"*Bitch*," she says, and flips the paper back at me.

Mrs. Garcia doesn't notice any of this because an extraordinarily tall boy sitting up front is asking her questions about the grading rubric.

I stay motionless, but can't resist a peek at Brianna Montaro's paper. She got an A-minus.

Maybe I'm not the bitch. Maybe Mrs. Garcia is. Maybe THE Brianna Montaro is, and she's just mad at herself.

Better to assume it's me, though.

"Knock it off, Brianna," a boy says to her.

He's sitting in the desk opposite THE Brianna Montaro. She is between us. He has dark hair, dark eyes, and is attractive even though he's not really dressed right for school in khakis and a button-down. A nice button-down, though. It is red and sits well on him. He looks . . . somehow above all this. Like he's just waiting for high school to end so he can become president.

THE Brianna Montaro turns to the guy. I brace myself, waiting for her to insult him.

She doesn't. She only stares.

"What?" the boy says.

THE Brianna Montaro just keeps looking at him. Freezing him with ice-cold princess powers.

"What?" the boy says again, agitated.

THE Brianna Montaro says nothing.

The boy shakes his head and mutters, "Whatever."

At last, THE Brianna Montaro speaks: "Well that was clever, Sam. Honestly, I expected more from a master debater."

She says it fast so it sounds like one word instead. Only then does she face front again.

The boy shakes his head.

We make eye contact.

He shrugs and smiles. On the outside.

I look at my desk.

And smile. On the inside.

# CADENCE

These three girls have another girl pinned against the bath-room wall when I walk in. One of the three is Brianna Montaro. I recognize her instantly, because everyone recognizes Brianna Montaro instantly. I think her given name, as it appears on school records, is THE Brianna Montaro, all caps. I think she's already been picked to be valedictorian, whatever that is, and it sounds important. She doesn't look like the boss in here, but then, all three of them might as well be clones. They're all pretty and they're all athletic and they're all old. Like, put-together, I mean. They are not, *for example*, wearing their older brother's old Kona board shorts, Doc sandals, and a Rancid *Ruby Soho* T-shirt like someone else is right now.

The girl pinned to the tile wall looks familiar, maybe, but I'm not sure. I don't have any classes with her. A black magic marker flashes like a blade in Clone #1's hand as they whirl toward me.

"Take a walk, freshman," #1 says.

"What're you doing?" I ask instead of taking a walk.

#1 uncaps the marker. I imagine I can smell its addictive fumes hovering over the smell of stale cigarettes, mascara, and pee.

"It's not your problem," #2 says.

THE Brianna Montaro doesn't say anything. She's got her arms crossed and stands a bit to the side, eyes darting between us. But she's with them, definitely. Maybe she's supervising, or doing research.

I make eye contact with the girl against the wall. She's scared, but not struggling. Clones #1 and #2 hold her easily in place with their hands, not straining either. The girl has clearly accepted her fate.

I watch as #1 methodically spells out A+ SLUT on the girl's exposed forehead. The letters are bold, sharp, perfectly shaped. I wait for laughter from Brianna, or the clones, but no one laughs. The girl against the wall shuts her eyes during the procedure, but she doesn't shake her head or shove them away or scream. Somehow that's the worst part, the way she just takes it without making any fuss.

I want to do something, but what? Sweet ninja moves? I don't have any of those. I could run shouting out of the bathroom, get a teacher or call SWAT, but I don't think they'll actually do anything about it. These girls seem like the kind of people who get away with stuff regardless of what a wee freshman might say about them.

"Nice," Clone #1 says when it's over. They release the girl and drop the marker to the floor.

The three of them muscle past me, writing me off as they go. I didn't interfere, and they don't think I'll tell, because no one tells, I'm pretty sure about that. It wasn't in the student handbook, but I still know. Brianna looks back once, at the end of their procession. She meets my eyes, super, super fast, and looks away again. I can't tell if she feels guilty, or embarrassed, or what.

The girl stays against the wall, eyes still shut, breathing shallow through her nose.

"You okay?" I ask.

The girl doesn't move, doesn't answer.

"I could get you some paper towels and soap. Here." I go to the sinks and start pulling out handfuls of paper towels, as thick and crisp as colorful kindergarten butcher paper. Seriously, who buys this stuff? "We can try to wash it off," I say. "While it's still fresh. Do you want some help?"

Her eyes have been replaced by orbs of hard, black ice when she opens them, freezing me in place. Then she breaks her gaze to reach down into a red backpack. She takes out a black beanie and pulls it carefully over her curly brown hair so that the rim meets her eyebrows, covering the graffiti on her forehead.

"That works," I say. "But really, we can—"

She shoulders the bag and makes her way to the door.

"I'm gonna go ahead and report them," I say.

"Don't," the girl whispers. Then she's out of the bathroom.

"Nice to meet you," I say after the door has closed. Sad face. Why do people do that kind of thing to each other? I mean, really, who feels better about themselves after something like that?

I consider reporting them anyway. I'm pretty sure I'm right about Brianna Montaro's name. I could bust her, if not the other two.

But it's their three words against me and the other girl's two. Three against one if the girl with the fresh Sharpie tattoo doesn't speak up. And I get the impression she won't.

So there's nothing I can do. Man that sucks! *People* suck sometimes.

But my day gets better when I come out of the bathroom a few minutes later and see Zach wandering down the hall in my direction. At last! I wave.

"Hi, Zach!"

He smiles right away. I could find my way in the dark by that grin.

"How's it going," he says, "um . . . Katie?"

"Cadence." I fall into step beside him. "But you could call me Cadie for short."

"Cadence, right," he says. "Cadie, Cadence. Got it. So what's up?"

"Some girls just wrote *slut* on this other girl's forehead in the bathroom," I say, since he asked.

"Wow. That sucks."

"Really does," I say. "I would have done some sweet ninja moves on them, but I'm out of practice."

"I'd pay a lot to see that."

"Cool! I'll set up a demo. What're you doing out of class?"

"Taking a message to the office. What about you?"

I hold up my green hall pass. "Bathroom break."

"What class are you in right now?"

"At this very moment, I'm in Walking Zach Down The Hall class."

"Don't take this wrong way," he says when we reach an intersection. "But you're kind of a doofblatt."

"What's a doofblatt?"

"Not sure. My mom says it all the time. I think it means, you know . . . a little crazy."

"I'll take it!"

"I'm heading this way," Zach says.

"And I'm heading that."

"All right. See you around, Cadie."

"See ya, Zach! I'm glad I got to take a class with you today, finally."

He laughs and goes off down the hall. I think he's shaking his head a bit, probably because I'm a doofblatt. I turn and walk back to my earth science class, thinking about the girl with the black beanie and wondering if there was anything I could have done different. I decide to ask Dad and Mom and Johnny when I get home, during dinner. They'll know.

# VIVI

The boy in the red button-down from Mrs. Garcia's class is also in my seventh-period math class. Our teacher, Mr. Donelly, lets us sit anywhere. I want to sit in the back, farthest corner, but AP potheads have already staked it out. I end up in the middle of the row, closest to the door. It'll do.

In hindsight, I realize the boy usually sits a few seats away from where I am. Today he gets there earlier and sits across from me. He could touch me from his desk.

"No hats in class," he says to me.

He smiles, too. He has 8.4 zits. They are the small kind that probably hurt when he touches them.

"I know," I say, then sink down in my seat.

He might be someone's boyfriend. Dangerous.

He *must* be someone's boyfriend. He knows answers in both classes. He is cute. Not hot. Brady Culliver is hot. I know his name now. So is Donte Walker, whose name I also know now.

But this boy next to me is cute. I have never seen him in jeans, not from the first day of school to now. It would be weird to see him in jeans, I think.

"I'm Sam. Well, Samuel, but only my grandmother calls me that."

I nod. Conversation must end.

"Are you going to leave your hat on?"

My hat. I have to leave it on. Can't take it off. Can't let anyone see. Should have gone home. Daddy hasn't gotten me a car yet, but he swears he will. I might drive it back to my real neighborhood if he does, where it's less safe but at least I know the rules. Maybe I could go live with his sister instead, my Aunt Marlene.

"There's something on your forehead," Sam says.

I pull my hat down further. It's slipped up a little, probably revealing the black markings. "It's nothing."

Sam reaches across the aisle and rests his fingers on the edge of my desk. "Are you okay?"

I nod. But I have to keep my mouth closed very, very tightly so I don't cry. It didn't help in the Dez; it won't help here.

"Hey," Sam says, quietly, like a secret. "You want to ditch? Go get coffee or something?"

Ditch?

The word feels like a spike. I don't ditch. Bad kids ditch. Dad will kill me if I ditch.

Except he'd have to be able to get out of bed first.

I scan the class. Will anybody notice? Will anybody care? What about Mr. Donelly? He'll take roll. He'll know I'm not here. He'll call my dad. I'll get in trouble.

Sam stands up, pulling his backpack over one shoulder. "Come on."

I shrink back. People look at him. He doesn't care.

"Come on," he urges again. "I know a place. You obviously need sugar. Probably chocolate."

My fingers tingle. *Ditch*. It sounds so bad. And chocolate . . . it sounds so good.

My forehead itches where the black ink is sinking in like a tattoo. Will it ever come off?

I pick up my bag. "Okay."

"Cool," Sam says.

We rush for the door and out into the hallway. I look at him for guidance.

"This way," he says, and holds out a hand.

I stare at it.

Then I take it.

Sam smiles, and we run. He guides me through hallways and breezeways until we reach the parking lot, and then we waltz right off campus and onto the street outside. I don't see the security guards anywhere. It's warm, but I don't care. Sam lets go of my hand.

"You haven't actually told me your name yet," Sam says as we walk.

He's right. Now that we are away from school, I can feel my throat loosening.

"Vivi."

"Civvy?" Sam says. "Like, a civilian?"

"Vivi." I try to be louder. "*Vivian*."

"Oh, *Vivi*," Sam says. "Okay. Cool. Vivian. That's a pretty name."

I tuck my chin into my neck for safety.

"So are you new?" Sam asks as we wait to cross a street. "I don't remember seeing you before."

I nod.

"Where are you from?"

"The Dez." I answer automatically, not thinking of how Sam might react. The Dez, a neighborhood with the city's most dense population but not a grocery store in sight, is mostly known for its bustling drug trade.

So I quickly add, "Desert Guadalupe." The G comes out as an H. It's the only trace of an accent I've got. My mom used to say that my Spanish words come out with "Mexican flair," like my dad's. All my English words sounds like I'm from the Midwest, like Mom's.

"Desert Guadalupe," Sam says, with the hard G. "That's not anywhere near here. How'd you end up at this school?"

I shouldn't even have spoken. "Where are we going?" I ask instead.

"Just over there. Jamaican Blue. Really good coffee and pastry stuff. You don't want to tell me how you wound up here?"

I shake my head.

"Okay," Sam says. "You're very mysterious—anyone ever tell you that?"

I shake again.

"Well, I'm pleased to be the first. Are you in any clubs at school?"

Shake.

"Oh. Well, I'm in debate. I'm really quite good."

He glances at me. I guess to see if I smile. I think I do, because Sam looks pleased.

"So don't ever argue with me. Also, I can talk a lot. I don't have to, but I can. Do you want me to keep talking? Because you don't seem to be in the habit of saying much."

I'll have to speak. I can't just keep answering with a yes-nod or shake-no.

"I don't," I say quickly. "Say much."

"That's okay," Sam says. "Because I rather like the sound of my own voice. I could go on and on and on. Here's the shop."

We stop in front of a single large window that reads JAMAICAN BLUE in painted letters. He holds the door open for me, the way Daddy used to do for Mom. Sam orders for me, something listed on the menu as a CHOCOLATE F*CKING EXPLOSION. It appears to be a kind of milkshake, but he orders it by saying, "She'll have a Chocolate Explosion." Then he wrinkles his forehead.

"Shoot. I just ordered for you, didn't I? Sorry, I'm trying to quit doing stuff like that."

"I'll forgive you this time," I say, hoping it's funny.

Sam does in fact smile. "Okay. Thank you. Won't happen again. Where do you want to sit?"

I wander off in search of a good spot while he places his own order. I already like this shop. It's dark, but cool in both senses of the word. I could get used to being here instead of school. I pick a tall table in a corner and sit down. Sam joins me a minute later.

"Okay, so now I'm plying you with chocolate and I rescued you from a boring math class," Sam says, kicking one foot up over his knee. "Now I get to cross-examine you. All right?"

I shrug. Sam starts to ask me something, but then a barista comes to the bar and holds up two cups.

"I've got a large Chocolate Fucking Explosion for Vivi and a large caramel latte for . . ." She hesitates. "He Who Shall Not Be Named!"

Sam gets up and takes the cups from her, then returns to our table. For the first time in many weeks, maybe months, I start laughing.

Sam looks pleased. "Did you like that? It's my favorite name to use."

I just keep laughing.

I *do* like that.

I might like *him*.

Grinning, Sam says, "So. Vivian. What brings you to our fine school?"

"My daddy. Dad! My dad." I look for a place to hide. But Sam doesn't seem to notice my idiocy.

"What about him?"

I drink my Explosion for strength. It works wonderfully. "He got hurt. At work. A beam fell on him. Like, one of those metal beams at a construction site."

"Wow, sorry. I'm going to be a lawyer—you want me to sue someone?"

"We did."

"No kidding. Are you rich now?"

"He bought a new house."

"So that's a yes."

I drink instead of answering. It is a yes. A huge yes. A seven-figure yes.

"I'm sorry," Sam says. "I shouldn't be asking you stuff like that, that's rude."

"It's okay."

Sam squints at me. "If it's really okay, then I have one more question. Were you this quiet before the money?"

I sip. Savor. Then shake.

"Was it the money or the move?"

"Money, move . . . and Mom." I peer into my tall glass of Chocolate F*cking Explosion, mesmerized by the swirls of chocolate sauce.

Sam urges me to keep talking with his sincere brown eyes.

"She left. Just before the accident."

"So she got nothing? That must make her mad."

"It does." I finish my drink. "Can I ask *you* something?"

"I'd be amazed and delighted."

"Why do you think that girl Brianna is so popular?"

"THE Brianna Montaro?" Sam says, and in that moment, I want to kiss him. "Is she?"

"Is she what?"

"Is she actually popular. I mean, by definition, that would mean a lot of people like her. What's a lot of people? Half the campus? Three quarters? She doesn't actually hang out with that many people. Too busy, for one thing."

"Okay, well . . . maybe popular is the wrong word."

"Sorry, I get hung up on specificity," Sam says. "It's a debate thing. I know what you meant. I was just thinking, popular means adored by many. I don't think that quite fits her."

When he smiles again, I do, too. I decide right then to be friends with Sam the rest of my life.

# DREA

I wonder if either of my parents ever wake up in the dead of night in cold sweats, thinking, *Just how badly have I screwed up my kid?* If they don't, they should. They really, really should.

My dad resents me. I can't prove it. It's just one of those things you pick up on by the time you're fourteen. Both of my parents are screwed up—but then, doesn't everyone think that? Plus, if it's true, what does that make *me*? I don't think they even wanted me, but I'm not quite stupid enough to ask and know for sure.

My father is a hypocrite. To supplement his income from running a community theater, he writes for health websites—articles with titles like "10 Reasons Water Is Good For You!" and "Exercise Right!" and "Why Forgiveness Is Healthy!" while smoking at least half a pack of Winston Lights per day, sometimes more during tech week, the week before his newest play opens. He never drinks water, and he never exercises, except taking our dog—a knotted, bedraggled thing named Gertrude—out for a walk once a month or so. And even then, it's probably to get away from my mother, and I can't say that I blame him.

I try not to bitch about them. Not to Kelly or anyone else. I know some people have it a lot worse than me. In junior high, my friends, who all went to a charter high school instead of here, they sometimes played up the bad stuff at their houses so they could have more drama to gossip about. I thought that was dumb, you know? Everyone has their thing or things that are wrong, so what? These are mine. They belong to me. I mean, it's not like my parents are alcoholics or beat me up or anything.

But it's like Dad can only think about what's important to him, and Mom keeps putting up with it, at least in small bursts, until she has a meltdown. My mother is supposed to be on medication for some kind of personality problem that I don't understand, but she rarely sticks to it. I also wonder about her diagnosis, because Mom has never actually been to a psychiatrist, just our family doctor. Her mood swings trace epic pendulum arcs from day to day, and it's only gotten worse. They don't look at each other much. They look at me, sometimes, and they look at the dog, and that's about it.

This is what I'm thinking about as I draw the point of an unfolded paperclip down a blank area of my right arm. The left is too scabbed right now; I needed a fresh canvas. The paperclip drags my flesh into miniature skin mountains, not cutting so much as scraping. Still, it hurts a little, and that's all that matters, you know?

"Are you going to take all day?" Kelly calls from outside the bathroom stall.

"Almost done," I say, drawing another ragged scratch down my forearm.

Instantly my stomach muscles unwind and the mental pictures of my parents dissolve. I refold the paperclip to something like its original shape and come out of the stall, rolling down my sleeves.

Kelly, in baggy brown capri pants, sandals, and yellow-and-white baseball tee, is standing against the sinks, arms crossed. I think, but would never say, that a skirt and blouse would make a huge difference in Kelly's presentation.

"You know that I know what you were doing in there, right?"

"Sorry," I say automatically.

"Instead of being sorry, you could just not do it."

Kelly doesn't sound angry, or even disappointed. She sounds matter-of-fact, and I'm kind of grateful. Kelly's tone strikes me as respectful, somehow.

We leave the girls' restroom together and walk to the parking lot. We get into Kelly's green pickup truck with the rusted fenders.

"What kind of music do you like?" Kelly says.

"All kinds."

Kelly turns on the radio. Something poppy comes on. "This?"

"I guess."

Carelessly, Kelly launches into singing along, startling me. Her voice has a depth and tenor to it that I never would have anticipated. She should have a YouTube channel, at the very least, where she just covers pop songs a cappella or something. The song ends, and Kelly stops singing.

"Do that again," I tell her.

"What, sing? No."

"How come?"

"You heard it, you tell me! Silly freshman."

"It was good."

"Aw, you're sweet," Kelly says, but obviously doesn't believe me.

I spend the rest of the drive begging and teasing Kelly to sing again, but she won't. When she pulls up to my house and I start to get out, she says, "Hey, freshman. Put some Neosporin or something on your arms, okay? It's all fun and games until you get a blood infection and die."

"Okay, Mom."

She doesn't laugh. "Just do it."

"Fine. See you later."

I get out and go into the house. Mom and Dad are both gone. I go into the bathroom and put Neosporin on my arms.

# CADENCE

I see Danny just as he's reaching the sidewalk beyond the parking lot after seventh hour, so I shout his name and start running after him. I must have shouted pretty loud, because he has his earbuds in and still manages to hear me. I'm glad he stops, because I'd sure look stupid shouting and running through the parking lot without someone acknowledging me.

"Hi!" I say when I get to him.

"Uh—hi."

"Where are you going?"

"Well, let's see. It's after school, so my current theory is home?"

"Cool! Where's that?"

"A galaxy far, far away."

"You want to hang out?" No one will be home at my place yet. Usually I'd hang out with Faith or Gloria or Liza, but not anymore. Big jerks! I miss them.

Danny freezes in place for about ten seconds before saying, "Sorry, what?"

"I said, do you want to hang out. Go get something to eat or something. Or go to the park—hey, we could go on the swings!"

"Sorry," Danny says again, "did you just ask me to hang out?"

"You are not the fastest thinker, Dan."

"It's Danny. *Did* you?"

"Yes. *Danny.* God, you're weird."

I don't mean anything by it, and I know I'm smiling when I

say it. Danny looks mad for a second, but then he says, "Yeah, well, you've got a pirate flag on your ass, so there. That makes you a butt pirate. Now who's weird?"

Well, okay, he's right, I am wearing my favorite shorts today. "Oh, you're still weird. And it's called a Jolly Roger."

"What?"

"The pirate flag. The skull and crossbones, it's called a Jolly Roger."

He holds up both index fingers. "That pink emblem adorning the backside of your shorts is called a Jolly Roger? And you don't find that to be a huge innuendo?"

"Huge *what?* Dude, are you speaking English right now?"

Danny comes close to smirking, but doesn't quite do it. "Okay. Let's hang out. You ever been to the Blue?"

"What's that?"

"It's a coffee shop. The Jamaican Blue. We could walk there from here."

"Okay! Lead the way."

We start walking down the sidewalk together. He doesn't put his earbuds back in, which I take as a deep sign of respect.

We walk about two blocks to a neighborhood I've never been to before, at least not that I remember. My house and my old school and my friends' houses are all in the other direction. It's kind of cool over here, though. Lots of red brick buildings and trees planted in the medians.

Right when he steps into a small parking lot in front of an L-shaped row of shops, I stop dead.

"Wait! This is Fifty-Third Street."

Danny stops, too. "Yeah?"

I point to a green-and-white street sign nearby, posted at a little one-lane side street that intersects Fifty-Third. "And that's Third Avenue?"

"Your powers of deduction are breathtaking. Truly."

"This is the corner of Fifty-Third and Third!" I shout at him. "Like the song! The Ramones song. Well, except their song is set in New York. And it's kind of about male prostitution. But, still! This is so cool."

"Let's back up to the whole male prostitute thing," Danny suggests, holding up his index fingers again.

"I thought you loved the Ramones!"

"I've *heard* the Ramones. Two different things."

I blow a raspberry at him and return to studying my new favorite place in the entire city. Here on the northeast corner of the intersection, there's a patch of grass blanketing a short hill. A young tree reaches out from the top of it, like a leafy hand pleading to God. The grassy area is maybe half the size of a tennis court or so, based on what I remember of the courts at school. The grass is bright and lush, almost impossibly green, really, considering how hot it is. The corner is a tiny oasis in the midst of red brick buildings and blacktop.

"Wow," I say, and take a picture of the street sign, which I send to the girls. Only Liza will care, but I send it to all of them, anyway. Then I send it to Johnny, who I know will appreciate it, and Colin, even though we don't talk much anymore.

"Can we go inside now?" Danny pleads. "It's effing hot. The Blue is right down here."

"Yeah, yeah," I say, watching a free trolley turn down a street less than a block away. Awesome! I'll be able to get here anytime I want by taking the trolley.

We cross Third Avenue and follow a brick sidewalk to a coffee shop. The air-conditioning is blasting on high right over the entrance, almost tearing my hair out. But, man, it smells great in here.

Danny heads straight for the counter, and I follow him. While he's ordering, I take in the whole scene. "The Blue" is lit low. Lots of tall, round tables with barstools line the walls and run down the middle of the shop. The walls are painted matte barn red and deep brown, and there's no ceiling, meaning the air ducts and stuff like that aren't hidden behind tiles or anything, they're just up there, all metally and black. The walls are dotted with smeared pastel art prints that I would totally hang in my room if there was any space left between the posters.

As I'm mentally redecorating my bedroom, I make accidental eye contact with someone from school. The girl from the bathroom. She's still got the black beanie over her head, pulled low. She's sitting with a boy I've seen around, but haven't met yet. When we see each other, her eyes open wide.

I give her a secret wave, low, by my hip, knowing she might not like that I recognize her, because people can be weird about stuff like that, like your presence reminds them of something bad. I'm grateful when her expression softens a little and she returns my wave. I'd love to go over there and talk to her, see how she's doing, but sometimes people don't like it when you do *that*, either. Like I said, they want to be left alone and not reminded that something bad happened. Plus, she's with that guy! I know if it was me and Zach sitting there, I wouldn't want anyone bothering me.

So I turn to the counter and order a blended iced coffee thing. Danny has a black iced coffee, nothing in it.

"Isn't it bitter?" I ask as we weave our way to an empty table.

"Does it show?" he says, slouching onto one of the tall barstools at a table near the door. "And I try so hard to be a ray of sunshine."

"I meant the coffee, doofblatt."

I get the impression he's trying not to smile, like he doesn't want anyone to see him happy.

So I say, "You don't want anyone to think you're happy, do you."

"Who said I was happy?"

"Well, what's up?"

He gives me the evil eye. Or at least the suspicious eye. "Why should I tell you?"

"Because I'm nice, dummy! Plus we're at a coffee shop, so we have to be all deep and stuff."

"Can't argue with that logic." He leans over the table, so I do, too, because this must be important.

"So last year, my friend Donald tells me that his dad will

pay us a dollar for every pigeon we kill at his garage. He's a mechanic, and all these pigeons have started roosting on his roof and crapping on everything. He works on a lot of high-end cars, and he's always got to clean up the shit right away. Sounds like a good deal, so I bring my pellet gun to school so me and Donald can go to the garage when school gets out."

"This school? I'm new, so I don't know."

"The Arts Academy, downtown," Danny says. "I was a freshman. So everything's going fine, right? Then during my speech class, this other friend of mine takes my bag and plays Keep Away with it. Except the gun falls out—"

"And it shot him in the face?"

". . . Uh, no, it fell out of my bag and broke. It was an air gun, not a Glock. It shoots one pellet at a time. You with me?"

"Oh, sorry. Jumped ahead. Go on!"

"So it is technically a gun, even though it only shoots point-one-seven-seven pellets. That's less than half the size of your pinky fingernail, probably wouldn't even penetrate your clothes, but they have to treat it like it's this big threat, like I'm a god damn terrorist or something. So while I'm trying to explain why I had the gun in the first place, they call my parents. Then my dad shows up, and he flips right out. I point out that he's the one who got me the pellet gun in the first place, but does he care about that? No. So I start getting mad, and I start shouting, and then everyone's telling me to calm down, and I'm telling them to shut up and leave me alone—"

He's starting to squeeze his plastic cup so much, it's going to spill bitter coffee out from under the lid. I try to point this out, but Danny's talking fast now and doesn't even hear me.

"And they're all saying, 'Calm down, Danny, calm down, you need to relax, Danny!' But I don't, and the more they tell me to, the more pissed I get. So then, *then*, after everything's settled down and I don't get kicked out or anything because, for the record, my school loves me, I start smoking out with Donald and some other guys a few days later because everyone had said to calm down. And I bought a couple tranqs from this other guy, so that I can stay nice and *calm* all day, just like everyone wants. I figure this is a great way to do it."

It's a stupid way to do it, but I don't say that to him.

"But we get caught and my mom flips out and my dad says, 'You've come to a crossroads, m'boy!' like he's this god damn Jedi godfather wise man, and the next thing I know, they're sending me to a shrink and putting me on drugs—drugs, Cadence! Think about it, the *irony*. And they pull me out of the Arts Academy and I end up here. At this school. With my sister who never liked me, anyway—and I can't wear what I want, and I can't take the classes I want because of *pigeons* and my god damn dad."

He's breathing hard and his eyes are open superwide and he won't blink. I don't move. I just meet his eyes and nod.

"That sucks," I say.

He doesn't respond for a second, then leans back in his barstool. The red flush in his face starts draining. "Yeah." He releases his death grip on his coffee.

"But hey," I add, "at least you're here with me instead of at home, where I assume you'd rather not be right now."

"True."

"We should do something tonight."

"Tonight? Like a . . . ?"

"No, not like that," I say. And I mean, I don't want to be full of myself, but for a second, I swear he looks disappointed. I hope not. I'm not someone he should be disappointed over. I try to come up with something that's not date-like.

"We could . . ."

Danny starts taking a drink of coffee.

"Oh! How about we go to the game?"

No kidding, he literally chokes on his coffee. He has to cough for like five minutes before he can talk again.

"Are you insane? A football game? I don't command language well enough to emphasize how much that is not going to happen."

I sip my drink to stall for time before saying, "Are you sure?"

Danny stares at me like he can't believe what I just said.

"Why?" he says. "Why would you choose that one thing?"

"I don't know. Because it's high school. It's part of the experience. What else would you be doing on Friday night?"

"Uh, anything other *than?*"

"Oh, come on. I'll even pay for you."

"Money's not the point."

"What's the point, then?"

Danny gives me a look like the answer to this simple

question is way too big for my wee freshman head to get. So I just stare at him, arms folded on the table, waiting for him to dazzle me with his reasoning.

Finally he says, with a big exhaled breath, "Okay. Fine. We'll go to the football game. Jesus. Are you sure we can't go on a date instead? Movie or something?"

I'm not sure how to answer him besides *no*. I don't think I'm the go-on-a-date type with boys like Danny. But then, I don't know exactly what kind of boy would ask me out. What I do know is that I hope it's Zach!

"I kind of have my eye on someone," I say. "Only, he maybe doesn't know it yet."

"Who?" He sounds like he wants to kill whoever it is.

"Doesn't matter," I say, to protect Zach. "So we'll go to the game?"

"Yeah, sure. Anything to be close to you."

I can't tell if he's kidding or not, or being sarcastic, or just what, so I decide to let it go.

# VIVI

Sam wears a watch, I notice. Nobody else at school does, not that I've seen. Some of the teachers do, that's it. It is very nice, with a rich chocolate-brown strap and a gleaming silver circle. He checks it and blinks.

"School's over," Sam says. "You need to head back?"

"Yes . . . but, wait a second."

On our way to the door, I veer in the direction of the table where the girl from the bathroom is sitting. She's with a boy who looks like he wishes he was a Hells Angel. She waved to me earlier, just a quick "Hi" sort of gesture, but didn't come over or say anything. I'm grateful for that. I didn't want to be interrupted with Sam, and I definitely didn't want her saying anything about what happened with the marker and all that.

But now, feeling better—stronger—I want say hi, at least. Sam follows along with me as I stop at their table.

"Hi!" the girl says. She's like a punk rock elf.

"Um—I'm sorry I was mean to you before," I say.

"Oh my gosh, are you kidding? No way! You totally weren't. I'm just sorry that—you know."

I tug my hat down again to make sure it's covering my forehead. "Yeah . . ."

"This is Danny!" she says. "He's new. I mean, I'm new, too, but he's a sophomore. Right?"

Danny nods, giving me and Sam suspicious looks.

"Vivian," I say. "Or Vivi. This is Sam."

"Hey," Sam says to both of them.

"Hi, Sam! I'm Cadence. Are you guys going to the game tonight?"

I blurt a one-syllable laugh. "No."

"Yeah, not a big football fan," Sam says.

"Me, neither," Cadence says. "We're just going to go check it out, see if it's really all that bad."

"You're a brave woman," Sam says.

"Thanks! It's just the one time. Scope it out, get the whole experience. So are you guys on a date?"

My eyes pop wide. I hear Sam take a big breath, and then not say anything. But finally he goes, "Uh, no . . . not at the moment."

"We just met," I say quickly.

"Although, I thought the afternoon went pretty well . . ." Sam says, using a pretend deep-thought voice.

"How about you guys?" I ask, just to make sure we're off the subject of me and Sam.

"No," Danny says, loudly. "What would ever give you *that* idea?"

"Don't be rude," Cadence says. Then she adds, "We're just hanging out."

"Well, maybe we'll see you around school," Sam says.

"Cool!" says Cadence. "See you guys!"

Danny tips his head back, because he is apparently way too cool to say goodbye. Sam and I say goodbye, and head out to the sidewalk.

"You know them from *where*, now?" Sam says, laughing a little.

I tug my knit hat down a bit again. "I ran into her in the bathroom earlier today. And . . ."

I really don't want to tell him the truth.

"And I was a little rude to her is all. Wasn't in a good mood." That's no lie.

"Oh, okay. So, um . . . it *was* a good afternoon, right? I wasn't kidding about that."

Surprised, I say, "Yeah! Yeah, it was fine."

That doesn't sound right.

"It was good," I say.

Sam nods once, grins, and we keep walking. "Cool. And, can we enter it into the record that you are a lot nicer than Brianna."

The comment makes my skin warm. "Oh yeah?" I say, in a desperate attempt at flirting. I don't think I do very well. "How do you figure?"

"Trust me, I know. She's my ex."

My warmth turns to ice.

# DANNY

I am in hell.

Or at least next door. How in the name of all that is holy and righteous and good in the multiverse did I ever let Cadence talk me into coming here?

Okay—I do know how. I know exactly how. She's cute, and I love the way she dresses and how her body fits into her clothes and the way her hair frames her face. The way she looks at everything around her like the entire world is a Christmas present. She's like an anime schoolgirl vampire slayer, all eyes and hair.

She makes the world look like maybe it's actually okay.

*That's* how. That's how I ended up at a football game.

"There's Zach!" Cadence says.

"Who?"

"Zach! Never mind. You should meet him."

Cadence's eyes, already preposterously large by any standard, get even bigger when she says his name. That must be the guy she's *got her eye on*. Great. "You're lucky I made it past the gate," I say. "You know that's money I can never get back?"

"Whatever. Get us some popcorn?"

"What?"

"Popcorn, Danny, popcorn! You have got to start paying attention to me."

Mentally, I strangle myself to keep from blurting out something stupid. I've been paying plenty of attention to her.

"Popcorn, right. For *who* again?"

"Me, if you don't want any. You don't have to, I was just asking. I've got money—"

"It's fine," I say.

"Awesome! Thanks! I'll meet you right back here."

And she's off, squirreling through the crowd shouting something that sounds like "Out 'n' at her!" which makes no sense to me whatsoever, and that's okay.

I step off the sidewalk to avoid the people crushing into the stadium. Mostly old people, like parents. But lurking under the bleachers near the fence, I see a kid wearing a purple-and-black plaid kilt. It looks like mine except mine is green. I can't help but walk over to him. It beats the looks I'm getting for, I can only presume, my T-shirt, which reads in white block letters: Drugs Are My Anti-Sport.

"Hey."

He scans me in that practiced way of career criminals. ". . . Hey?"

"You like MacDougall Clan?"

The kid grins, putting out a hand. "My brother."

We shake, which feels kind of weird and kind of cool at the same time.

"You ever seen them live?" I move to stand under the bleachers with him, shoving my hands deep into my hip pockets. Just regular old jeans tonight. My only pair, really. I wonder if Cadence has noticed they're not black, or if she cares.

"Last year," the kid says. "Got my jaw broke in the pit."

"No shit?"

"Not a drop."

He's scanning again, like he's either looking for someone in particular, or not wanting to get snuck up on. It occurs to me that his back is to concrete; no one can approach him from behind. Maybe he really is a criminal.

"You can't exactly see the game from here," I say.

"Posit," he says. "Teenagers are more depressed and angry now than at any other time in this fine nation's history."

*Posit* means something like, put up a topic for debate. I think. I'm not sure what else to say, so I opt for a safe, neutral, "Okay."

"Consequence: they will do anything or *take* anything to alter these feelings. Result: they will pay any price just to survive from day to day. Conclusion?"

"Um . . . no idea, man."

Acting pleased with my answer, he says, "Conclusion: there's cash to be made selling stuff to pathetic losers who come to football games. Are you cool?"

It takes a second to process all that, but then it sinks in, and I say, "Yeah, I'm cool."

"Thought so. You're Danny Jennings."

"How'd you know that?"

"If I didn't make it my business to know that, I wouldn't have this lucrative job under the bleachers, Danny-boy."

I glance around. In this three square feet of space we're technically alone, but there are literally hundreds of adults everywhere else, and at least two uniformed cops wandering around.

"So it's safe under here?" I say.

"So far, so good. It's the irony they can't handle, see. Surely I wouldn't be doing anything illegal here, surrounded by so many people. Get it?"

"Right. So what do you have?"

"You in the market for something?"

"Might be. Yes."

"Tell you what," Pete says, scanning the area again before reaching into the waist of his kilt. He palms a tightly rolled joint over to me with the liquid efficiency of a real pro.

I quickly slip it into my pocket. This will be nice for later. I haven't had any all summer. Honestly I hate the taste—it usually makes me want to throw up. But at least I stay not pissed for a while.

"You let me know how you like it," Pete says. "If you want more, find me."

"Where?"

"Jesus, dude, look at me. I'm not hard to find."

"How do you know I'm not a cop?"

Pete stares into my eyes. "Because I'd kill you."

He means it.

Except then he laughs.

"Just kidding. I know who Danny Jennings is. That's enough for me, man."

I don't care much for that response, but it beats getting

threatened with death. "Cool," I say, feeling stupid. "See ya around."

"Almost certainly. Later, Daniel-san."

I don't bother correcting him. I prefer Danny, period, the end. But whatever. Anything's better than Dan. I start to head back out to the sidewalk, but then stop and face Pete again.

"Hey, man. Do you wear your kilt to school?"

"Of course I do. I'm not a pussy."

Wonderful.

I vaguely remember that Cadence wanted popcorn, so I head for the concession stand. There's two long lines already. God damn. I keep my hands in my pockets, trying to look casual and not like I have a joint the size of my pinky in there.

While I'm waiting in line, I look around for Cadence. I spot her on the other side of the field, the home side. She's talking to some guy who's sitting in the front row. I don't recognize him.

Fuck. Fine, whatever. Guess it doesn't matter. Why am I standing here like a god damn turd buying popcorn for a girl who made it clear we were not going to date—and at a football game, of all places?

Hell with this. I walk back down the sidewalk toward the ticket booth to get out of this god damn stadium, but I pull up short when I see Pete still lounging around near the visitor bleachers, and a girl wearing way-too-short shorts walking furtively away from him. *He* doesn't seem to have a line, at least. I guess popcorn's more popular than what he's selling.

I snake through the crowd in his direction once again.

"Back for more?" Pete says.

"When are you done for the night?"

"Why, you want to make out?"

"No. But I just bought something from this guy under the bleachers and felt like I could use it right about now."

Pete smiles. "I like you, Daniel-san. Let's mosey."

I turn and leave the stadium—and Cadence—behind.

# CADENCE

I work my way through the crowd as everyone looks for a seat. "Coming through, coming through!" I call as I squeeze through them to get to Zach. "Make a hole!"

People get out of the way, or they don't. It takes a couple minutes for me to get to the home-side bleachers.

"Zach! *Zach!*"

He looks surprised to see me, but then he totally *smiles.* Awesome!

"What's up?" I lean against the short chain-link fence across from him. He's scored a great seat in the front.

"Just waiting for the game," Zach says.

"Who are you rooting for?"

"Uh . . ."

"Trick question! Just kidding. Unless you transferred from the Titans' school. You didn't, did you?"

"No. No, I'm a Spartan, born and raised."

"THIS! IS! SPARTA!" I shout, raising a fist.

That gets the attention of the first few rows. Some people give me You're Crazy looks, some people laugh, but a few shout it back at me or call out "Aroo!" which is so awesome.

Zach starts laughing out loud, and I love the sound of it.

"Can I just ask you something?" Zach says.

"Sure!"

"You're not . . . I mean, this is really you, right? You're not like *on* something."

"You mean drugs?"

"Well—yeah."

"No! Of course not. This is really me. You can ask my brother, or my parents, they'll tell you."

"Your brother go here?"

"He did. He graduated last year. Johnny Fuller, you know him?"

"Never met him. But everyone kind of knew him, I think. What's he up to?"

"Nothing, really. He said he's figuring himself out. He might also be lazy, except he has too much energy for that."

"Too much energy. So that's how you're related."

"Probably!"

The band starts playing an old rock and roll song from I think the fifties, but I can't remember the name of it. Our band sounds good, I like them. I watch them play for a few seconds, liking how the big brass tubas reflect the overhead field lights.

I turn to Zach to ask if he likes the band, too, when three girls come walking over. I recognize all three. They're the ones who drew on Vivian's face. And it looks like they all know Zach.

"Hey, Zach," Brianna says.

"Hey, Bree," Zach says.

The others say hi, and he says hi. I am not seen. They sashay down the front aisle of the bleachers before climbing stairs at the far end. They find seats at the top and start cheering our team to victory. Their shirts are artfully torn and knotted, showing off teeny tiny tummies and huge grown woman boobs. Well, everyone's showing off but Brianna Montaro. She walks with her shoulders rolled forward a bit, like she doesn't actually want anyone to be staring at her chest. But if that's the case, why wear such a revealing shirt? I am so confused.

"So you know them?" I ask Zach.

"Acquainted, mainly. I've got a couple classes with Bree."

"Oh, yeah! THE Brianna Montaro, right?"

"Yeah, why does everyone say it like that?"

I lift one boot, rest the sole against the chain-link behind me, and cross my arms badassedly. "Remember that girl I told you about who got that stuff written on her forehead in Sharpie? Brianna was in there. She was one of the ones who did it."

"What? No, come on."

"Scout's honor."

"That doesn't seem like her."

"Well, okay, she didn't actually do the writing, but she was in there with those other two when they did it. I would totally turn them in, too, except the girl who got wrote on told me not to. Her name's Vivi."

Zach, looking like he's not sure whether to believe me or not, starts to say something. But then a security guy in a yellow shirt yells at me to keep the aisle clear. "Sit down or move along!"

"I gotta go," I say. "I didn't mean to make you mad or anything."

"No, no, it's cool," Zach says. "I'm just surprised is all. Do you mind if I ask her about it?"

"Better not, I think. I mean, I can't stop you, but it might turn into a big thing."

"Sure, sure, that's cool."

The guard yells at me again. I put my foot down and step away from the fence. "Well, I think *you're* cool, so there."

"Thanks."

"No problem!" I wave and Zach nods back at me. He's got a little smile on his face, so that's good, right?

Happy with how that all went, except for the whole Brianna Montaro part, I cross behind the back end of the field. I look for Danny at the concession stand, but I can't find him anywhere. So I try looking around the gate where we came in. No Danny. Sad face!

I go back to the concession stand again. Still not anywhere. I need to put a bell on that kid!

I go back to the home-side bleachers. "So, hi again," I say to Zach.

"Hi again."

He seems pleased. Awesome!

"Can I sit here with you?"

"Sure." He scoots to one side and I squish myself next to him.

I spend the whole game with Zach. The team is losing, big time, but I think *I* kind of win. Well, except for Danny disappearing. Jerk!

So to make myself feel better, I jump right in and ask Zach, "You want to go out sometime?"

"Out, like, a date?" Zach says, like he's not sure he heard me.

"Sure! Or whatever it's called. I don't really know, I'll be honest. I've always gone on these group things with a bunch of people, which is all my dad would let me do, but now I think maybe he'd change his mind, since it's high school. Oh, sorry if this was a little out of nowhere."

Zach smiles in a weird way. I can't figure out what it means. I'm not very good at that. Telling what people are thinking from their expressions.

"Don't take this the wrong way," he says, kind of slowly, like he's not sure I can keep up. "But do you mind if I ask how old you are?"

"Oh! Fourteen. I'm a young'un. My birthday was the day before school started. My parents had to decide whether to make me the little kid or the big kid when I started school, and I ended up being the little kid."

Zach's smile changes again. Not in a bad way, I don't think.

"Gotcha. Uh . . . so . . . why don't we see where the year takes us? Maybe take some time. You know, *on* campus?"

"Sure! That's cool. Thanks!"

"No problem." Then he laughs a little, and I laugh, too, and we watch the game. Score!

Score for *me*, I mean. Our team doesn't score much at all.

# COACH

Culliver looks good. Too thin, but good. Walker is ready to eat the flesh off the Titans' bones. The Spartans need the win. He talked to Steve Butler about it earlier in the day, and Steve agrees: they need a win to start the season.

Brady needs it. Coach needs it. The school needs it.

He's distantly aware that the band is playing "Louie Louie," and it sends a fresh shot of adrenaline into his bloodstream. They play it the first game of every year. The band director has been here longer than Coach, longer than the last three principals combined. Coach isn't one to mess with tradition.

The Titans receive.

And the Titans score.

"God *damn it*," Coach says.

## FINAL SCORE

| Titans | 28 |
| SPARTANS | 06 |

*Humankind*

# DANNY

"I need a new phone," I say during breakfast Monday morning. "I lost mine last week, and I've looked everywhere. Or some-one took it."

"Suffer," Dad says.

So I try Mom.

She says, "I'm sorry, Danny, you just have to keep looking for now, or wait until we can get you new one."

Magnifico.

So I take something of Pete's at random and walk to school. Whatever I took, it slows me down. A lot. Which is nice. I traded some of my pills for some of his, and now it's like a game to see what'll happen when I take one. Or two. By the time I reach the parking lot, I do not give a good god damn about . . . let's see . . . yep. *Anything.* It's sort of freeing. I can't wait to see where this sort of freedom leads me today.

Maybe I'll try out for football.

# DREA

"Oh thank God," Kelly says when I climb into her truck Monday morning. "Someone I'm not related to."

"Rough morning?" I ask.

"Didn't I tell you?" Kelly scowls as she pulls out of my neighborhood. "I think my mom had my name legally changed to 'Pick Up The Baby.'"

I wrinkle my nose. "Sounds serious. Should I just call you PUT-B for short?"

Kelly laughs, which brings a smile to my own face. "You know," she says, turning left, "for someone in so much pain, you have the strangest ability to make me laugh."

I barely hear the last half of her sentence. "What?"

She blinks. "What."

"I'm not *in pain.*"

Her eyes widen as we roll to a stop at a light. "Um . . . yes you are."

"Why? Because I—" I gesture wildly because she knows the rest.

Except Kelly's not buying it. "Say it. Go ahead. See? You can't even say it. You cut yourself with razor blades, Drea."

*Not* just *razor blades*, I think, but choose not to say it because it sounds stupid even to me. Kelly accelerates through the green light, a little faster than usual for her.

"Healthy people don't do that," Kelly adds, quieter, but like she still wants me to hear it.

I don't like this. I do not, do not like this. "Maybe I should just walk from here."

"Oh, grow up," Kelly mutters. This time I can't tell if I am meant to hear it or not.

But I did, that's all that matters. "What the *hell*? Why are you even talking to me if I'm such a little kid, huh?"

Which sounds very much like a little kid and makes me blush, I can feel it. I want my **paperclip**.

I wait for Kelly to pull over and tell me to get out and walk already, which I don't actually want to do, and not just because school's still a few miles away. I wait for her to yell at me, but she doesn't do that either. Instead, she turns on her stereo and searches for a particular song without taking her eyes off the road. When the song starts, it's slow and melodic, and her voice cuts through my anger. I don't recognize the song, and I don't look at her, watching the city go by instead. Everyone's in a hurry to get to work and school, places they don't even want to really be.

We come to another light, gliding to a gentle stop in time with the last lingering note of the song.

I don't realize she's crying until I hear her sniffle. I turn to face her, stunned. Kelly never struck me as a crier. She's not wailing or anything, just twin streams of tears rolling down her face, her nose stuffy.

"I thought you were a ghost," she says.

"Huh?" I say, because, what else is there to say?

"The first day of school in the cafeteria," Kelly says, wiping her nose with the sleeve of her baseball shirt. "I could see your hair from like miles away. It looked just like my friend Chloe's. She dyed hers, but still. I just waved before I could even stop to think."

"You didn't mean to invite me to sit with you?"

Kelly shakes her head, and makes a sharp right into a Starbucks parking lot. "No, it wasn't like that, I just mean I *had* to see you. Talk to you. It was so weird at first."

I take that in. "So where is Chloe?"

"Portland. She graduated last year. We used to sing together, but then she moved and met this guy and won't call me back anymore and Mom had the twins and . . ."

She wipes her nose again.

"Coffee?" she asks.

I nod.

Kelly takes us through the drive-through, which has a long line so we have to sit there forever, not talking, while I try to figure out what this means, if anything.

She orders two tall hot coffees, nothing in them, without asking me. It's a bit annoying, but under the circumstances, I'm not going to complain, you know?

Back on the road toward school, Kelly finally says, "Nobody sees me. And the ones who do are either asking me to wipe up baby shit, or calling me stuff like Mister Kelly or Kelly the Man or 'chickdude.' It's not a good place to be. You were nice to me. And you trusted me with your—" She mimics my earlier gesture. "You know."

I nod again. I get it. I get not being seen. But I don't know how to say it.

Instead, I say, "All right. Thank you for the coffee."

"You're welcome. Are we okay?"

"Yeah."

"Cool."

We drive into the school parking lot and Kelly pulls into an empty space. "Quite the odd little friendship we have brewing here, huh?" she says and slowly grins, holding up her coffee. "*Brewing.* Get it?"

I laugh out loud and it startles me, because I have not heard my own laugh in a long time.

# DANNY

"So someone tell me what the play is about," Mrs. Garcia says in English first period, and I can tell I smile. But very, very, very slowly. I am

MELLOW.

"Revenge," a kid says.

"Good. What does Hamlet want?"

"Revenge!" three or four kids say. They must think this is one of those surprise extra-credit games.

"Ah, does he?" Mrs. Garcia says in that sly way of a teacher who's hooked a class. "Think about it. If Hamlet merely wants revenge for his father's assassination, if that were his only goal—what would he do? What would *you* do?"

"Pop a cap in his ass," someone says sarcastically.

"Yes!" Mrs. Garcia says over the class's laughter. "I can't tell if you were guessing or not, Miles, but you're right. If all he really wanted was revenge, Hamlet would kill Claudius as soon as he spoke to his father's ghost. But he doesn't. So what else is going on here? Anyone?"

"He wants the king to know who did it," I say. It feels like the words come out in a thick syrup.

Everyone turns.

Gasp!

The kid in back exists!

And can speak!

Glory be!

"Good, good," Mrs. Garcia says, gliding closer to me. "Keep going."

I shrug. This is stuff I got last year at my real school. "Everyone loves Claudius. Everyone thinks he's this hotshot. But he's not. And only Hamlet knows the whole story."

"Excellent!" Mrs. Garcia says. Virtually apoplectic that I might be

LEARNING SOMETHING.

So I play along. What the hell. Maybe she'll bump up my grade. "And another thing. Hamlet's not about to kill himself. That's a myth. Or maybe just bad teaching."

I don't mean it to sound insulting to Garcia, but some of the dumbasses go, "Ooooo!"

Jesus, what is it with these people? Are we in kindergarten?

But Garcia only smiles, and she means it. "I agree. Why do you think that?"

"Well, for one, just like if he only wanted revenge, he'd kill Claudius. If he just wanted to die, he could do it. No one can stop you if you *really* decide to kill yourself. Plus, he spends so much time making people think he's crazy—setting up the play, staging the fight with Laertes . . . he's not going anywhere anytime soon. He's got business with the king."

For some reason, the classroom is silent when I'm done. God, now what'd I do?

"That," Mrs. Garcia says, "is very astute. I hope you all were taking notes."

Grumbling, moaning, papers shuffling. Great. Now they're pissed.

Well played.

Get it?

PLAYED.

Jesus.

# BRADY

Mom says his name is Pat. Patrick.

"Do you know his last name?" I ask.

"Oh, shut up," Mom says.

Patrick is sitting at the kitchen table. He smirks. Takes a slow drag off a menthol. I want to shove it into his face.

"Get my money from Dad yet?" I ask. "It usually comes today."

Mom flaps her arms. Sighs. Rolls her eyes. The most stressed out person on the planet. "You know we need that for rent," she says.

"Or food."

"Yeah, or food."

"Or menthols. Or a hit."

Arms flap. Eyes roll. "Brady, I swear to God."

Patrick says, "You should be nice to your mom, pal."

"You're not my pal."

"But I'm the next closest thing you got to a dad, so I say be nice to your mom."

I make a fist under the table. Smile. Ask, "Is that right?"

# COACH

Brady Culliver doesn't show up for weight room third period Monday. God damn.

Coach calls Donte over before D hits the showers. "Heard from Brady?"

"Not yet, Coach."

"See him over the weekend?"

"Not since review. I been picking him up at Starbucks in the morning, but today he never showed. I went by his place, but nobody answered."

Coach nods, fighting an urge to spit his worry and anger against the shower room tile. After their smothering by the Titans, the Saturday morning game review was a somber gathering. A bunch of dispirited Spartans acting nothing like their namesakes.

"No texts, nothing?" Coach persists.

"Sorry, Coach. I been trying."

"All right. Look, track him down, will ya?"

"On it. Might not be till sixth, though."

"Sure." Coach gives D a firm grip on one shoulder before retreating into his office. Brady barely spoke during review, even when spoken to. Coach took it easy on him; maybe too easy, he thinks now. Maybe the kid needed a kick in the ass. Every player is different. Opening the season with a loss has hit everyone hard. But there's plenty of room to come back if they can all keep their heads in the game.

*That includes you*, Coach thinks.

It doesn't occur to him until lunch that Brady Culliver isn't the only no-show today. Danny Jennings was missing from PE second period.

God damn.

# DANNY

*Athleaders.*

This is an actual word they use. Oh my moist and chewy God, they really do. Athleaders. Athletes Who Lead.

My second phoneless Monday continues with usual fanfare as I move between bodies to get to my locker after third period. A bunch of Athleader football players are headed my way. Glorious. I brace for impact.

"Skinny little faggot," one of them whispers. He's wearing a school jersey with his name on the back. Walker.

Times have changed. It used to be they could just shout it and no one would care. But now "faggot" has supplanted the other F-word as the worst possible thing you can say in public. So they have to whisper it, like the church kids do when they talk about Jesus.

Skinny little faggot. It's the best these pole-smokers can come up with. I should put on more weight, like Dad said. Get really huge, really enormous, because *fat faggot* has that sort of sibilance to it that *skinny little faggot* lacks.

I stop and turn.

"What, am I the only piece of ass you can get, you colossal virgin?"

See, it's all about hitting them where it hurts. And that one hurt, I can see it on his face. But I guess I'll be hurting in a second as the Athleader comes barreling at me with murder on his mind, chewing hard on his lower lip. Nobody questions his hetero virility; no one, I say!

The attack is stopped by none other than Dr. Flores, our principal, as he appears in the hallway. The giant Athleader falters and spins quickly to walk the other direction.

Dr. Flores looks down at me and says, "Daniel, right?"

"Danny."

"Well Danny, there's someone I'd like you to meet."

And that's how one week in, I'm talking to the school shrink. Dr. Hanson's office is in the admin building, one of a whole hallway's worth of tiny rooms. Interesting that the athletic offices here are larger than the offices of people charged with running the entire school. Priorities, indeed.

I stretch out in a yellow stuffed chair, crossing my feet and banging them together. The chains on my shoes bounce and jangle. It takes three seconds for this to annoy the secretary, who sends me Mean Old Lady vibes over the tops of her rimless glasses.

I stop bouncing. She hasn't done anything to me.

A few minutes later, Dr. Hanson pokes her head out. "Danny? Come on in."

I slip into her office and sit in the vinyl seat across from her desk. She has pictures of dogs tacked to a corkboard. I don't know what kind. They're not yippy dogs, anyway. Too big. And Dr. Hanson's not hard to look at. Her hair is too long though. I like it short. Like Cadence's.

*Cadence.* God, I can't stop thinking her name, or saying it when no when can hear.

"How are you feeling today, Danny?" Dr. Hanson says, smiling.

"Magnifico." I cross my ankle over my knee.

Still smiling, she says, "Sarcasm doesn't become you."

"Sure it does."

Her grin fades. I regret it, but only for a second. She takes out a notepad.

"I was just getting ready to call you in. I guess Dr. Flores thought sooner would be better, hmm?"

I click my teeth and shoot her with my finger. *Click, bang.*

"I've got your health records here . . . how're the meds treating you?"

*Like a skinny little faggot,* I think.

"Fine," I say.

I do not add that they fetch a fair price from Pete, who is apparently going to buy his way through my entire allotment. Pete's got a booming business charging twice what he pays me for them. It's a fair deal, and puts money I need in my pocket. Plus I never take the god damn things, anyway. He's traded a few with me already. I've built a good stash of some nice pops. Everybody wins.

"No side effects?"

I pretend to consider, while actually trying to recall everything I've read online about the side effects of my prescriptions. "Headache," I recite slowly. "A little dizzy sometimes."

She nods seriously, buying it. Jesus.

"How about your emotions? Pretty regular stuff?"

I nod-frown-shrug, all one motion.

"How's school?"

My stomach clenches.

"Splendiferous," I say after a pause, and force a smile.

She rewards me with a laugh. It breaks my concentration so I make a mistake. "Why am I the one on medication?" I ask. "Why not them? What did I do?"

"Who?"

"Them," I gesture pointlessly to a wall, and beyond it, the school and the wide world. "Everyone else. I mean, I get called all sorts of heinous shit, but when I defend myself, I get dragged to the school psych. No offense."

"None taken. So, you're having trouble with some other students? Or teachers?"

Am I having trouble? Well, let's see. Where should I begin?

I decide not to begin at all. What's the point.

"No, of course not," I say. "Here? Certainly not."

Dr. Hanson gives me an exaggerated, *I'm studying you closely* sort of look. "Who are some of your friends?"

"I don't know. This guy Pete. This girl Cadence. That's pretty much it right now."

"Do they relax you? What I mean is, is it stressful to be around them?"

I think about Cadence. That smile of hers, those ridiculously round eyes, and how she never has a bad thing to say about anything. How does she *do* that? "No," I say, accidentally honest. "I like being around them."

"Good," Dr. Hanson says. "I wonder if maybe you need some more of that. Have you thought about getting more involved at school? Are there any clubs that sound interesting?"

I snap back to reality. If that's what this is. "Is there a mime club? I could just be sort of quiet and white-faced and annoy the shit out of . . . oh, wait. Just described my normal day. Drat the luck."

But she seizes on it. "There's drama. You could try that. There are auditions tomorrow after school for a little show, I think. Would you consider at least checking it out?"

"I suppose . . ."

"Just give it a shot. It will you do you some good. I bet you're really good at it."

"That was never a question."

She doesn't know what to do with that. I slap my hands down on the arms of the chair. "My work here is finished."

"Danny, wait."

I wait.

"Listen," Dr. Hanson says. Earnestly. "In three years, none of these people will be in your life anymore. You can forget all about them, stop spending all this time being angry with them. You're young and have your whole life to look forward to. Try not to waste it on things that don't matter."

"Like sports?"

No response.

"Just checking. Bye now."

Dr. Hanson looks like she's not sure I'm allowed to leave, since I was hand-delivered by the principal. But she relents and gives me a pass back to class.

En route, I catch a poster advertising for the auditions. The "little show" Dr. Hanson mentioned is *Hamlet*. By some unknown scribbler named William Shakespeare.

A "little show." Good God. What are the qualifications for her job? Robust illiteracy? Basic western cultural ignorance?

I miss my real school.

# VIVI

"How was your weekend?" Sam asks as he falls into step beside me on the way to lunch.

I sidestep away. "Okay."

"Bad day?" Sam says. "You look upset."

I shake my head and walk faster. Sam keeps up.

"Do you want to have lunch? I mean, together."

I veer to one wall, cutting people off. No one yells at me, though. Sam follows along until we're out of the way of foot traffic.

"With Brianna?" I say, not too loud, but loud enough so he hears me.

"*Brianna?* No. Not by any stretch of the imagination." And instead of getting mad or defensive, he smiles.

I consider his answer for a second. "And . . . you're not going out anymore?"

"Oh my God, Vivi, no. It was a year ago."

THE Brianna Montaro walks by just then with a group of her friends. They all look alike to me. Brianna happens to see me and Sam standing together, and gives us a double take. I move just a little bit closer to him, and make sure she sees me do it. Sam doesn't notice her because his back is to them.

After they've turned a corner, I gaze up into Sam's eyes. He is still smiling. Then I look down at his hands and, carefully, like I might get burned, take one of his in mine. I feel him watching me do it. Once I've got his hand in mine, he tightens his grip, just a bit.

Not looking up, I say, "What're they serving today?"

"Nothing delicious."

"Okay," I say. "Can we eat it outside?"

# CADENCE

I run into Danny heading for the doors leading out to the student parking lot. He's walking with a guy wearing a kilt. A kilt! I don't know whether to be impressed or to make him go home and change before someone beats him up. But it's exactly the kind of thing I could see Danny wearing, so it kind of makes sense they'd be hanging out. Danny, on the other hand, is only wearing some jeans and a plain black T-shirt. I barely recognize him without his armor!

"Danny!"

He stops, one hand on the handle. I can't read his expression, but then Dad says I usually don't anyway. I don't know if that's a good thing or a bad thing.

I run up to them, my bag banging into my kidney with every step. Ouch. I hope he appreciates that.

"Where you going?"

With a shrug that seems kind of forced, he says, "Ditch. Go get high."

"Dude!" the kilt guy says.

"It's okay, she's cool."

"Clearly not as cool as you are," I say, making fun of him.

Danny doesn't get it. "You want to come?"

"No. You know ditching is against the rules, right?"

"Come on," Danny says. "It'll be fun."

"Nah. I laugh enough, I don't need help." To the kilt guy, I say, "Hi, I'm Cadence, by the way."

"I've heard," Kilt Guy says, and it's kind of smarmy. Danny gives him a warning look. Hey, maybe I'm better at guessing looks than Dad says!

"What's your name?" I ask.

"Pete. What's yours?"

"Cade . . . I just told you!"

This makes Pete laugh. I can't quite tell if I'm supposed to be in on the joke, or if he's making fun of me.

So I go, "Well, don't get caught and don't do anything too stupid," and start to go to class. Except suddenly Danny yells my name and comes running up to me.

"Hey," he says, all serious. "He was just messing around. Don't be mad."

"I'm not mad."

"Are you sure?"

"Danny, if there's one thing I'm absolutely sure of, it's that I would never lie to you."

"Really."

"Really! I don't lie. It's stupid."

"Okay," he says, like he doesn't believe me. Then he says it again like he *does*. Then he says, "So come with us then."

"I don't ditch, either."

"You *haven't*. That's not necessarily the same thing."

The warning bell rings. Great, now I'll be late. I *guess* I could go with them. It's an art class, not my best subject but not one that will destroy my career if I get a B or a C. At least they're asking me to hang out, which is more than I can say for anyone else so far.

And it's only this once, right?

So I say, "Well, it's only this once, right?"

Danny says, *almost* smiling, "Yep. Come on."

I'm gonna make that kid smile one day if it kills me! We go back to the double doors where Pete is still waiting. He doesn't seem to mind that I'm tagging along. We rush out to the parking lot, and I follow Pete to an old blue CR-V. Danny hurries into the back seat. Wow. Mister Chivalry, who'd've thunk it?

So I get into shotgun. Pete puts the car in reverse without looking behind him, and already I'm scared for my life. I pull my seat belt on, and notice Danny doing the same. Pete, not so much.

After a squealing left-hand turn out of the parking lot, Pete takes us to the open road. He snaps his phone into a stereo adapter and asks me, "You like Floyd?"

"Who's Floyd? I don't think I've met him."

In slow motion, Pete turns in the driver's seat to gape at me. Oncoming traffic? Pshaw, they'll get out of his way.

"GEE-zus!" he says. "Are you . . . *Dude!* Okay. That's it."

Pete, still not caring much about traffic, starts swiping through his phone. A minute later, a song starts. At least, I think it's a song. There's just lots of bells and alarms going off, like a school day wake-up call from Hell.

"Wow, this is just great," I say. Sarcastically.

"Shut up," Pete says. "Just listen, all right? No talking, just— *God!* Just listen."

So I shut up and Just Listen while Pete swerves around cars to get to Taco Bell.

# DONTE

With an unspoken go-ahead from Coach to not worry about my sixth-period elective, I drive my new-old car straight to Brady's, thinking about that punk-ass kid in hallway earlier. It's been pissing me off all day. Man, he's a lucky little bitch. That mouth on that kid needs some serious closing. I'll figure what's up with B, make sure he's cool, then maybe next week sometime, me and B will have a chat with him.

Brady's neighborhood is a wreck. My own won't be making the cover of *Hot Shit* magazine anytime soon, but it's kept up. People care where I live. Out here, caring is like trust and hope. No one can afford them.

I pull up in front of B's house and take a look around before getting out of the car. The street seems empty enough, but bad things can happen quickly. Lots of people around here need a hit or some cash, and they're not afraid to take it.

Jogging to the front door, I give my chin a confident lift and narrow my eyes, hoping to look badass enough to keep back any potential threats. I pound on the door.

"Hey, Brady!"

No response. I pound again with a hammer fist, and the cheap wood trembles.

"Brady, man! It's D, open up."

Damn. Nothing. I try the doorknob, and while it turns easily, the wood seems stuck; square-peg-round-hole. I give it a little shove, and it cracks open.

"B?"

The house is quiet, but it feels like there's someone here.

"Don't anybody shoot me, all right?" It's only partly a joke.

A yellow sheet hangs as a curtain in the front window, covering up shattered and tattered blinds. The sagging couch is cratered with cigarette burns. Two Chinese food takeout boxes sit on a garage sale coffee table, crumbs calcified at the bottom.

I move cautiously toward the kitchen. And I find out Brady is dead.

"B!"

Brady looks up from his position on the floor. Not dead. He's sitting against the fridge, hands limp on his lap. The kitchen table is on its side, and one wooden chair is utterly shattered. Brady's fingers bleed, and there's a cut over his left eye.

"Sup, D."

I take stock of the kitchen real quick, and listen hard. We seem to be alone.

"Hey, man," I say. "What's going on?"

"I gotta be nice to my mother."

I hunker down beside B. "That right?"

"That's what Pat said. He actually said I need to be nice to my mother."

I don't bother asking who Pat is. Odds are he's another of B's mom's boyfriends-slash-sugar daddies. Mostly that means any guy she's willing to blow who'll spend money on her. Keep her up on whatever she's smoking or drinking this week.

"Like he's my dad," Brady goes on, staring blankly at the

tips of his shoes. They're from last year. I recognize a tiny blue star penned there by Brianna at lunch during first semester of junior year.

Some kids already have a second car by now. Not a lot. But some. Some of our friends.

They sure as hell have newer shoes.

"Mom took Dad's check again," Brady says. "Can you believe that shit? I'm the one guy in the world whose dad actually pays up, and she goes and takes it. Every time, man."

"You're bleeding, B."

"Oh, I beat the shit out of 'im. Can't throw a football, but I can beat his sorry ass."

"He call the cops?"

"Kiddin' me? Asshole's prolly got warrants five states deep."

"We gotta fix your hands, man," I say, eyeing the blood dripping down Brady's fingers. I can see now it comes from scrapes on his knuckles. Like they say, I can't help but wonder what the other guy looks like.

"Those are money makers right there, huh?" I say. "We gotta keep them taken care of. 'Cause you *can* throw the ball, man. Trust me."

Brady doesn't answer.

"I gotta get you back to school. Coach is asking."

That shakes Brady enough to get him on his feet. I make him wash his hands in the sink, where piles of food-encrusted plates sit. Something brown and crisp pops off the edge of a bowl and falls into the drain, and for some reason, it makes me gag.

I find a passably clean rag in one of the kitchen drawers, and tell B to push it against the cut over his eye, saying, "We'll clean it up in the locker room."

"Yeah, okay," B says.

Together we leave the house and get into my new-old car. I drive through Taco Bell on the way back to school. Cheapest food on the run. Brady takes his share and tears into it, and neither one of us says anything because we don't have to.

# CADENCE

Pete screams along with a "Floyd" song that warns us all that we're one day closer to death.

"Well this is cheerful," I shout over the music.

Pete giggles insanely.

Danny says, "So, what, you're saying the Ramones are cheerful? Because beating on kids with a baseball bat, that's delightful. The Ku Klux Klan kidnapping babies? Ah, another wholesome classic."

I turn down the volume. Pete snaps, "Hey!"

I ignore him and turn in my seat to look at Danny, sitting behind the driver seat. "I thought you didn't like the Ramones."

A super fast expression zips past Danny's face. Like guilt, or surprise, or something. I don't know. Then he gives a little fake I'm-totally-badass sniff and looks out the window.

"Been listening."

"Been listening, huh? Well, good. I'm glad to see you're finally getting some good music into your life."

Pete says, "Floyd is all you need to know. Ever."

"You're the boss." I face forward again, pretty pleased with myself.

Pete drives us through a Taco Bell. I wonder when the getting high part happens, but I'm not about to ask. Maybe they've forgotten about it. That would be awesome.

"Ah, shit, would you look at that?" Pete says. "Right behind a meathead mobile. We'll be here for days."

"Say what?" I ask.

He nods at the car in front of us in line at the drive-through. "Coupla sportos. Donte Walkins and Brady Gulliver or something. Figures. They'll probably clean the place out. Gotta bulk up for the big game and all."

"Got to keep their energy up for date raping the cheer team," Danny says.

"They do?" I twist around to look at Danny. "I mean, they really do that?"

Danny coughs. I think like it's supposed to be a laugh or something. "Pretty *sure . . .*"

"'Pretty sure' isn't the same as sure. If you're sure then you should report it."

Now he won't blink. He just stares at me. "That's—that's not the point—"

"It is the point. You can't joke about things like that. Okay?"

Danny looks away. "Great, sure. Okay, wait, how about this: they are the kind of fetid assholes who *would* do something like that—is that better?"

"I don't get it," I say. "What'd they do to you?"

Somehow it gets really, really cold in the car, and it's not the air-conditioning.

"I gotta get high," Pete says, shaking his head.

Danny's glaring at me like I kicked his puppy, but he doesn't say anything. I turn back around to face front.

The boys in the car in front of us are handed a Taco Bell bag the size of a grocery sack. I have never in my life seen an order that big. They pull out, and we move forward. A grumpy girl hands Pete a bag, and off we go, Pete cranking up his "Floyd" while we drive. Nobody says anything, and I get the feeling it's my fault, but what did I say that was so bad?

Pete drives us back toward school, but instead of going all the way there he pulls into a parking lot attached to a city park. There aren't many people around, probably because it's still pretty hot out, but every once in a while someone rides by on a bike.

Pete passes the bag of food to Danny, who pulls out a steak burrito. He glances at me, pretends like he didn't, then lifts the sack my way.

"Want any? It's soft tacos."

"Okay. Thanks."

Danny shrugs fast, like it doesn't matter. That kid, I swear.

"Holy *crud*!" Pete roars. "How do you mess up a bean burrito?"

He's scowling at the wilting burrito in his hand. I start laughing. Danny successfully manages not to.

"No, I mean, for real," Pete goes on. "Fried beans. Tortilla. Done. How does someone screw that up, I mean, *gee*-zus!"

"Maybe someone pissed in it," Danny offers.

Pete thinks about this for a second, then takes an enormous bite to test Danny's theory. He sloshes the food in his mouth for a minute before talking around it. "Nah, I don't taste any piss."

That sends first me then Pete into laughs. When the food's gone, Pete rolls down his window and lights up a joint. Gross. I roll my window down too. So does Danny.

"This bother you?" Pete says, barely, in that holding-your-breath sort of way.

"Don't know yet." I cover my nose and mouth with my T-shirt. "I can puke on your floor, right?"

"Be my guest."

Pete passes the smoke back to Danny, who I think looks at me first before taking a long hit from it.

Boring. I start thinking about the two boys who'd been in the car in front of us, wondering if they do this, too. Or maybe they drink a lot. That's what TV and movies make it seem like. Then I think about the kind of girls they probably date, and if it's really true they all go out with cheerleaders. Then that makes me think of the girls from the restroom who wrote on Vivi's forehead.

The joint is half gone by the time I ask, "Do you guys know a girl named Brianna Montaro?"

"Psh, yeah," Danny says. "She's a slut bag."

Pete laughs, and it's that stupid pothead screech like Johnny used to get. It bugs the crap out of me. Danny does not laugh. He's starting to look sleepy.

"How do you know her?" I ask Danny.

"Hangs out with my sister and people like that. You know—slut bags."

Pete laughs again. So I ask him, "You know her, too?"

"Yeah. Since like, kindergarten," Pete says. "Total tight-ass. She got kind of cool for a bit sophomore year, dating this one guy, but then she turned all bitch-face again. Even worse than before, actually."

"Sounds right. They're all alike. One big happy-ass sorority." Danny looks at his shoes like they've done something wrong to him. "Why?"

"Just curious. It seems like everyone knows who she *is*, but no one *knows* her."

"That's deep," Pete says, and belches.

I can feel Danny giving me some kind of stinkeye, but I don't look back. If he has something to say, he can go ahead and say it.

# DANNY

Tuesday morning after a shower, I put on a collared shirt and a tie. A navy jacket that I think fits pretty well. Nice pants, and my only pair of dress shoes.

It has the desired effect.

"What's the occasion?" Mom says when I come in for breakfast, instantly suspicious.

I pour cereal. "Must there be one?"

Mom sighs, as if I've given her a terrible migraine. Surely, not I!

Dad minces no words as he comes sprinting in. He stops short upon seeing me, closes his eyes, and says, "God damn it, now what?"

"Good morning, Father!"

"I don't know," Dad mutters. "I just don't know."

"Can't a guy look nice once in a while?" I say, adding milk to the bowl.

"Stop it!" Mom says. Whoa. "What are you up to?"

"Maybe I'm trying to earn a promotion."

"To what?" Mom says—

—just as Dad tries to stop her. "Don't ask him."

"Well, I figure if you see me put forth some effort, like you always say, then maybe before Christmas comes around, you'll let me go back to my real school."

"No," Dad says.

"Oh, because things are going so swimmingly at this one?"

"Because it was a privilege you abused," Dad says. "It's way the hell out and gone from home, but we took you, Danny. Every day. Then you lost control of yourself, and now this is what happens."

"You're the one who *gave* me the—"

"I'm not having this conversation." Dad takes his enormous ring of keys off the peg on the wall and goes out to the garage. Without even telling us he loves us.

The agony.

I walk to school—as usual—and get honked and yelled at—as usual—this time for wearing the tie. Gosh, it's like you can't please some people. I light a cigarette from a pack I got from Pete, and don't flick it away until I'm practically inside the school. Nobody notices. Or maybe they do, and I don't notice them noticing. Either way.

But other than that, it's a pretty calm morning for a change. I almost don't know what to do with it. Then I get nervous, thinking that maybe it's some kind of calm before a storm. Turns out I'm right about that, because right after my third-period bio class starts, a student assistant comes in and summons me to Dr. Flores's office.

*Dun dun dun!* At least the class doesn't do that *Ooooo!* bullshit. I'll give them points for that.

The TA takes off on some other errand so I pop one of Pete's pills and roam the halls in the general direction of the admin offices. There's a girls' PE class going on downstairs in the gymnasium, and I find myself in desperate need of a water balloon launcher. Of course, the windows don't open and I wouldn't use plain water to fill the balloons . . . but it's fun to think about and I'm still smiling a little when I walk into admin and take a seat outside Dr. Flores's office.

I clear my throat and sink down into the stuffed yellow chair, left ankle over right knee. When the principal's door opens, it's not Dr. Flores I see. It's a uniformed cop.

I stop smiling.

"It was just a cigarette," I say, thinking that must be what got me here.

"Daniel Jennings?" the cop says.

"Uh—yeah?"

"Come on in."

He steps aside. The secretary doesn't look at me. Like how you pretend to be distracted when your friend is getting yelled at by his parents.

So I Come On In, and the cop closes the door behind me. Dr. *Floor* is clearly not having a good day. I take the time to point this out to him.

"Have a seat, Danny," Dr. Floor says.

"Thanks, I'd rather st—"

"Sit down."

Okay, so it's like that then. I sit. "Like the tie? I'm turning over a new leaf."

I'm the only one who finds this amusing. The cop holds up an iPhone in a red case, decorated on the back in black Sharpie:

The MacDougall Clan logo, and assorted straight-line curves and other doodles.

"Is this your phone?"

"Yeah!" I say, relieved. "I've been looking for it since last week, where'd you find it?"

"You have not had this phone all week," the cop says—like it should be a question but it's not.

"Uh—yeah?"

"Starting when?"

"Monday. Last Monday."

"Any way you can prove that? Did you file a police report?"

"Because a lot of kids who lose phones file police reports. Jesus, dude. No, I didn't."

My wit is lost on him. "You tell anyone you lost it?"

"My mom and dad. This girl Cadence. I was trying to get her number 'cause she's super cute, and—"

"We can check with his parents," Dr. Floor says to the cop.

I look from him to the cop. "Can I have my phone back?"

"No," the cop says. "Right now it's being held as evidence."

That word is serrated like a blade. "Evidence of what?"

"There's a nude photo of a boy on this phone," the cop says. "Know anything about that?"

"*Jesus*, no! Why would I have—what kind of boy? I mean, are you talking about like a little kid or something, because, dude—"

"It's another student," Dr. Floor says to me. "Elias Clarke. Do you know him? Was it a joke?"

"I've never heard of him!"

I can't tell what the cop is thinking as he studies me. I hold up my hands. "Look, I have no idea what you are talking about. That is my phone, but I lost it last week. So help me God."

"It's child pornography," the cop says.

Yeah, this is a little worse trouble than I'm used to. "Good to know, except that I didn't do it, and I still don't know what you're talking about."

The cop and Dr. Floor trade a glance. "Okay," the cop says. "We're looking into it. You'll probably get a call from a detective before too long."

"Great. Except *you have my phone.* Genius." I'm starting to feel the same way I did last time I was in a principal's office with a cop. The rage is building.

"You can go back to class," Dr. Floor says. "I'm sure we'll get it worked out. But, Danny, a nude photo of a boy in the school showers is a very serious crime, even if you only meant it as a joke."

"Whoa, back up," I say. "It was taken here? In the locker room?"

Dr. Floor leans forward, ready for my big confession. "That's correct. Do you want to add anything to your story?"

So I lean forward, too, elbows on my knees. "Dr. Flores," I say carefully, "do you really think. I spend. One *nanosecond.* In the locker room showers. Of this fine institution?"

I see doubt cross his face like a shadow.

"Do you want to ask the coach to confirm?" I keep going. "I can't sit through a gym class, much less spend time in the locker room. Come on. How many times have you seen me right here in your office during PE, for fuck's sake?"

Dr. Floor makes some noise and looks at the cop. "That is true."

"Okay," the cop says. "Like I said, we'll be investigating. Thanks for coming in."

Dr. Flores hands me a hall pass with a reminder not to swear. I take it and walk out. I go out into the hall, which is empty. Across from me, taped to the wall, a yellow poster announces auditions for *Hamlet*.

Shakespeare's greatest revenge play! the poster reads.

"To be or not to be . . . in this place for one more minute," I say to the poster.

My pill kicks in right about then, and I feel better. Mostly.

The bell rings, and the halls flood suddenly with foot traffic. The way this pill makes me feel, whatever it is, I just want to float along with the crowd, or maybe be lifted up on top of them like at a concert.

But then there's the quarterback. The old QB himself, Brady Shitbag Culliver.

Need I say more?

Apparently a meme went out that I didn't catch, seeing as how my phone was stolen to take kiddie porn shots in a place I would never enter lest I burst into flame.

The meme must have said something like, "Call the Jennings kid a skinny little faggot at every opportunity," because that's what this QB calls me as I pass him in the hall. Just like last time. Same method, too: passing in the hall, spoken quietly so as not to catch the ear of anyone who might actually have to do something about it.

So I stop. Pivot.

"Explain something to me," I say over the noise of people rushing to get to class.

It takes QB a second to register I'm actually saying something back. I don't think he's used to it.

Good. So much the better.

"If I wore padded tights," I say, loudly, "and smacked guys on the ass, and dove into big piles of huge, sweaty men, and afterward spent time naked in a shower with them all, you'd call me a . . . what?"

The hall crowd slows, then stops to watch. It's like an old filmstrip losing power and freezing on one frame. The football player looks about ready to explode.

I may have crossed the line. No, wait . . . I am pole-vaulting over that motherfucking line because that's what needs to happen here. It stops. I'm deciding, right now, I'm not taking this shit anymore.

And it's about time, right? The good news is, I'm so high right now that I don't feel a thing. Not even an inkling of nerves, not a whiff of self-preservation. Hopefully, when he smashes my face to crimson pulp, I won't feel that, either.

I simply and gloriously do not give a galactic shit.

"Seriously," I say. "What would you call me? Say it nice and loud so everyone can hear."

The guy shakes. I can literally see him quaking.

"No?" I say. "Nothing? What, you don't want to say it now, or you just can't process things fast enough? You must ace those standardized tests, huh?"

You could hear a number two pencil snap in the silence. Then a hand lands on my shoulder. It's a teacher. Mr. Butler. Or Bladder, or Ballsack, or something. Same guy who interrupted us last time, now that I think about it. His button-up is lavender today.

"You should get to class, Danny," he says, very softly.

"Oh, sorry, I'm having a conversation right now." I do not take my eyes off QB.

"You should really get to class." The teacher's hand tightens on my shoulder.

I decide I'm done with jerk-off teachers, too.

I look pointedly down at that hand on me. "And this is assault. I haven't done anything wrong. I'm only asking our star Athleader here when he thinks it is appropriate to use the word 'faggot' in a sentence. Using small words, of course."

"It's never appropriate," the teacher says. He tries to pull me away. "Now, it's time to go to class."

I pull my shoulder back. His hand glides off. "Don't touch me, dick."

I get a few gasps for that one. Meh. The downside to these pills is, since I don't care about anything, I don't care when I get a good reaction, either. Bummer.

"So come on, I'm waiting," I say to QB.

The hand lands again. It means business. It's Business Hand.

"Let's go," Mr. Bladder says.

"Whatever you say, boss," I say, and let him turn me around.

"*I'll see you later!*" the star Athleader says.

"You see me now, nothing's stopping you," I call back. I pause for just the right length of time before adding, "Candy-ass bitch."

Not because that's something I would normally say. To anyone. It's just not in my oeuvre. The thing is, I know what buttons to push. I could've called him any number of great things, but *candy-ass* . . . now that's a symphony. That's the thing that will stick with him. That's the thing that will drive him into the red.

I walk away from Mr. Ballsack and head for Hanson's office. Mr. Bladder tries to stop me.

"I'm going to see the shrink," I tell him. "She'll explain everything, I'm sure."

Mr. Bladder escorts me to her office nonetheless. When I get there, they hold a hurried, whispered conversation in the hallway while I sink into the chair opposite her desk. So cushiony. So soft.

"Danny. *Danny.*"

I open my eyes. Holy crap, how long was I asleep?

"Wake up," Hanson says, sitting at her desk with a sigh.

"You bet, Doc."

"Let's start with what I sincerely hope is the easy question. What are you wearing?"

"Clothes."

"Danny . . ."

"What."

"Those aren't your usual clothes."

"But I'm a teenager." I can tell my words are coming out slowly. I wonder if she notices. I wonder if I care.

Mmm . . . nope.

"I'm experimenting with many different styles of self-expression. Isn't that what we're supposed to do?"

"Sometimes you are very upsetting, Danny."

"And sometimes you give me a hard-on, but I elect not to tell you about it."

Dr. Hanson laces her fingers together and leans forward over the desk. "Not only is that immature and offensive, it's also criminal. I could have you suspended for that comment, right here and now, no question, do you understand that?"

Ah, hell. She's not kidding. That's some true shit right there. I shift gears to throw her off: "Why don't you call my parents? See what they think of that idea."

"Danny . . ."

"And actually, I think you have to have a trial or something. Or a hearing, with the school board and everything. You really have time for that?"

"If you don't stop using provocative language, yes."

"Fine. No one's stopping you. Although now that you mention it, how is kicking someone out of a school when they don't want to be *at* that school considered a punishment?"

"Have you been taking your medication?"

"Religiously. Can't you see how calm and rational I've become?"

"Danny . . ."

The slowness disappears from my voice. It comes out strong now. Hell yeah.

"*What?* Jesus, you keep saying my name with ellipses, finish the thought! What do you want? I changed my clothes, I didn't lose my temper on that assjack in the hall, what the hell do you want? Everything I try gets shot down, so what do you people want? Huh? Spell it out, and I'll do it, just leave me the Christ alone!"

Well, she lets that sit for a while before saying, "Auditions start today. Are you going?"

"That's why I dressed up."

She can't tell if I'm serious. Thing is, I am. More or less.

"Stop trying to figure me out," I say. "I'll do the math for you. I had this great school, and I want to go back to it. The end, close the file. Send me back, Doc."

"I'm glad you'll be trying out."

"Magnifico. Lovely chatting with you." I get up and walk out. Because the truth is, they can't really stop you from doing that. I think about taking another pill, except now I'm getting jazzed up. Blood's pumping. Screw it. I'm going to the audition like this. It'll be fun.

Something has to be.

# AFTER SCHOOL

A lot of schools don't care about their speech and theater departments. This one? Is no different. Except over the last decade, since Mrs. Tanner began teaching, this department has an 8-2 record of placing at state competitions. Four times, they won first. Best in the state.

Everyone knows that Day One of auditions for the fall play is for the kids with heartbreaking lisps, or who can't speak louder than a whisper, or who have body funk that's too hard to overcome. It's for the kids who can barely read but think they are ready for Hollywood. It's also for kids who don't want to be in the play at all, but stay after school because there's air-conditioning and the AC doesn't work at their houses.

Day Two is for the real royalty. The red-carpet walkers. The ones who already have auditions lined up out of town for Juilliard, for The New School, for Carnegie Mellon, for other coveted institutions of higher learning for the arts. They *attend* Day One, sitting in the back row of the auditorium and clapping politely for schlubs like Kelly The Man who don't stand a chance of getting cast. But everyone who's anyone knows that Day One is something of a sham.

That's how it's been every year, as far back as even Mrs. Tanner can remember.

Until today.

At first, this Day One is like all the others. There's the usual slew of nervous freshmen, nervous not because they are cold-reading Shakespeare in front of their peers, but because they are freshmen without a Place. Without a Group or Set or Clique or Gang. They are moorless, wandering the halls during normal school hours, still trying to remember where all those big-kid classrooms are.

There's the usual group of other underachievers; bored, many of them, having nothing better to do. There's Kelly, of course, who everyone knows, because she will probably be awarded Least Likely to Take a Hint at the annual and unsanctioned Most & Least Awards held at the drama club president's house each May. Kelly is too tall, too heavy, and too awkward a gal, one who actually looks like the word "gal" still applies. She is remarkable in only one aspect, and that is her utter unremarkableness.

But today Kelly is reading with a new kid. Her audition is as abysmal as any of her auditions over the years, but after the first line is spoken, the day goes in an entirely unheard-of direction.

This new kid, wearing a *tie* for reasons known only to him, bursts onto the stage and stands beside Kelly, full of kinetic energy unlike anything anyone has ever seen. He pulls on faces and accents like they are hats; off with one, on with another. He hits cues others don't even know exist. He goes off-book but returns right back to it just in time to give poor, bewildered Kelly a cue. Once Kelly gets her line choked out, he's off again, riffing and improvising and quite literally bouncing off the walls. At one point, he makes a joke about aliens, and tears a hole in his shirt, an alien chest-burster popping forth. A few of the seniors might have thought to make the joke, but had they torn their clothes in the process, they'd have slunk off stage, embarrassed.

Not this guy. He just widens his eyes and keeps on going. He turns his fingers into an alien hand puppet, shrieking for blood.

No one has ever seen anything like it. Mrs. Tanner is beside herself with hysterics. Someone in the back row whispers loudly, "Who *is* that?" and a small girl wearing a Ramones T-shirt several rows down turns and says, "Danny Jennings!" before facing the stage again and laughing at his antics.

Jennings's is the first ever standing ovation for a cold reading from a script. The president of the drama club, Jason, and his upperclassmen club officers don't know whether to join in or murder him and hide his body in the prop closet. He's made them all look like wannabes.

It is unfortunate that the play Jennings has just auditioned for is *Hamlet*, which is not known for its comedic bits. But no matter; everyone knows he just won a part, probably a decently sized one, too, because as they say, *If you can do comedy you can do anything*, and *If you can do Shakespeare you can do anything*.

Danny Jennings just did both. Quite suddenly, Day Two of auditions isn't such a big deal anymore.

*He* is.

"Let's go," President Jason is heard saying, and he leads his troupe of players from the theater to the loading dock beyond the auditorium scene shop to smoke. A lot. Fiercely.

Danny Jennings disappears as quickly as he appeared, as if in a puff of smoke. Kelly looks stunned and embarrassed as she and a freshman girl wearing long sleeves gather their bags and slink out of the auditorium.

"Next!" Mrs. Tanner calls, but no one gets up. Who would want to follow Danny Jennings?

# CADENCE

It takes awhile, but I finally find Danny at lunch on Wednesday sitting outdoors by himself behind the cafeteria. There's six or seven other people here, too, all of them alone, all of them cranky looking. One guy, who could fit three of me inside his shirt, is sitting under a tree drawing on his arms with a black Sharpie. He's *really* good, so I tell him so. He looks up like he's surprised, then gives me this very adult-looking nod that I think is meant to say both *Thank you* and *It is, isn't it?*

I should talk to him sometime. He might be fascinating.

But right now, I'm on a mission. I walk up to Danny and sit down on a short concrete wall beside him.

"Dude! Your audition!" I say, setting my plate down on my other side. The other students dart their eyes at me. I'm not supposed to talk back here, apparently.

"What about it."

"I loved it!"

Danny's eyes snap wide. "You saw it?"

"Yeah! I tried to track you down to tell you but you got out so fast I couldn't find you."

Danny frowns for some reason and mumbles something about having things to do, then opens a paperback copy of *Hamlet*.

"Seriously, man, it was so awesome," I say, because it's true and I want him to know that. "Everyone's talking about it."

"Who's everyone?"

"I don't know. People in classes and stuff. A lot of people."

"Am I popular now?" he deadpans.

Oh, boy.

"Danny, I'm gonna level with you," I say after a sip of my soda. "Sometimes you are exceptionally difficult to get along with."

"Only sometimes?"

"Okay," I say, and stand up. "You know, I just wanted a friend. That's it. All my girlfriends moved or got pregnant or got caught getting high so it was just me. But whatever, that's cool. I'll find someone else. Ciao, baby."

I shoulder my bag, pick up my plate, and head back toward the cafeteria doors.

I've almost made it when I just barely hear him behind me. "Wait."

I almost don't. Just to show him. His voice is so quiet, I could easily pretend I didn't hear it.

But I'm big dopey sucker, so I stop instead and turn and say, "What."

He looks around, then nods to his side, like I'm supposed to come sit next to him again.

I almost don't. But, *sigh*, I am a big dopey sucker, so I go back and sit down.

"Sorry," he says.

I cross one ankle over my knee and sit up straight. I'm trying to fix my posture. "About what, exactly? Be specific."

"You're going to make this a thing, aren't you."

"Yes."

He grits his teeth. I can see his jaw clenching. "I'm sorry I'm such an asshole."

"Well," I tell him, "I didn't say—"

"I'm sorry I suck at *sports*."

Uh-oh. Now *he's* the one making this a thing. "I'm sorry I like to wear clothes that no one else in the galaxy likes. I'm sorry I like music no one else has ever heard of. I'm sorry my sister is such big bossy bitch, and I'm sorry my mom doesn't give a fuck about any of it. And my *dad*, well. Fuckin' forget about it."

I bite my lips.

"Is that specific enough?" he says after a minute.

"Yep," I whisper. It sucks when he goes off like this. Like I'm not being his friend or something. But I'm also not going to point it out right now.

"You can go if you want," he says. "I don't mind. I understand."

"You wouldn't mind, or you wouldn't care?"

He thinks about that. "Oh, I'd care. You have no idea."

"Then I'll stay."

I pull a sack of trail mix out of my bag, open it, and start munching. I offer it to Danny. "Some?"

He doesn't answer, but he picks out a few cashews. My favorite.

Ah, well. I'll let it go. He looks like he needs a favor. And cashews are supposed to be an antidepressant or something,

I think, so it's probably good he's having them. Because seriously, I've never met anyone quite so unhappy as Danny.

But I get it. Sometimes things are tough. It's just that sometimes, I don't think he thinks it's tough for anyone other than him.

# DANNY

They post the cast list on Friday. Kind of like how people are fired on Fridays so there's less likelihood that they'll return to shoot up the place.

The list gets taped to Mrs. Tanner's office window after first period, and draws a crowd. Apparently, there are no surprises written on the column of names and parts assigned.

No surprises except for me.

DANNY JENNINGS ...... LAERTES

Cool, I guess. Didn't expect it, but, hey, I get to swordfight and die on stage. Not bad.

Looks like everyone else got what they wanted. Well, maybe not everyone; there're a couple sad souls—freshmen, I assume—who look downcast. Yeah, well, life's rough.

I turn to go and bump into the drama club president, Jason, whose face I only know from the big-ass black-and-white head-shot adorning Mrs. Tanner's office window along with those of the other club officers. President Jason is trying very hard to look humble, having naturally been cast as Hamlet. I wonder if everyone sees past it as easily as I do. When he sees it's me, he says, "Oh. Hey. Uh . . . congratulations."

I almost smart-ass him, but then pull back. "Thanks."

"You know, she's never cast a sophomore in a role like yours before."

Am I supposed to genuflect? But again I hold a sarcastic

comment back. This is the first not-sucky thing that's happened to me here. "Oh. Well. Cool."

He leans a little closer so no one else can hear and whispers, "*So don't fuck it up.*"

I can't help smiling as I say, "Wouldn't think of it, Lin-Manuel," and shove past him. Dick.

By the time I get home, though, I'm still liking the idea of Laertes. He's not actually in the show for a lot of it, but he gets to do all the cool sword stuff at the end. I think that'll be fun. Too bad Jason gets to kill me, but whatever.

I decide to make the announcement over dinner, where the whole damn family can give me some fucking credit for Getting Involved. So that night, right after we've all served ourselves and sat down, I say, "I got ca—"

That's as much as I can get out between my sister going off about softball season and how she and her best friend are probably in competition for shortstop.

"So I got—"

Strike two. Big Sis has much more important drama to discuss. Sports drama, of course. How we are related, I do not know.

I time my entry again, and this time I simply bellow, "I got cast in the play."

At last, they all turn to me.

"What?" Mom says.

"*Hamlet.* I'm playing Laertes. I get to swordfight with

Hamlet at the end. And get summarily killed, but hey, look at me, I'm getting involved."

"You're *what now*?" Dad says, mouth full of cooked carrots like orange guts.

"I got cast in the show."

"What show?"

Jesus. Patiently, I say, "*Hamlet*."

"Where at?"

"Broadway, Dad."

"Nobody likes a smart-ass."

"Oh, but I do."

"Nobody needs one. I sure as hell don't." He jams beef into his mouth.

"Well," I say, and spear two carrots with my fork, "try to contain your excitement."

"I think it's wonderful," Mom says, giving Dad an At-least-he's-not-in-prison look.

Dad sighs and removes his glasses, abandoning his food altogether. "When is it?"

"It opens October twenty-fourth."

Big Sis says, "Isn't that a Friday?"

"Yeah. So?"

"There's a game Friday."

She says this as if it is the most natural thing in the world. Like she just can't make herself comprehend that the school probably has more than one event.

"Right," I say. "Sorry. Forgot."

I do not mention the performances on Saturday.

"But now that I'm showing school spirit and, I hasten to add again, getting involved, can I please get a new phone?"

"What happened to your old one, again?" Mom says. "You haven't found it? Have you looked hard enough?"

"Well, that's an interesting story and one that I don't care to go into. But suffice it to say it got stolen."

"Well then we'll just wait till you can be more responsible," Dad says.

My head falls back. I check the yellow ceiling for God. Nope. Still not up there.

"Do you know when you lost it?" Big Sis asks, smiling like this is her best attempt at being nice.

"First day of school."

She just lets that sit there and keeps on stuffing her big old sporto face. Since no one else has anything to add, she mumbles something like "Hope you find it." And that's it.

Magnifico.

I finish dinner thinking primarily about Cadence; that she came to the audition, that she might come see the show. She didn't have to come watch me, but she did. That's got to mean something. That's got to mean she's interested in me. And Big Bad Zach or whoever didn't make everyone in the whole auditorium laugh. I did. Well, that is, everyone except President Jason, kingshit of the drama department himself, who looked like he wanted to kick my ass for daring to be cast in the show.

Oh, golly, no. Being hunted down by drama geeks. I'm in such peril.

## FINAL SCORE

| | |
|---|---|
| SPARTANS | 29 |
| Mustangs | 50 |

*Daytime Dilemma (Dangers of Love)*

# CADENCE

I should probably be more bummed about having to go to school on a Saturday, like a normal person. But the truth, and I am totally okay with it, is that I'm just not the smartest kid in school. I mean, I can read and I can pay attention for most of a class, but I guess things just don't quite stick all the time.

Sat School is short for Saturday School. I'm sure the term is meant to make it sound cool, but I doubt many people are buying it.

"I'm here for earth science," I tell Mrs. Cornelius, the librarian, when I get to the library.

Mrs. Cornelius points to a table, where I'm kind of surprised to see two girls I actually recognize. One of them auditioned with Danny on Tuesday. The other is Vivi, the girl with the maybe-boyfriend, Sam.

Vivi's sitting on one end of the table and the tall girl's on the other side. I sit across from Vivi and say hi. She looks up from an English textbook and smiles.

"How is Sam?"

Vivi's smile turns girlie-shy, making me laugh. "Good. How's . . . I'm sorry, is it Danny?"

The tall girl whips her head around. Uh-oh.

"Danny, yeah, he's good," I say quickly. I don't want the tall girl to get upset. "Listen—"

But I'm too late. She cuts me off. "You mean Danny Jennings, from the drama department?"

I slide around in my chair to face her. "Yeah. He's a friend of mine. Your audition was really good."

She grunts. "It's okay. You don't have to kiss up. He walked off with the audition, I know it."

"Well, he *was* pretty funny."

"Uh-huh, noticed that." She turns back to her science book.

"But he couldn't have been without you there," I add. "It's not like he was by himself up there. He needed you to work with him."

She studies me for a minute before shrugging, with a little laugh. "If that was a lie, it was a pretty good one. Thanks."

"You're welcome! I'm Cadence."

"Kelly."

"Hi, Kelly! This is Vivi, do you guys know each other?"

They don't. Now that I've got two older and more experienced women to talk to, I shift in my chair to kind of see them both. "Can I ask you guys a question?"

"Only if it's about chemistry," Kelly says. "I'm not good at English."

"Actually, it's about boys."

Kelly laughs out loud, making Mrs. Cornelius snap her fingers. Kelly lifts her shoulders in an *Oops!* response, and creeps to a chair closer to us. "I doubt I can help. There's not a line of gentlemen callers at my door. But I'd love to hear the question."

Vivi nods, too, and just like that, we're all in cahoots. I don't know what a cahoot is, but I think this is one.

"There's a guy I like, but I haven't really told him yet. He's older. And tall. Holy crap, he is so freaking tall, you don't even know."

Vivi tilts her head. "Brown eyes? Sort of dark blond hair? But doesn't play sports or anything?"

"Right! His name's Zach."

"Zach Pearson. I have a couple classes with him. He seems like a nice guy."

"You know him? Totally tell me everything!"

Vivi laughs. Only this time, she doesn't try to stop it. I think she should laugh like that more often. "Nothing to tell. I know English isn't his best subject, but I think he's an artist or something. Maybe into engineering or architecture. I'm just guessing, here."

"Guesses are good!"

"Have you talked to him?" Kelly says. "That's usually a good start."

"Oh, sure! We talk. When we see each other, which isn't often. He's a junior, so we're not usually on the same sides of the buildings."

"You could just tell him you like him," Vivi says, but quietly. "It's scary, I know. But maybe being direct is best." After saying it, she kind of looks to the side like she just thought of something.

"Boys like direct," Kelly adds.

"Hmm. Direct. So just ask him out on a date? Because I

kind of did that once and he said we should just hang out on campus first or something."

"He might be right. Maybe start with lunch," Kelly says. "Hang out in the cafeteria, or someplace like that. Get a sense of how he feels."

"See if you can make him laugh," Vivi says, snapping back into the conversation. "That's huge. And if you think he's funny, you need to laugh, too."

"I can do that!" Since we're on the topic of boys and laughing, I can't help but think about Danny. Danny, who for some reason wanted to go out with *me*.

"Okay. Now, what if another boy likes you and you don't like him?"

"Well, that takes me out of the conversation," Kelly says, but like a joke.

"Is the boy Danny Jennings?" Vivi says. "Sam heard he shot up his old school."

"No, he didn't. He brought a BB gun to kill pigeons at his friend's dad's work. The dad was going to pay them to do it. The BB gun fell out his backpack and he got in trouble. That's all."

"Oh," Vivi says. "That makes a lot more sense."

"But he's crushing on you?" Kelly says.

"Maybe. I don't know. He's just a friend. But he's also sad. Like, I've never seen him smile, not once. Sometimes it looks like he wants to, but he, like, fights it."

"Well, his sister's a giant pain, so that might be part of it," Kelly says. "Her and all her little clique-y prom queens."

"Like THE Brianna Montaro," Vivi says, doodling something in a blank notebook.

"Yes!" Kelly says, pointing a finger at Vivi.

And Vivi replies right back, "Right? What is *up* with her?"

"Wait a sec," I say. "People always say her name like that, THE Brianna Montaro, I don't get it."

Vivi snaps her mouth shut and keeps doodling. Kelly says, "She's got some kind of complex about being the smartest person in school. Like if she's not valedictorian, it will signal the apocalypse or . . ." Kelly trails off, glancing at Vivi. "Hold on, did you say Sam a second ago?"

Vivi's entire body seems to tense as she says, "Yeah."

"Sam, as in, the Sam who used to go out with Brianna?"

Vivi scowls. "Yeah, why?"

Kelly leans back. "Oh. Okay. Well, A, you got a good one. Congratulations. But B, for the rest of us, now we have to deal with Brianna. They went out for five or six months last year, and, man, it was like night and day with her. I don't know what kind of business he was giving her, but it was sure keeping her calm."

Vivi's scowl gets worse, so Kelly hurries to finish. "But then it ended and she went full-on dark side. I don't think that it had to do with Sam, though. She's the one who broke it off."

Vivi is silent for a sec, then says, "*Good.*" Real short and sharp. It makes me and Kelly both laugh, and then Vivi grins.

"It would be a real shame if someone else was first in our class," Vivi says.

"It would indeed," Kelly agrees.

One of the Sat School teachers comes over and politely asks who is tutoring and who is studying. I tell him I suck at everything, so Vivi and Kelly say they're helping me with English and earth science, which they actually do. But then after Sat School shuts down, Kelly drives us to Jamaican Blue and shows us photos on her phone, talking about some friends who've all graduated.

I'll be honest, I'm only half listening. Part of me's thinking about how to talk to Zach more, while the other part's trying to figure out how to not hurt Danny's feelings and still be friends.

# VIVI

Sam always walks with me to seventh hour. On Monday, we split up halfway there and head to separate restrooms.

I check my face. Hair. My new shirt, the first since we moved.

I look good. Screw Brianna Montaro.

I'm just closing my stall when the bathroom door opens. Voices and general chaos waft in behind whoever enters. Sounds like more than one person.

"So, what's it like?" I hear Brianna Montaro say as a faucet starts up.

I freeze. She must be talking to her friends.

Keep still.

Don't move. Last time I was in here alone with her, I got pinned to a wall and had *slut* written across my head.

"Vivian?" she says. "I asked you a question."

Oh, God. God, no.

"What's it like?" The water shuts off. "Being white trash, I mean?"

Stay quiet.

Say nothing.

Besides . . . they're only half right. Ha ha. Joke's on you. My dad's Mexican, so I'm only white trash on my mom's side. Ha ha . . .

"Do you have, like, special trash-only barbecues?" she goes on, and the two clones laugh. It must be the same two from the other bathroom a couple of weeks ago. Stay quiet, Vivian. Stay quiet.

Except, instead, I say, "I'm not."

No!

Stupid, stupid, why? Shut up!

"You're not what?"

"*I'm not white trash.*"

In my head, I sound like a Norse Viking at the top of a granite mountain, wielding a battle-ax and bellowing my rage.

In this smelly bathroom, it's more of a mouse fart.

"Um, yeah, you are," one of the Brianna clones says. "Oh my God, you guys! Did you know that when people like her move into neighborhoods around here, the value of our houses goes down?"

Brianna sucks in a dramatic breath. "Is that *true*?"

"Oh, yeah, my dad talks about it all the time," the clone says. "Vivian, I'm not making fun of you, by the way. I'm not *bullying* you. I'm just telling you how it is. People like you move in, and the rest of us suffer for it. It's a fact. Look it up."

The bell rings, and I listen to them walk out of the bathroom together. My new shirt is now a rag. Might as well clean toilets with it. Right, Mom?

When I finally come out of the restroom, Sam is leaning against the wall across from me. He smiles. "So, hey, I was thinking—"

I race past him to the parking lot—gone in sixty seconds. I can't face him. Not now. Because what if they're right about

me—and because *he* used to go out with *her*, what if *he* thinks
the same thing about *me*, and—

I run.

# DANNY

I'm dead.

I'm lying on the floor, looking up, and all I see is darkness. That's all that's waiting up there. Just the dark.

But then the stage lights brighten, and Mrs. Tanner shouts, "Yes, much better! Go ahead, Danny, take it from your last line."

Still on the stage floor, I hold my paperback script up above my head, scan it, and set it back down.

"It is here, Hamlet," I say, making sure my voice is loud enough. Jason, playing Hamlet, crosses over to me and kneels by my right side. He lifts my head in both hands, cradling my upper body. "Hamlet, thou art slain. No medicine in the world can do thee good. In thee there is not half an hour of life. The . . . shit!"

I grab my script again. Jason mutters, "Don't worry, you got it. How'd you memorize it so fast?"

"Inherent genius." I read the lines to myself two more times and go on: "The treacherous instrument is in thy hand, unbated and envenom'd; the foul practise hath turned itself on me."

Damn, this shit is kind of fun! So fucking melodramatic, it's great.

"The king, the king's to blame!" I shout at the end of my speech, and then flop over, totally dead.

Jason carefully sets me down and goes on with the show. I have to try hard not to smile as I hear him kill Gertrude.

It's after six when I get home, and I don't even feel like

taking a pill or anything while I fake swordfight with Hamlet in my room. I stay in there, slashing and cutting with an imaginary rapier until I hear Dad get home a little while later.

And I do mean *hear* him.

"It's child pornography!" Dad screams in the kitchen.

Oh, shit. Here we go. I shake my head and go out to explain. "So, hey—

"Have you lost your mind?" Dad shouts.

For one moment, I am one hundred percent sure he's going to deck me. He doesn't. But, man, does he want to.

"I take it you heard about my phone."

"You're god damn right I did! Jesus, Danny! What is the matter with you? What am I doing wrong?"

Whoa. He's really going off the rails. I choose not to answer his question directly, though the temptation is overwhelming.

Mom tries to help. "Danny," she says to me, "it's against the law."

"Yes, I know. Fortunately, I didn't take the picture, so. Yay."

"You are out of that damn show," Dad says, his face red. "You are going to school and coming straight home and doing your god damn homework—and that is *it* until I say otherwise."

"Well," I say slowly, carefully, "that would be fair, except, again, I didn't do it."

Mom shakes her head, clearly Disappointed In Me. "It was on your phone, Danny."

"Which someone stole."

"We're done," Dad barks. "You're either at home or you're at school. That's it. Jesus, we'll probably have to find a god damn lawyer."

"So is now a bad time to ask for a new phone? Because the police still have mine."

"Danny," Mom says. Still Very Disappointed.

I lift my index fingers for emphasis. "You *are* kidding, right?" I say, quite honestly. "You're joking with me."

"It's a felony, Danny," Dad says. "And not the fun kind, either. This is the kind of thing that follows you around the rest of your life. Jesus Christ, child pornography. You really are out of your mind."

I clear my throat and fold my hands in front of me so I don't swing at him.

"Just so we're clear," I say, unable to even look him in the face because

I

AM

SO

PISSED.

"It's your contention that I—*I*—was in the *locker room*, with a phone that I told you multiple times was lost, and took a picture of a naked kid, and then posted it online. Because that's the kind of thing I routinely do."

"We don't know what you routinely do," Mom says.

"Except get into trouble," Dad adds. Brilliantly.

I nod slowly. "So, then, you are completely uninterested in the truth."

"What I'm *interested* in is the police not calling me at work," Dad says.

"Because that is becoming routine," Mom jabs.

"Touché." I'm amazed they can't see the forge-like heat of my rage emanating off my skin. Surprised it's not burning them.

I back up, slowly, carefully, no sudden moves.

"Just for the record," I say, "I did not do this. I am innocent. Even Dr. Flores believes me. I think. This is not something I would ever do. I have no interest in doing it, I don't see the humor in it, and I don't fancy people thinking of me as a pedophile. I also like to think that somewhere deep down in those primitive brains of yours you know I'm telling the truth—"

"Danny—" Mom says.

"—but the reality is, you have no interest in whether I'm telling the truth or not. And that, folks, is pretty much the part of this I will take to the grave."

They don't even bother yelling at me as I walk carefully to my room and close the door.

# DONTE

After weight room, me and Brady head for the showers. This one crazy fat kid who's always drawing stuff on his arms and legs escaped a bit early, probably precisely so he could avoid this moment, when the athletes come in to get cleaned up before the next class starts.

But I'm not in the mood to give him shit. I only ever do it for laughs, anyway. It's not that it means anything. You got to be able to laugh at yourself, in my opinion, otherwise this world's gonna make you crazy.

I see faded black marker on the guy's left arm, some kind of vine drawing. It's kind of stupid to be all drawing on yourself, but the work is good. I can admit that to myself, anyway. And now that I think about it, the kid really has lost some weight. Good on him.

We take fast showers, then head to our lockers. The fat kid is almost done getting dressed, standing by the long bench between rows of Spartan-blue lockers.

"You fat shit," Brady says out of nowhere.

The kid doesn't answer. He slows down, like Brady's comment has dunked him in water, making every movement a struggle. But he doesn't look over, doesn't respond.

Another guy—I think his name is Zach—walks past, drying his hair. Zach's new to weight room this year, and it's not working for him.

Zach glances at us and disappears around a row of lockers. Then he backs up. "Hey, man," he says to Brady.

Brady turns and pulls his shoulders back. This Zach kid is tall—tall enough he should be playing basketball, but too skinny. Me and Brady can take him if we need to. Or want to.

"What?" Brady says.

"Look, not for nothing, but you're like the king of the whole school," the Zach kid says. "Everyone looks up to you. And this is what you're going to do with it? With that kind of power?"

"You trying to tell me what to do in my house?" Brady says, taking a pointedly slow and menacing step toward Zach.

Zach just looks disappointed. "Really? Your house? Come on."

In that second, I see what Brady doesn't. Zach's not looking for a fight, but he won't back away from one if one starts. There's no way for this to end well for the team unless someone steps in.

"It's cool," I say, putting myself between Brady and Zach. "We were just messing around, it's cool."

"Cool," Zach says easily. "Hey, have a great game Friday."

In my mind, I respect it. Zach said it with casual sincerity. He wasn't kissing up like a lot of people might.

"Thanks, man," I say, and punch Zach on the arm. Not full strength, but enough to let him know that me at full strength would be a reckoning. Got to keep things in perspective.

Zach nods a bit, then goes on his way. By that point the fat kid has snuck away, anyway. I notice it, but Brady doesn't. He's still scowling after Zach.

"Lucky little bitch," Brady says.

"He's cool, don't worry about it. You all right, man?"

Brady says nothing for a bit. Then he swings hard at the nearest locker, denting it. Then he swings again. And again. Soon he's shouting. Cursing, swearing. Words I know very well but have never strung together in quite this order, or with quite this ferocity. Brady tears into the row of blue lockers like they're linemen.

I take a step back, putting myself in the walkway between rows. A few heads poke out from farther down, and I raise a warning hand: *Don't come over here.* They need no more urging than that. They either pull back into their rows, or leave the locker room entirely, heads down. *No, sir, didn't hear or see a thing.*

A bell rings, and Brady's head snaps up. He steps away from the lockers and drops down onto the center bench, breathing hard. Blood drips from his hands onto the concrete floor.

I don't budge. I'm pretty sure the locker room is empty now.

It's quiet right up until the final bell for next period. Seven minutes of silence, broken only by the heavy breathing of my quarterback.

"Okay?" I say at last.

"I'm gonna kill someone," Brady says.

"All right. Want any help?"

"No."

And then he grunts something like a laugh. I can't help snorting too, laughing at the stupidity of it all. Brady looks at his wrecked hands.

"Coach's gonna kick my ass."

"We'll wrap them up," I say. "I'll get the ice and shit."

"I don't know if I can throw today at practice."

"Sure you can, man."

"I don't know, D. Swear to God. I don't know."

"It's the Wildcats Friday. We can mercy rule those suckers."

Brady grunts. Our team forced a mercy ruling against the Wildcats last year, and afterward we partied so hard not one us made it to practice Saturday morning. Coach never said a word about the missed practice; just gave us all a stern look Monday after school and said, "Keep your heads in the game. What kind of game is this?"

"Man's game!" the team shouted in unison.

"What kind?"

"*Man's game!*"

It was one of those Hollywood moments, and I figure Brady wants to relive it again this season—probably as badly as I do.

"Be right back," I say, and head to the first aid closet for the gear.

I'd never admit it, but for a minute there I was actually scared. I've never worried about whether or not I could smoke Brady, because we're friends. And because Brady keeps losing—or at least not gaining—any weight.

But back there at what's left of the lockers . . . man, if Brady cut loose like that on a guy, it wouldn't be easy to get him down.

By the time I'm done wrapping Brady's hands, I still haven't decided whether or not to tell Coach what happened. Brady doesn't ask if I will or not.

# CADENCE

I'm not supposed to leave campus for lunch because I'm a wee freshman. But the security guard at the gate doesn't seem to care enough to check IDs. Pete drives me and Danny out of the parking lot and that's that. This guy isn't that worried about security, I guess! I feel very grown-up and responsible, right up until Pete speaks.

"I been thinking," he says as he lights a joint. "We need really good names for our dicks."

Oh, dear. I could have stayed on campus, had my nice reduced-price lunch. But no. I elected to hang out with these two again.

"Some really badass names," Pete says. We turn right and head for McDonald's. *Gag reflex! Blegh!*

"For mine, too?" I ask him. I'm in shotgun again.

"Oh, no," Pete says, totally serious. "I'm just talking about me and Daniel-san. I mean, unless you *got* one. Then, yeah, that's cool."

"I don't. But thanks."

"So what do you mean?" Danny asks, taking the joint from Pete. "Like, Hulk?"

"Yeah. Or like . . . Rock Jack! That's totally my dick's name."

"Or, how about Fluffy?" I say.

Now I know why Pete lets me tag along. I crack him up. I mean, he can't even breathe. What the heck, it's the only time anyone laughs at me like this. Meaning, in the good way. "Or . . . Professor Flaccid?"

He howls. I check to see if Danny's smiling. Hmm . . . looking out the window. Maybe trying not to smile!

"No no no," Pete says, waving his hands in the air, the steering wheel a mere nuisance. "I got it . . . Doctor Boner the Third."

"This is great," I say as he chokes to death. "I'll get home today, and my dad will say, 'What did you do in school today, Cadence?' and I'll say, 'Sat around with two of my friends who got high and talked about what to name their penises,' and then he'll say, 'Really? Where do they live? I'd like to remove their spinal cords with this ice cream scoop.'"

Pete stops laughing.

Danny says, "Really? He'd say that?"

"Something like it, yeah. He was in the navy, remember? He's kind of badass."

"Did he swab the poop deck?" Pete says, and he's off again, rolling around in his seat in hysterics. The person trying to take our order at the drive-through is unimpressed.

"You're ridiculous," I say to Pete.

"That's what my dad tells me," Pete says. "Only he says 'recockulous.' Like, replaces 'dic' with 'cock,' get it?"

"Uh . . . yeah," I say. "Is he like a stand-up comic or something?" Come to think of it, that might explain some things about Pete!

"Nah. He writes video games. Like, the story worlds and

stuff. You guys want any? I got a shit-ton of them at home. I don't really play much."

"Sure," Danny says.

"What do *your* parents do?" I ask Danny, since he never ever talks about them.

"My mom's a real estate agent," he says.

"Ugh, boring," I say. "What about your dad?"

Danny sits back in his seat, shutting his eyes. "You wouldn't believe me if I told you."

"Catholic priest!"

"Good guess, but no."

Pete manages to order three Happy Meals. Fitting, somehow. Then we go to that same parking lot at the park.

Pete finishes off the joint, chucks the end out the window, and opens his Happy Meal. Unwrapping what passes for a cheeseburger, Pete says to Danny, "You got any more Adderall coming you want to trade?"

"Working on it," Danny says, quiet.

Pete turns on his stereo so we can listen to more "Floyd," singing along, more stuff about life and death.

"I don't get it," I say, reaching to turn down the volume. "What is it with all the drug stuff? I'm not judging, or I'm not trying to anyway, but like, really, explain it to me."

"What, you never want to just check out for a while?" Pete says. "It's like recess, dude."

"If you say so."

"She doesn't get it," Danny says, eyes closed. "She's Cadence. Everything's all glitter and unicorns in her world."

"*Awww!*" I say sweetly. "You could go ahead and fuck yourself if you want."

That sure gets his attention. Danny blinks rapidly at me while Pete freezes with his cheeseburger halfway to his mouth.

"S'matter?" I say. "I can't say any F-bombs in my glittery unicorn world? You're not the only one with problems, Danny. You're not the only one who wants a recess every once in a while. My mom and my dad and my brother drive me crazy sometimes. Johnny gets so depressed we can't get him to leave his room for weeks. My dad's done stuff for the navy he's not even allowed to talk about and we know it drives him crazy. I have to go to this school where everyone's so mean to each other all the time. Then there's *you* guys, who I like a lot, but all you want to do is get high and jump in on the meanness! All I did was ask a question and you had to go all dickhead on me."

Danny doesn't say anything. His expression is way too hard for me to read. Pete makes a theatrical show of turning the volume back up on the stereo so it won't seem like we're not talking to each other.

When we get back to school, there are *two* security guys standing at the parking lot entrance, and they're checking every ID of every person in every car coming back onto campus.

Curses. Foiled again. Happy Meal, indeed! I'm busted for being a wee freshman off campus, and Pete gets busted for being the big bad junior driving the car with the wee freshman inside it. Danny gets in no trouble at all.

Fortunately, Pete isn't upset by the fresh new referral he got handed, although I'm not happy about mine. But then, I knew what I was doing. My bad. We'll have to put in an hour of detention after school this week. I figure I'll do mine today, get it over with. Pete says he'll probably skip it all together, because there's a chance our referrals will just get lost in the system.

Danny doesn't say anything.

So I figure, whatever, not my problem, I've done nothing but be nice to him, I don't need to sit around being a punching bag for his drama. "Do I got Everlast stamped on my forehead?" Dad says sometimes when me or Johnny or Mom get bitchy. "Then don't beat me up."

# VIVI

I ditch the entire morning's worth of classes, car shopping with Aunt Marlene. The salesman is dubious at first, but Marlene's no fool. She convinces him that we are not only serious, but we also have cash. So by the time the bell goes off to end lunch, I'm driving into the student parking lot with a new model year Chevy Camaro. And this car—oh, this car, she is nice to me. She purrs along the streets, taking turns smooth as a sports car should. She's red. *Caliente* red. Cops-more-likely-to-pull-you-over red.

But while I love my new car, it doesn't help. It doesn't change what they said, or what they think of me. It won't fix my parents being apart. Nothing will fix that.

I brought it home first to show Daddy, still high off the new car smell. Daddy looked at it from the window of the downstairs guest bedroom where he is staying while he heals. He didn't say anything for a long time. I thought he was angry.

He wasn't. He put his arm around my shoulder and said, "Things are different, *mija*. We'll be okay."

I thought it would make me feel better. Shove that white trash crap right back into THE Brianna Montaro's face. Into all of their stupid faces. I'm going to get straight 100s this year, and steal that valedictorian right out from under that . . . *bitch*.

I want to believe him when he says we'll be okay. I just can't yet. I haven't even told him about me and Sam.

Sam.

I still have to talk to him. I've got to, before it's too late.

He texted me all yesterday, and then again this morning, between classes based on the time stamp. Walking to sixth hour, I know he'll be there, in Mrs. Garcia's class, and I have to talk to him. But should I tell him the truth, tell him exactly what his ex said to me? I don't know.

Sam isn't paying any attention to Mrs. Garcia. I know this because he keeps staring at me, but pretending not to. *I* pretend to listen to Mrs. Garcia. Pretend not to know that Sam is watching me.

Sitting beside Brianna Montaro makes my stomach hurt. *She* is not pretending to pay attention—she really is. She scribbles furiously in a notebook, and I know she's recording the entire class on her phone, artfully hidden in a blouse pocket. Is that against the rules? I don't think so. Having a phone out is, though.

While I'm watching her, Brianna Montaro shoots a wicked glare my way. Except not at my face. At my desk. Not cheating—we're not having a quiz or test. She wants to see what I've written for notes.

What I've written so far is: HAMLET, REVENGE, GUILDENSTERN, a small heart, and SAM.

"For all Hamlet's talk about revenge," Mrs. Garcia is saying, "the truth is, Hamlet also wants the throne. So while he does technically get his revenge on Claudius, Hamlet doesn't obtain what he's really after, which is his father's place on the throne of Denmark. Hamlet loses."

Brianna Montaro snorts, quietly. It's like she's empathizing. Saying, *Yeah, Hamlet, I always lose, too.*

Whatever.

"Hamlet ultimately loses everything because of his single-minded pursuit of vengeance," Mrs. Garcia says.

"Is that the—what's it called—theme?" Zach says.

"Maybe," Mrs. Garcia with a teacherly shrug. "What do you think? Does vengeance ever come without cost?"

It's been almost exactly twenty-four hours since I talked to Sam. He's the best thing that's happened to me since the move. But how can I tell him what happened in the bathroom yesterday, what Brianna and those girls said about me? This isn't like the Sharpie thing. We didn't know each other then, and I didn't know he was Brianna's ex. This is . . . personal.

Because the truth is, maybe she was right. Maybe I really am what she said. I feel like an imposter as it is, living in that house, in that neighborhood, where my dad's skin color and name and accent scare and confuse the neighbors. I can see them imagining weed trimmers and portable, gasoline-operated leaf blowers in his hands.

It doesn't matter which half of my race those girls attacked. It all feels the same.

And Sam did go out with her. He saw something he liked, right? What if this whole thing with him and me is fake? What if he's really just one of *them* in disguise? So I can't talk to him. I'm too scared, too embarrassed. What if I told him what happened, and he starts laughing at me, or worse? What if this one good thing that's come out of the move is going to be taken away?

Except—

Except Sam hasn't given up on me. Not yet. I can see it in his face while I'm pretending not to watch him watching me.

But he won't wait forever. He *shouldn't* wait forever.

I have to fix it. I can't risk losing him because of something I did. If he's not for real with me, fine. But how stupid would it be to chase him away if he *is* for real?

So I resort to middle school tactics: I start writing a note.

*Dear Sam,*

*Please don't be mad at me. Something happened yesterday before 7th hour and I don't know if I can really tell you what—*

Right then, the PA system crackles to life, cutting off my thought process and Mrs. Garcia's lecture.

"Faculty and staff, your attention please," says Dr. Flores. "We are now in hard lockdown. All outside activities are canceled. All students and staff in classrooms are to remain there. If you are outside, return to the school building immediately or proceed to the designated alternative gathering point. The code word is notebook. The code word is notebook."

"Oh, great," Mrs. Garcia sighs. "Okay, well, everyone up here and sit down, I guess."

Somehow, when we all stand up, I end up at Sam's side. My heart beats fast. "What's going on?" I say to him as we all shuffle to the front of the room.

"It's just a drill," he says. "They have these code words for when it's a drill and when it's the real thing. I guess 'notebook' means drill."

My heart slows down. Then it speeds back up as I realize Sam has my hand in his. Like nothing happened. Like I haven't been ignoring him.

"Okay, okay," Mrs. Garcia says, sitting us all down with our backs against the wall. "No talking."

No one obeys her.

"Mrs. G!" someone stage whispers. "Mrs. G!"

"Yes, Patty."

"If you get shot, will there still be a quiz tomorrow?"

Mrs. Garcia laughs. So do we. Tension breaker.

"There will be now, thanks for reminding me," Mrs. Garcia says, and everyone pretends to get mad at Patty.

Sam and I sit side by side, our entwined hands hidden between our hips.

"I'm sorry," I say, barely audible. "About—everything."

He squeezes my hand. "Will you tell me what happened later?"

I don't want to, really. But I say, "Yes."

Another squeeze. We're okay. I'll have to tell him what happened, but we'll be fine.

I look at Brianna Montaro.

She is reading a paperback of *Hamlet* fiercely and writing in her notebook. Like she's angry the drill has interrupted her learning time.

I decide I will ace the next quiz.

"Whoa," Sam whispers.

I turn to him. "What."

"You just got a really intense look on your face."

"Oh. Just—thinking." There's still a low buzz in the class-room from all the whispered conversations, and Mrs. Garcia is leaning her head against the wall as if grateful for the break. I scoot even closer to Sam. "Can I ask you something?"

"Absolutely."

"That Friday a couple weeks ago . . . when we went to the coffee shop . . ."

"Yeah? Hey, I won't order for you again."

I laugh—short and quiet. "It's not that. It's . . . why did you do that?"

His expression turns serious. "Wait, the ordering thing?"

"No, I mean, why did you ask me to do that at all? To go?" I lower my voice even more. "Was it to get back at *her*?"

Sam relaxes, like that's a much easier question. "No. No. You just looked like you needed copious amounts of chocolate, that's all."

I feel stabbed in the stomach. "That's all?"

"Ah, no. There's, um . . . there's more."

I like the direction that's going. The stabbing feeling goes away as I whisper, "Well, lots of people *do* need copious amounts of chocolate, I guess. Look at Mrs. Garcia."

Sam laughs—long and loud. Loud enough for Mrs. Garcia to open her eyes and frown. Sam waves an apology.

"Fair enough," he whispers.

Doodling on my notebook cover, I say, "You said there was more?"

He keeps his voice quiet as he says, "Well . . . you're very pretty."

That doesn't suck to hear.

"But also," Sam says, then pauses with a strange little smile on his face. "Also, I liked the way you take notes."

I can't even respond to that. Sam's little grin gets bigger.

"You write freehand faster than I can type," he says. "And you hardly even look down at your notebook while you do it. Like you can daydream and take notes at the same time. It's the weirdest thing. Weird cool, I mean. Did you not know you did that?"

Truthfully, I say, "I had no idea."

"Yeah. It's sort of intense. Like it just comes easily to you. That's intriguing."

Trying to be covert about it, I glance at Brianna again. She's still madly flipping pages and scribbling notes. She looks *angry* at the text. I've never felt that way before in my life, that I can remember.

"So, I was intrigued," Sam goes on. "That, and the afore-mentioned 'pretty' part."

I want to say thank you, but somehow it feels wrong.

But I'm spared having to say much of anything because Dr. Flores's voice comes over the PA. "Your attention, please. The lockdown has ended. The lockdown has ended. Please return to your classrooms. This has been a drill."

We go back to our seats. I try very hard to give Brianna Montaro a confident smirk. I don't know if it works or not.

I sit straight and attentive in my desk, making sure to give Mrs. Garcia my undivided attention.

There's a quiz coming up.

# COACH

"You two," Coach says to Donte and Brady. They're in the hall between sixth and seventh period, standing by their lockers. The flock of pretty, underclassmen girls crowded around them scatters when Coach approaches. He enjoys the effect he has, though his two players clearly do not. But they give him their attention.

It's good to be king.

"My office," he says.

The boys follow without complaint. The bell rings, but none of them care. This is official coach business. He's got a whole pad of passes for just such an occasion.

They swagger into his office. Coach hurls himself into the ancient office chair and pulls his wallet from a desk drawer.

"Here," Coach says. He yanks a gold-colored Starbucks card from the wallet. He hands it to Brady, but looks at Donte. "You got that new car, right?"

"Hell yeah," Donte says. "Got a nice system in it, too, good bass—"

"Yeah yeah, I know about the bass," Coach says, feigning anger. It makes Donte grin. "All right, take this, go get me a, uh . . . get me a cup of coffee and a doughnut or something. Then you two heroes get whatever you want."

The boys trade surprised and thrilled glances, but don't ask questions. They hustle out the door with hurried *Thanks, Coach*-es over their shoulders.

*You did that right,* Coach tells himself. *God damn if you mess things up sometimes, but that one you did right.*

He picks up the phone to make a report to the facilities guy. Someone beat the almighty crap out of some lockers in the boys' locker room, and they'll need replacing. He hopes it doesn't come out of his budget, but has a feeling it will. It always does.

# DANNY

President Jason and Mrs. Tanner are in her office in the drama department when the bell for seventh period rings. I ignore it. I mean, how much more trouble could I possibly get in, right?

Jason looks pissed as fuck, sitting on an old vinyl couch from the seventies.

I don't ask. I have business.

Mrs. Tanner looks up from her desk and smiles. "Hey, Danny. What's up? Shouldn't you be in class?"

"I have to drop out of the show." It comes out in a robotic voice, dry and monotone.

Her face falls. Jason looks up with a scowl. At the exact same time, they say, "What?"

"Sorry," I say in that same tone. "Nothing I can do about it. Good luck."

Jason jumps to his feet like he's going to square off with me, but of course he doesn't. "You can't just do that! People are counting on you!"

"Everything's fine, though, thanks for asking," I say. "Take it easy."

Mrs. Tanner says my name as I walk out of the office. Jason, on the other hand, calls me an asshole.

Yes, because *I'm* the asshole in this scenario. Jesus Christ, fuck you, too, Mr. President.

I almost go back in. I almost tell them both the whole

sordid, stupid fucking story. But I don't. Why bother? Nothing's going to change.

Thanks, Dad. Well done, sir.

I spend seventh period in a bathroom, which stinks like . . . everything a high school boys' bathroom stinks like. I really should just go home. But I've got to try and at least fix things with Cadence, if nothing else. That might at least be a nice way to end the day.

Probably shouldn't get my hopes up.

# VIVI

Seventh period. Last class of the day. Not my favorite either, and not because it's math but because Mr. Donelly is so old-fashioned that he still makes people come up to the board to solve problems. Does he keep a switch in his desk, too? Slates and chalk?

Mr. Donelly scans the class. "Let's see . . . Vivian."

I freeze. Try to hide. Shrink. Ungrow. Travel back in time to before I took a breath in this world.

It doesn't work.

"Can you come up and complete the graph?"

A trillion eyes pierce me. Their invisible blades pin me to my seat.

I try to form words. Nothing. Try Spanish instead. Nothing.

"Vivian?" Mr. Donelly says. He holds the marker out, like a dog treat. As if that will work. "Do you not know the answer, or do you not want to come up?"

The answers to these questions are, in order, *Yes, I know the answer*, and *No, I do not want to come up*.

Then magic happens.

Sam stands up, arms straight down at his sides, and shouts, "I volunteer as tribute!"

Half the class starts laughing. Many even hold up three fingers, pressed tightly together. When others see them, they join in, still giggling.

"All right, all right," Mr. Donelly says. "I get it. You win. Sam, come on up."

Sam marches to the front of the class and takes the marker. Mr. Donelly sits on the edge of his desk, eyes me, and says, "He's a keeper."

The class laughs again. I keep growing in reverse.

But not quite as fast as a moment ago.

When class is over, I take Sam's hand the instant we're out of the room.

"You're awesome," I say.

"Thank you," he says. "So, now that we're all friendly again, can you tell me what happened yesterday?"

"You want to come with me someplace?" I say instead of answering.

"*Any*place." His hand tightens on mine for a second.

We pass a kid sitting in the hallway near the library doors, knees drawn close to his chest and arms folded over his stomach. I recognize him from the Jamaican Blue coffee shop. He starts to glare at us as we walk past, but then stops.

"Hi," I say.

"Hey," he grunts.

He and Sam trade nods, but that's it.

We keep walking, right past the library windows. I see Brianna Montaro alone at a table with a textbook open in front of her, plus her phone, an iPad, and a notebook. She's staring down at the textbook with her head in both hands, pulling her skin tight around her face. Something in the book is driving her crazy.

I don't realize that I've stopped to watch her until she looks up, right at me, like she sensed my gaze somehow. I expect her expression to be bitchy. Instead, for one second, maybe before she realizes who it is she's looking at—me, the A+ SLUT herself—her eyes are pinched and haunted.

We hold each other in our sights for a moment. She turns away before I do.

*Good.*

"What's up?" Sam asks.

"Nothing," I say. "Let's go."

We head for my new car, its red paint shining under the sun. Sam says, "Whoa. This is . . . a car."

"Do you like it? Smell inside."

Sam climbs in behind the wheel. "Oh my. Yes, a guy could get used to this. Very easily. Holy crap, is this leather?"

"The best money can buy."

"Can I drive it?"

"No. I don't know. Maybe. Okay."

"Vivi?"

"Yeah?"

"I'm totally screwing with you. I wouldn't drive this thing on a bet." He gets out and shuts the door. "Uh . . . I didn't just lock your keys in your shiny new car, right?"

I jingle them.

"Good," he says. "Because that would have been a really awful way to end a Tuesday."

I smile.

I *smile*. At school.

"Hop in," I say to Sam as I get behind the wheel.

"Gosh, I don't know . . . okay!"

He gets in beside me, and I peel out of the parking space. I'm being stupid, but it feels good. People glare. I like it.

But then I drive carefully out of the parking lot and onto the street.

"Is this what you were doing this morning?" Sam asks as I drive.

"Yes. With my Aunt Marlene."

"Wow. Does your Dad know?"

"Yes. I showed it to him this morning. He likes it."

"Well, this is nice." Sam takes a moment to admire the interior again before facing me. "All right. So, yesterday. I don't necessarily need you to apologize or anyth—"

"Sorry."

"Now, see what you did there? I wasn't even done." He smacks my knee, smiling.

I smile, too, a bit ashamed and a lot grateful.

"You don't have to apologize. I just want to know what happened, if I did something wrong."

"No. It was me. Me and that stupid . . ."

Sam waits. We come to a stoplight.

"My mom works at a car wash," I say as we drive north.

"Okay?" Sam says.

"It's . . . you'll see in a minute."

Sam nods, and sits back in the leather seat. Twenty minutes later, we're parked in front of my house, with Sam's side facing it. I park on the street, not the driveway, because with Sam in the car, I feel like a visitor, not a resident.

"This is where I live now."

"Oh," Sam says, eyebrows whisking up. "So, your mom *owns* a chain of car washes across the developed world. That's what you meant to say. Right? Because, and I don't say this very often—holy *shit* that's a nice house."

It's a monstrosity. That's what I think.

But Sam's not stupid. Still looking at the house, he says, "So this is from the lawsuit."

"The settlement from Dad's accident, yeah," I say. "I swear to God, I think he picked a neighborhood and just bought the most expensive one he could. I don't even know when he could have come to look at it."

"So then your mom . . . ?"

"She left us," I say, staring at the house, alternating my focus between it and Sam's head, like a movie camera. "Then Dad got hurt. And when he got this place, he couldn't . . . God, he could not *wait* to give her the change of address. He was *thrilled*."

"Okay, so . . . I don't get it. I mean, I get your dad wanting to show off for the woman who left him. What's this have to do with whatever happened at school yesterday?"

"Brianna Montaro."

"What about her?"

"When I was in the bathroom, she came in with her little group—"

"I saw them go in, yeah. Brianna's the *nice* one, believe it or not."

"They said when I moved here, their property values went down. I don't even know what that means."

Sam's face becomes fierce. Not an expression I've seen on him before.

"Brianna said that?"

"Her or one of the others. They all sound alike."

"See, now I'm pissed," Sam says. "Really, sincerely, righteously pissed. How can someone . . . ? Damn. I'm sorry, Viv. No wonder you took off."

I nod a little, wondering if I should tell him what else they said.

"Does she embarrass you?" Sam says.

"Sometimes. Yes. I'm afraid to go into the restrooms now. I don't even want to be here anymore, I never wanted to be here. I want to be back in the Dez with my friends and my aunt. Everything *sucks* here except . . ."

My voice drops.

"Except for you."

Sam, who has been studying my house, turns slowly to face me. He looks into my eyes, and I can't read his expression. I just told him more than I ever, ever wanted to. And I'm almost glad. Mostly scared. But still glad.

"Wow," he says softly. "Okay. Well. First off, thank you for trusting me with all that. Seriously. And second? I was actually asking about your mom."

Oh.

My first thought is, *God, am I stupid.*

My second thought is, *That's hysterical.*

A snort escapes. Then one high-pitched bark. Then: laughing. Hard.

Sam looks uncertain for a moment, then he starts laughing with me. It's so ridiculous and so stupid and so . . . so . . .

Sam leans in and kisses me.

And—it's so . . . *so* . . .

Yes.

# BRADY

Pay for my Trenta iced mocha and two muffins with Coach's scratched-up gold Starbucks card. Donte gets a Venti mocha frap and a croissant. I call him a pussy.

Most everyone is gone by the time we roll back up to school with Coach's tall coffee. People are rushing to get off campus. I wonder what that feels like. To be in a hurry to get home.

Walk to Coach's office and hand over his coffee. He says, "Didn't you guys get anything?"

Me and Donte grin. Our stuff didn't last the ride. Coach laughs. Says, "All right, get dressed out, we got a short day."

We start to go. Coach says, "Brady."

I stop. Donte keeps walking. Coach has this voice that he can use. We all know what it means: sit down and shut up.

I sit across from him.

"You wanna tell me what you did to your hands, chief?"

Shit. He didn't say anything before we left to get the coffee. Thought he hadn't noticed. Or didn't worry about it.

"Accident," I say.

"Oh," Coach says. "All right. You know anything about what happened to the lockers? Looks like they've been beat to hell."

I stare at my bandages.

"Look a man in the eye, son."

I lift my chin. Look him in the eye.

"Anything I need to know?"

"Naw," I say. Then I say, "No, sir."

"We got a hard game coming up. Can I put you in?"

I flex my hands. They ache, but not bad. I make tight fists.

"Yes, sir."

"All right. Get dressed out."

I stand up.

"Hey, you got my card?"

"Oh, yeah." I reach for my back pocket and pull it out. The gold plastic shimmers under the fluorescents.

Coach waves a hand. "Hang on to it for me."

I stand there.

"It automatically reloads when there's less than ten bucks on it," Coach says. He shuffles through some papers on his desk. "You can just, you know . . . use it for whatever. Give it back to me at the end of the year. When you graduate."

I clench my teeth hard enough to bust a football between them.

Charity. It's charity. Coach knows it. I know it. I bet everyone knows it.

No. Wait. Coach don't go around talking about his players. Not to anyone. My secrets are still safe. Except for Donte. But Donte's not talking. No way.

*Just take it*, I tell myself. *Don't tie up your panties. Just take it.*

"Cool," I say to Coach. Coach only nods. Guess we have an understanding.

"One more thing," Coach says when I reach the doorway. "I want you to come over for dinner next week. Week from Thursday. Can you do that?"

"Yeah, sure."

"All right. We'll see you then. Now get the hell out of here, we gotta practice."

I get the hell outta there. Stow the card in my locker for after practice. I'll need it.

# CADENCE

At the end of detention, which is in this glass-walled room inside of the library that everyone calls the Fishbowl, I say goodbye to the leather-jacketed guys and one tattooed girl who spent the hour with me. Fascinating people. I'd like to talk to them someday, because we couldn't talk in detention, of course. I bet they have interesting life stories. The girl had the Serenity Prayer from AA tattooed on the back of her left calf. I recognized it because Dad still goes once a week.

I walk into the hallway, and there's Danny, sitting across the hall with his knees up and arms crossed. He reminds me of a little boy because of the expression on his face. Sort of pouty but stubborn.

Seeing Danny makes me stop dead. I'm not sure I want to talk to him right now. But then someone bangs into me from behind.

Whoever it is says, "Watch it!"

"Sorry," I say, automatically, and take a step to one side.

That should be the end of it. It's not. Sad face.

THE Brianna Montaro is alone this time, so that's something. At least she doesn't have her pack of hyenas with her. But she cruises past me, looking at me over her shoulder like I just curb stomped a koala bear.

"Look out, bitch," she says as she goes.

I don't bother replying. I'm more interested in what Danny wants.

Danny, on the other hand, watches Brianna for just a second, then leaps to his feet.

"Hey, uh—Brianna. Right?"

She stops. Studies him. "What."

Danny holds up his hands, as if to show he's not carrying any weapons. He smiles. Smiles! It's as I'm processing that fact that it dawns on me he's not smiling for real. He's disarming her, setting her up. Uh-oh.

"Hi, sorry, I don't mean to bother you, I just noticed you had something in your teeth, is all. I thought you should know."

Naturally, Brianna runs her tongue over her teeth in that way any person would when someone tells them they have something in their teeth.

"Did I get it?" she asks after a second.

Danny frowns in a friendly way. "No, not quite . . . it looks like a . . ." He points, gingerly, toward her face. "Like a . . . little . . . sperm stuck in there. A little quarterback sperm, maybe."

It takes THE Brianna Montaro a second for Danny's insult to sink in. I'd laugh myself except it really is pretty crude.

"You're an asshole!" she shouts.

The game is on. Danny's usual, narrow-eyed glare comes back full force.

"Then you must want to lick me," Danny says. "That's what you ladies do to them, isn't it? Lick their assholes?"

Her jaw falls open with almost audible snap. "Oh my *God!*"

"Ah," Danny says. "A popular refrain of yours. Right up there with 'don't stop' and 'oh baby.' Yes? No? Am I in the ballpark?"

He is really enjoying himself, and part of me is sort of happy because he's doing it to defend me, just like Johnny or Dad would. But another part of me feels like telling Danny to stop.

Brianna's face turns red. "Fuck you!"

"*That's* the other one I was thinking of," Danny replies, snapping his fingers once. "Also? Fuck *you*? Not on a bet. I wouldn't *touch* you, you giant walking herpie."

Danny wins. Brianna gasps, and her whole body stiffens up. She walks away like she's on stilts. I wonder if she'll cry, and if she did, if I should feel good or bad about it.

But then Brianna stops and turns to face Danny again. I am entirely forgotten.

"No wonder your family hates you," she says.

Danny's tough-guy, smart-ass face drops, his eyes going to half-lid. Honestly, there's a second there where I am positive he's going to run over and clock her right in the face.

Brianna sees she's won, and spins around to make a quick exit before Danny can come up with anything else to say.

When she's turned a corner, I walk cautiously up to Danny. I approach from an angle in front of him so he won't be startled, and I don't stand too close, just close enough to make sure he knows I'm here. We stand there, facing the direction Brianna went.

"That was kinda brutal of you," I say.

"Thanks." He says it without opening his mouth, somehow.

"It wasn't a compliment. But still, thank you. She knows your family?"

Danny doesn't answer right away.

"My sister goes here," he says finally, his lips barely moving. "She has balls."

"Which kind? The sports kind or the boy kind?"

Like a sheet being whipped off a new work of art, Danny's face relaxes.

"Both, most likely," he says. "Nah, she's a meathead Athleader, that's all. Softball and volleyball. She's kind of a C-word."

I don't know whether to believe his sudden mood change. "What's a C-word?"

Danny eyes me. "Carnivore. She eats meat."

I can tell by his eyes that I'm missing something, but man, I am just not smart enough to figure out what it is. So I let it go.

"What were you doing out here?" I ask him, readjusting my bag on my shoulder.

"I was waiting for you."

"Why?"

"To . . . tell you . . . that . . ."

I hold up a hand. "Wait. Don't even say it. You were going to say 'I'm sorry,' right? For all that crap in Pete's car about my unicorns and glitter?"

"That had been my plan."

"Well, don't. I have a better idea. Stop *needing* to say it. Okay?"

". . . Okay."

"Cool." Without thinking, I give him a quick hug. "Thank you for defending me."

I can feel him wanting to hold me closer, tighter, but resisting. Maybe I shouldn't have hugged him. But he stood up for me. There's a good guy in there, somewhere.

# VIVI

I've lost track of time. All I know is I'm sweating and a little breathless, sitting behind the wheel of my new car with Sam all splotchy faced beside me.

I don't know what to say. I've never been kissed like that before. It started simply enough, just him moving in and me responding with a quick peck.

But that quick one . . . I don't know if I really felt a static shock, maybe from the new upholstery or something, but there was definitely something electrical. I don't remember a lot after that. But my lips are tingling and parts of me are on fire.

Sam at last clears this throat and adjusts his clothing, sitting up straight.

"For the record," he says, and his usually lawyerlike voice cracks just a little. "Any time you want to do that, and I do mean any time, feel free."

"Sounds good," I manage to say.

We both blow out breaths at the same time, which makes us laugh again. Not quite as big as before, but it doesn't matter. We're feeling good.

And now that we're feeling good . . . I can tell him more. It's as if our kissing opened a vault.

"You asked about my mom."

Sam sits up even more. "I did."

"The answer is yes. I'm such a bitch, but yes, she embarrasses me."

"I wasn't trying to make a moral call on it. I was just curious."

"No, but it's true with Dad, too. Differently. But still. He embarrasses the hell out of me."

I turn toward Sam, now that I'm mostly sure I won't attack his face with mine again.

"It's like, he sold out and ran off from everything that defined us. Traditions. History. Made us come up here so we could be like . . ."

Sam either grins or grimaces. "You can say it."

"No I can't," I say. "But you know what I mean."

"People like me?"

"People like *her*."

"Brianna."

"Yeah. So that's embarrassing." I sigh. "But look at this car. It's awesome. And I love it. I love that it's quiet here. I love that I could sit outside at night without counting the cars across the street swinging by for drugs. Some traditions and histories *should* be left behind."

"Definitely."

"So knowing where Mom works now, and the fact that she left, which you're just not supposed to do, ever . . . God, Sam, part of me wants to drive this car to her car wash and watch her detail it, and be like, 'See what you missed?' What kind of shitty person *am* I?"

"You're not. She bailed, you're pissed. You should be. That's normal."

"Then why do I feel so terrible?"

"Because it's a terrible situation. But I don't see that you did anything wrong here. For what it's worth."

It's worth the world. I can't quite make myself say it out loud, but I hope Sam understands.

"And as far as Brianna goes," Sam adds, "she's just . . . well, she's a lot of things. Driven is the biggest thing. Ambitious. That's mostly her mom and dad, though. She's got to be first at everything. The whole family's like that. She pushes herself really hard. I kind of respect that part—"

I glare.

"—but only as far as it goes," Sam says. "I'm driven, too. But I also understand the value of a good cup of coffee during sixth hour every once in a while."

I think I'm in love. But that's something else I'm not about to say. "Do you still think about her?"

"Not really. I feel bad for her sometimes, maybe. Her parents are kind of on the harsh side, to say the least. They made us break up."

"So you didn't want to."

"Well, no. Not at the time. But, Viv, it was last year. And when she broke up with me, she didn't just end it. She cranked the bitch up to eleven. I don't miss her, and I don't think about her. I think a whole lot about you, though."

That'll do. "You want a ride home?"

"Sure. Can we do that whole kissing thing again soon?"

I don't say anything. But I think the heat emanating from my face is all the answer he needs.

# DREA

Kelly and I leave play rehearsal together and go to Kelly's old pickup truck. She drives me home, which is sort of our tradition now.

When Kelly pulls up in front of my house, she puts the truck in park and says, "Listen, do me a favor, huh?"

This is new. "Um—okay."

"Don't cut yourself today, all right?"

My stomach shrivels up. She hasn't brought it up recently.

"I'm not trying to make a thing out of it," Kelly says. "Just, you know. Give it a day. Don't do it again today or tonight. Can you go that long?"

"I guess," I say. No one's ever asked me to stop cutting. But then, no one knows I do it, either.

"That would be cool," Kelly says. "Thanks."

"Um . . . sure," I say, because I don't know what *else* to say.

"I just don't like the idea of you getting hurt," Kelly says. It feels weird, so I open my door and hop out. I don't want her to be my mom.

"I get it," I tell her. "I won't. All right?"

Kelly nods quickly, like she can tell I'm not super comfortable. I say goodbye and head for the front door as Kelly drives away.

"I'm home," I say, standing just inside the doorway.

Silence.

Without consciously deciding to do it, I scream into the depths of the house.

"*I'm home!*"

The word "home" ricochets through halls and rooms like a rifle shot, you know? Pinging off doors and ceilings. The effort forces my eyes closed, and the clenching of my stomach half bends me over.

Silence.

I rub my neck. My vocal cords must be hanging like raw strips of meat at the back of my throat.

I go to my room, turn on some music, find a paperclip, and hold it in both hands for a very long time. Wondering: *If I do it, will Kelly find out?*

Before I can, I hear someone coming through the front door. It is either an ax murderer or Dad, because Mom always shouts "Hello" —though not quite as loud as I just did. My throat still hurts.

I get up and go to the kitchen, where Dad is getting himself a Coke. His short brown hair shows natural highlights in the fridge light.

"Hey, Sweet," he says, not looking at me.

"Where's Mom?"

"Dunno."

"Do you care?"

Dad pauses, sips, and—still not looking—says, "Dunno that either. Why?"

"No reason. Just have some—choices to make."

Finally he looks at me, and smiles a little. "Oh yeah? Like what?"

I tug the cuffs of my sleeves down past my wrists.

"Nothing."

# CADENCE

I meet the boys Friday night at Fifty-Third and Third. We get coffee to go from Jamaican Blue, then Pete drives us to a middle school he used to go to. We sit in the dark in the middle of the soccer field, because in the city this is one of the only places where you can hide in plain sight, as long as the sun is not up.

"Definition of a stoner," Pete says, carefully packing his bowl. "One who or that which stones."

"Sure you don't want to try it?" Danny asks me.

"I'm sure. You both look ridiculous."

Pete glares at me. "You can totally not be here if you want."

"I know."

"If you're staying here, can you at least not talk shit about us?" Pete says.

"I'm not. I'm being honest. Your clothes are going to reek, you'll laugh for a little while, like no one on earth has ever laughed before without having drugs in their body, and then you'll be hungry. Then there's those bong zits you get on your cheeks. Where's the fun part?"

"You just described it," Pete says, and laughs.

"I can laugh and munch out without getting high first," I say. "Zits, too. Those just show up regardless."

"That," Pete says, "is your loss." He lights the bowl and inhales deeply. He immediately coughs like his lungs are going to burst.

"Yep," I say. "That sure does look like fun. Boy, howdy."

Pete tries mightily to say something, and I can tell he's pissed, but he can't stop coughing. That makes me laugh.

"Are you all right?" I say after a full minute of this. "Can you breathe?"

Pete keeps gagging, but he nods. He passes the bong, which is made out of a Mrs. Butterworth's bottle, over to Danny. Danny glances at me with narrow eyes while Pete starts clearing his throat and gesturing like he wants to say something but can't. "Go ahead," he finally rasps.

Danny keeps his eyes on me for a second longer, and I raise my eyebrows at him.

"You heard him," I say. "Have 'fun.'"

Danny inhales from the bottle. He doesn't fare much better than Pete. But then Pete takes the bottle back and smokes again. *And* coughs again.

Boys are hopeless. I suppose I could have stayed home and read, but it's Friday. All of my girls are incommunicado still, and I can't help but wonder if maybe we've just been apart too long now. Maybe Danny and Pete are my new best friends. It sort of feels that way.

Ten minutes later, the boys are on their backs in the grass, and Pete is giggling stupidly. If I wasn't worried about them getting home safe, I would have taken Pete's suggestion and just left, I swear. They are plotting ways to humiliate the many people they don't like at school.

"What's that—what's that one kid's name?" Pete says, still giggling.

"Oh yeah, that one," Danny says. This reply is, apparently, comedic gold. It sets them both off laughing. *This* kind of smiling doesn't count, I decide.

"The—the football player, what's his name?"

"There's eight hundred of them," I say. "Which one?"

"There are thirty-six," Danny says. He's not laughing now. "Plus two out for the season with injuries. That's varsity. JV has twenty-eight, but the juniors on varsity can be moved down to play JV, so the roster changes sometimes."

Pete pulls himself up to a sitting position, and we both stare down at Danny. His eyes look closed, but it's kind of hard to tell in the dark.

"How do you know that?" I say.

"Especially high?" Pete says.

Danny doesn't answer. Pete shrugs.

"Okay, so what's that guy's name . . . the quarterback guy?"

"Brady," I say. "Brady Culliver. They call him B."

"Because that's all they can spell," Danny says.

"How do you know his name?" Pete asks me.

"I listen."

"Okay, so he's on the list," Pete says. "Now who's the other one?"

"Donte," Danny says. "Donte Assjack Walker. I'm not sure that's his middle name, though. I'm just making that up."

Pete thinks this is hysterical.

"The other players just call him D," I say. "I've heard that, too."

"Wait a sec," Danny says. "So Brady is *B*. And Donte is *D*. So together, they're . . . B and D?"

"Um, I guess?"

"Which is short for 'bondage and discipline.' You know that, right?"

"Short for—huh?"

Whether it's because he's high or just that he understands the joke, Pete starts laughing all over again and tells me, "Just Google it. But not at school. Or where your parents might find it."

"Okay, well, that tells me pretty much all I needed to know. Why do you hate them?"

The two boys look at me like I just asked if the earth was round.

"They're just football players, not kitten assassins," I say.

"Meaning, they don't kill baby cats, or they aren't kittens who *do* assassinations?" Pete says. "Because that could be a really cool anime or something."

"They're just people. Same as you."

"Objection," Danny says. "I beg to differ. People have basic inalienable rights. Or they're supposed to. The right to self-expression, the right to wear what you want. The right to be left alone. Things like that. So maybe they are people, but let's *not* pretend they're the same as us."

"Danny, you're so mad, why are you so mad? You're all hostile about these guys when you don't know anything about them."

"I don't know any . . . ? *Excuse* me? Are you joking?"

"Danny—"

"Listen to me." Danny gets to his feet as if towering over me will make his statements true. "I studied this shit. In February 1960, four African American kids sat down at the 'white' counter in a café. And the white folks weren't super happy about that. Over the next week, a bunch more black kids showed up to support those first four kids. It was all part of the Civil Rights movement, and it was within our grandparents' lifetime. Got it? Now—you know who showed up to try and throw those kids out of the café? The *football team*. Not the drama department, not the artists, not band, not choir. Not the chess team, not the debate team, or the math club, or yearbook, or Sat School tutors. The football players. So what does that tell you?"

"That it was 1960 and people were being stupid?"

Danny stares at me for a long time before grunting and throwing his hands up in the air, letting them crash back down against his leg.

"Are you *truly* that naïve?" he says, and wanders a few steps away, pacing in circles.

"You asked," I call after him.

"Ah," Pete says, waving him off. "He'll be fine. He's just high."

Pete cracks himself up with that one, except he's the only one laughing. I sit back with my hands behind me and elbows locked, crossing my ankles and knocking my feet together.

"I gotta leak," Pete says. He gets slowly to his feet and wanders into the darkness.

Danny stops pacing and stands a few yards away, arms folded and chin down.

"You're mad at me?" I say.

"No. I mean, maybe, but—no. Frustrated. Ready to beat the shit out of something."

"I hope you don't mean me. Because I can take you."

"Because I'm a skinny little faggot?"

"What?"

"Nothing. Never mind."

"If I hear you talking like that again, I will seriously put the hurt on you, Danny."

Danny snorts. Is he smiling? Hard to tell in the dark. Probably not. Still. Pete shuffles back out of the darkness. "Ha," he says. "You didn't even see me coming, did you? I know what I'm gonna be for Halloween now. I'm gonna be a *ninja*. I got the weapons and everything."

"You have ninja weapons?" I ask.

"Of course I have ninja weapons!"

"Like what?"

He shows off two or three useless martial arts moves. "I've got nunchaku! And shuriken! *Hikeeba!*"

"Isn't that when you don't do something you were supposed to?" I ask. "Shirking your responsibilities or something?"

"Shuriken, not shirking."

"I give up."

"Perhaps you would enjoy the taste of . . . *my nunchacku! Waaaa! Watchah!*"

"You are such a doofblatt."

"What's that doofblatt stuff?" Danny says. "Where'd you get that from?"

"My friend Zach."

"Oh, your friend Zach, huh? And how is your good friend Zach?"

I start to say I don't know, because I don't. I haven't seen him around. Except Danny's tone makes me mad, and I've kind of had it with him tonight.

"All right," I say, and stand up. I brush grass off the back of my shorts. "That's it, I'm out. You are being a huge pain in the ass, and I don't have to sit here and take it. Love ya, bye."

"Hold on," Danny says.

"No. I'm not going to hold on. I asked you to stop doing things you'd have to apologize for, remember? But here you are doing it all over again. I don't even know why I came out here with you guys. It's just about getting high and hating people. I don't get it, sorry. I'll stay home and read a book or hang out with my brother and his friends or . . . stick knives in my face."

"I hate them," Danny says abruptly.

"My brother's friends?"

"The people at school. All of them. I hate them. You were right about that. They say and do all kinds of heinous shit and nobody ever calls them on it. I think you know that's true. Somewhere inside, you know that. You don't have to hate them, too, that's cool, whatever, but I would love it if you'd at least pretend for me once in a while."

He shakes his head a bit, looking at the ground.

"That's all," he says, and sits straight down, cross-legged, with a big huff.

Pete looks from him—

to me—

to him—

to me.

"Jesus," he says, finally, pulling out cigarettes. "Would you two have sex already?"

I cross my arms. "No. I've got another idea."

## FINAL SCORE

Wildcats                    12
SPARTANS                    06

*We're a Happy Family*

# BRADY

Coach has a dining room table. But it's covered with real estate brochures. Skim through a couple on my way to the kitchen. Big houses. Five or six bedrooms. Outdoor floodlights. Gravel yards raked out perfect.

I want one someday.

Coach brushes past. Smacks a hand on my shoulder. "Come on in, Brady, have a seat. You ever had Monica's pasta sauce? You can stand a fork in it."

I sit down. "Sounds good."

Coach's daughter walks in. Sits across from me. Smiles. "Hey, Brady."

"Hey."

"Glad you could make it."

I don't know what she means. Maybe just being nice. Or maybe she's *really* glad. Coach's daughter is hot. That's just the way it is. Which sucks. Not me, not nobody, is gonna move in on her. Still. I like that Coach's wife sits me across from her at the kitchen table. Amy's got a tight blue sweater on. Hair's pulled back smooth in a long ponytail. Good thing no one can see my lap while we're sitting down. I got a huge rager.

Monica puts spaghetti on the table. I smell oregano and garlic. Get a bunch of spit in my mouth from it.

Coach rubs his hands together real quick. It's a signal. I know what it means. We all bow our heads a little.

"Thank you for food, thank you for guests, thank you for family," he says. "Amen."

We say amen. Closest to church I ever get. Never seen a Bible here. But there's a small stone cross on one bookshelf in their living room. Coach never talks about God or Jesus or anything. Don't know why they do this dinner prayer. Don't care. Pray all night every night if it meant coming home to this.

I want to live here. Even if it meant Amy would be my sister and we could never hook up. That's okay. It would be worth it. Can't ever hook up, anyway.

Coach dishes out pasta. It's so freaking good.

"Slow down, Brady," Monica says. But she's smiling. Like she likes how much I like it.

Start my second bowl. Coach says, "So how're the grades?"

"Okay," Amy says. Takes a drink of iced tea. Wraps her lips around a straw to do it. I have to shift in my seat to keep my rager from pinching in my jeans.

Amy keeps talking. "I need to write a paper tonight for English on some werewolf or something. Pretty boring."

"Beowulf?" Monica says.

"Sure, I guess," Amy says.

Monica shakes her head. But she smiles, too.

Coach says, "Well, that's great. But I was asking Brady."

"Oh. Oops," Amy says.

Coach bumps his elbow into mine. "So?"

He doesn't sound mad. But he wants to know for real. I think he can find out for himself if wants. Could ask at the office. Just wants to see how I'm gonna answer him.

"They're okay," I say.

Coach picks something out from his teeth with his tongue. Doesn't say anything. I know what that means when he doesn't say anything. On the field or in the locker room or in his office or at his own dinner table. It means *Try again.*

I don't have a rager anymore.

"Better," I say. Take another big bite.

"Hmm," Coach says. That's all.

Amy saves me. She asks me, "So what're you going to be for Halloween?"

"Nothing," I say.

"Loser."

"What're you gonna be?"

"Oh, a volleyball player."

Everyone laughs. Amy helped take the team to Divisionals last year.

"Loser," I say.

"Come on," she says. "Come up with something. But not football player. I mean, how lame would *that* be."

We all laugh again. I almost start crying. Because this is what it's supposed to be like. This is it. I just want this.

Is that so wrong, Mom? I just want this.

"Maybe, uh . . . Superman," I say.

"Oh yeah! Then I could be Wonder Woman."

It takes less than a second to imagine her in tight blue underwear and a tight red top. That's all I know about Wonder Woman. My rager comes right back.

Did she mean something by it? Like we should go out together as a superhero couple? But I can't ask. Not here. Maybe at school. But Coach still wouldn't let that happen. No way.

He's not looking at me. But I can tell he still sort of is.

I focus on dinner. Hope for my rager to go down.

# DANNY

With the money I'm making from Pete, I buy one of those prepaid cell phones. It's not much, but it'll text. I use it to ask Pete for a ride. When I tell him where, he gives me a bunch of shit about it, but I don't care. I'm just a lucky sonofabitch that Cadence will still talk to me. Jesus, she's right. I've got to stop putting myself in positions where I have to apologize to her.

Maybe that's why she told me to come to her house for dinner. When she said last week that she had an idea other than sex, suffice it to say that dinner was not what I had in mind. But what if it means she's starting to like me differently now? I can't not find out.

No one notices when I leave. Or if they do, they don't say anything. Dinner smells good, too. Well, whatever. Anything Cadence makes will be better. I know it.

Cadence's house is small. Smaller than mine. It's in an older part of town, the type of place where I expect to see cars up on cement blocks, or graffiti on every sign. As it turns out, I only see a couple of blue-marker scrawls on a light pole, on top of a square of darker gray paint where the city has already covered up previous graffiti. But while most of the yards we drive past aren't exactly manicured, there's no trash in the street. Most of the properties have fences—short chain-link or flimsy wood. Some are even white picket. Many of them also have plastic lawn chairs, or dilapidated benches, or upturned milk crates on their porches.

"What's your plan, hotshot?" Pete says as he stops the car

in front of Cadence's house. There's a short wooden fence encircling the front yard. It's in good shape, but unpainted. A detached garage sits about ten feet from the house. Red light illuminates a drawn shade on the garage door, and I think there's movement inside, but I can't tell.

"Hell if I know," I tell Pete.

"You owe me ten Adds for this."

"Five."

"Ooo, bargaining now."

"It's a seller's market."

Pete smirks. "So you need a ride later or you staying the night?"

"Golly gee. Probably a ride, I'm thinking."

"Cool. Well, get on in there."

I open the door, but don't get out. "What the hell am I doing here, man? Must be a masochist."

"I don't know, dude." Pete starts to light a cigarette, but stops; I asked him not to smoke until after I got out, so I wouldn't stink when I got inside her house. "If you like her, you need to make a move. Just, you know . . . say something to her. Say words!"

I slide my legs out of the car and stand up.

"Words are for suckers."

I shut the door. I can hear Pete laughing inside.

He drives off while I follow a concrete path up to the front door. Cadence's dad opens it as I climb the wooden steps up to her porch.

"Howdy," he says, and pushes open the screen door with a hand the size of my skull. We're the same height, but he's shaped like the Kool-Aid Man.

"Hi," I say. I step into the house.

He lets the door shut behind me. The front room is narrow and long, running almost the length of the front side of the house. Straight ahead is the kitchen, and I don't see anyone in it, but I can smell some kind of spicy meat cooking.

"Danny, right?" Cadence's dad says.

"Yes. Yes, sir."

"Don't call me sir. I'm Chuck. Dinner'll be ready in a minute. Have a seat."

He's not being a dick, exactly. But he doesn't smile at all, either. I guess I have no room to bitch.

I turn to face the living room, and only then do I see Cadence. "Oh! Hey. Didn't see you." I don't know what to do with my hands. They shoot into my pockets, but that doesn't feel right, so I cross my arms, and that feels worse. Fuck.

"I find that hard to believe," she says, grinning.

Cadence is sitting on a purple couch, bare feet propped on a white coffee table. Magic pours from her lips—no, bubbles. She's dipping a pink wand into a blue bottle of bubbles and blowing them into the living room.

Her smile makes me wonder if she's on something, and her antidrug bit is just a cover. No one looks that peaceful for real.

Do they?

"Sit down, you look spooked," Cadence says.

"No," I say automatically. "I mean, no, I'm not spooked."

"It's okay," Cadence says. "We're still sort of recovering."

"From . . . ?"

"This wasn't always the best neighborhood," Cadence says. "It was really downhill for a while, when I was little. But it's coming back. People are working. Starting to care again. There's places not far from here where you probably don't want to be after ten or eleven at night, but mostly it's okay."

"Oh."

"You live in a nice place, don't you?"

"It's okay."

Compared to her neighborhood, yes, it's a nice place. A place where people can spend thousands on decorating their god damn garages, filling them with stuff so they can't even park in them anymore. So what? Guess what a chocolate-covered turd tastes like.

What's happening inside, that's what counts.

I sit on the edge of an easy chair, then wonder if it's "Chuck's" and move to a wooden rocking chair instead. I do not rock. No pun intended.

Cadence's mom walks out of the kitchen, drying her hands on an orange dish towel. I know it's her mother not just because that would be logical, but because they damn near look like sisters.

"Danny?" she says, smiling. "I'm Audry. Nice of you to come over."

"Thank you, nice to meet you."

"We're about ready, if you want to come grab a plate. You ever make your own quesadilla?"

"No, uh-uh."

"It's fun. Come on in here."

Cadence and I both get up. She points to the kitchen doorway. "Guests first."

"Ladies first."

"I'm not a lady. I'm a mature young woman."

Audry says, "I'd like to weigh in on that!"

"Mature young women first," I say.

Cadence bolts in front of me, and—I smile. She's the only thing in the world that can make me do that. I just don't want her to know, in case things don't work out.

Automatically, I start to watch her ass as she walks ahead of me, but caution is the better part of lust, and I lift my eyes very fast so Audry won't catch me checking out her daughter's body.

There are places set out at the kitchen table. There's no room for a dining area like that at our place. On the counter are the makings of a Mexican feast: black beans, homemade pico de gallo, grated cheese, warm tortillas, shredded meat, sliced jalapeño peppers, and a sautéed mix of bell peppers and onions. At the end of the line is a red quesadilla maker, like a big two-sided grill.

"Load 'em up," Chuck says, walking into the kitchen from another doorway that looks like it leads to a small bedroom or office. "Go ahead, Dan."

It's all I can do to not correct him. I loathe the name Dan.

But I follow his orders, because he sounds like he's used to people doing just that. I get a plate and start piling cheese onto a tortilla. Cadence falls in behind me while Audry puts bottles of water on the table and a glass pitcher of something red.

"Cadence said you worked on a submarine," I say, sprinkling beans on top of a bed of cheese.

"That's right," Chuck says.

"That's pretty cool. What, um . . . what'd you do on it?"

"Don't worry about it."

He might be messing with me, Daddy polishing the shotgun and all that. But I can't tell, and I'm not taking any chances. So I focus on dinner.

After all our quesadillas are finished cooking, Audry brings a dish of the pico to the table. I spoon some onto my plate and dip a tortilla chip into it. The chips and salsa are homemade.

The salsa is freaking awesome. We always have bottled stuff like Tostitos or Herdez at home. I could eat a bowl full of this like soup.

"Wow," I say, feeling like a dork but unable to stop. "This is great. What's in it?"

"Nail clippings," Audry says.

It actually takes a second for me to see if they're joking. When all three of them laugh, I choose to believe it's because she was kidding. And even if not, I don't care—I'll take the clippings because this stuff is incredible.

That's when the pain hits.

# DONTE

"How's the rice?" Mom asks.

I can't help laughing. We have rice almost every night. Sometimes noodles. But always one or the other.

"Mmm!" I say, exaggerating. "So good, Mom, so good."

Mom laughs right back at me. But then Ramon, being the seven-year-old that he is, says, "I'm sick of rice!"

"Hey," I say quietly. "Don't worry about it, boss."

"I am, I am, I am!" Ramon shouts, throwing his black plastic fork down. He jumps up from the table and picks up one of his plastic guns with the orange tip and fires it at the table.

"I don't like those things," Mom reminds him. "Put it down and come back to the table, Ramon."

He does, crossing his arms and sits there being pissy in that way only seven-year-olds can be.

Mom closes her eyes. She's sick of rice, too. We all are. We're sick of kung pao chicken, and orange chicken, and Mongolian beef, and everything else that Pei Wei has to offer. There are only so many combinations. A couple of weeks ago, Amy suggested we have Pei Wei when she and Brianna and Brady and me and some other friends were all out for lunch together. I almost threw up in the new-old car at the suggestion. We went to In-N-Out instead. I bought for everyone.

I take Ramon's black plastic dish and hold it up over mine. "All right. I'll just eat all yours then . . ."

"No, no, no!" Ramon screams, reaching for the dish.

"All right," I say again, putting the bowl back down. "But you gotta eat it, okay? You want mine instead?"

"It's all the same shit," Ramon says.

Mom's eyes flip open. Before she can do anything, though, I sit up tall in my chair and bark, "*Hey!*"

Ramon freezes in place.

"We don't talk like that," I say, aiming for firm but not angry. I know I can scare the kid when I want to. Right now, I don't want to. "Right? We don't talk like that?"

Ramon pouts, doesn't answer.

"Ramon? Let's go, boss. We don't talk like that, right?"

"Okay," Ramon says.

"Tell Mom."

"Sorry, Mom."

Mom rubs Ramon's arm. She still does that to me, too, sometimes. "Thank you, baby."

Then she glances over at me and says *Thank you* with her eyes.

I shrug it off, like it's no big thing. Sometimes, I hate that between me and my little brother we've got two dads running around somewhere. Then other times, I sincerely do not care about those bastards. Why would I want to know anything about my dad? Asshole took off, he can stay gone. Same with Ramon's dad. I've met him a few times. Useless piece of shit is all he is. Ramon's better off without him, but he still comes crawling around, demanding his rights to see the kid. I think he uses Ramon to get sympathy and scam younger women who don't know any better.

I scoop up yet another forkful of rice. This—*this* is a man's game, never mind football. Man's game is taking care of your kid, taking care of your family.

I watch Ramon eating pieces of white rice one at a time.

"You're a good man," I tell Ramon. "I like that. I want to be like you someday."

Ramon sits up a little straighter and actually eats a piece of broccoli. Me and Mom exchange looks. It's a good dinner after all.

# DREA

Mom is having one of her meltdowns. When I walk into the kitchen, I see two bowls shattered into ceramic jigsaws on the floor. Mom must have thrown them while I was in the shower, because I didn't hear them break, and usually I do. Usually I do.

Even as I'm assessing the damage, Dad steps past her and walks around the shards in his bare feet to open the fridge.

"Why won't you look at me?" Mom cries in a throaty, snot-clogged voice.

Dad peers into the fridge like a doctor studying an x-ray. "Because I'm looking for a Coke."

Mom makes a choking, gargling moan. I think, *God, don't ever let me be like this.* I don't know who I hate more. My mother, for making such a melodramatic ass of herself, or my dad for not giving a crap and not at least pretending—*acting!*—like he cares enough to do something about it, you know?

"I just . . ." Mom starts to say, and I know where it's going: "*I just can't do this anymore!*"

She says this approximately once a month. Sometimes more. She has been saying it since as far back as I can remember.

Dad sighs. "Pull yourself together, and we can talk."

Mom makes an effort to stop crying.

"After I finish the set design for the show," Dad adds.

And smirks. So pleased with himself.

Mom's emotions jump past crying and straight to damn

near psycho. "*Do you know what?* Do you want to know something?"

Dad shrugs.

"I screwed Dustin!" Mom howls, triumphant. "How about that? Huh? Whaddya say to that?!"

Her face is red, puffy. I think she's attempting to appear—what's the word?—*exultant*.

Instead, she looks stupid. Dustin is the stage manager over at the theater. I'm 98 percent sure he's gay.

Dad appears bemused. "Okay."

He always says that. Just that way. Like it doesn't mean a thing, like it does not and never will bother him, no matter if it's true or not.

My father's response brings immediate retaliation. "*I hate you!*" Mom screams. "I hate your guts! You *incomparable prick!*"

She rages on, creating combinations of profanities I could never have dreamed of. Dad watches her for a few moments, taking sips of his soda. I hate him for that. He's just letting her go, not making any move to calm her down. He might even be enjoying it. I want to try to help, to say something to her, but what?

Mom collapses against the kitchen table, heaving, clawing weakly at the tabletop as if shot. Tears run out of her eyes as she moans and weeps. Dad takes a sip. Walks past her and into their room. Shuts the door.

My parents, ladies and gentlemen. Let's hear it for them.

I walk back to my room, too, experiencing one of those

moments when you wonder why you were even born. This is not, I am sure, some self-pitying, selfish-teenager thing. I really want to know why these two obviously useless assholes had decided to conceive *anything*.

Maybe they didn't mean to. That would explain a lot.

I call Kelly. She arrives right away, ready to defend me against all invaders, foreign or domestic. She's decked out in black cutoff boys' dress pants and a tank top tie-dyed into a rainbow. Her colorless hair is pulled back, except it's cranky and doesn't appreciate the hair tie, so most of it spills around her round cheeks, anyway. The first thing out of Kelly's mouth is, "What happened?"

I'm not sure where to even start. I've been asking myself that question for fifteen years.

# BRADY

"Come on in here," Coach says after dinner. Amy and Monica clear the plates. They don't look at me. I get a bad feeling. Maybe it's all the pasta. There's a pie on the kitchen counter from a restaurant. I wanted it all to myself. Now I don't know.

Follow Coach into his office. It's nice. Big leather chair behind a desk. Autographed football sitting on a stand that's on top of a bookcase.

Coach sits behind his desk. "Sit down, son."

I sit.

"You wanna play in the NFL? Be a starting quarterback?"

"Yeah."

"No you don't."

I get mad.

"Not like that, you don't," Coach says. "You don't have the fire. You say 'yeah' because you think I want to hear you say 'yeah.'"

I'm not mad anymore. He's right. I know it.

"But I don't want to hear that. That's not what I want. You know what I want, son?"

"No." Looking at my shoes while he talks. Can't look up.

"I want whatever's gonna be best for you. And if you don't mind my saying, what's best for you is getting the hell out of this town."

Now I *do* look up. Into his eyes.

"There it is." Coach kinda grins and leans back in his chair.

"There's that fire I was talking about. You don't care about playing for the NFL, you care about getting out of here."

". . . *Yes*." Comes out like a growl.

"All right, then. Now we're being honest. So I'm gonna tell you what you're gonna do. You want me to do that?"

"Yes, sir."

"What we need to do is leverage your resources. You know what that means? It means you're gonna take what you got and put it to work. So, first, we're gonna get you fed. We're gonna get you bulked up. I'm sick of you not getting enough to eat."

I clamp my teeth together. I'm sick of it, too.

"And you're gonna study. You're gonna get As and Bs in every single class."

"But I—"

"What're buts for?"

"Sissies."

Coach grins. Nobody else says "sissy." Coach says he's trying to bring it back. Says it's a great word to describe some people. Maybe he's right.

"So you're gonna study, and you're gonna get the grades. Then you're gonna be at practice, and I'm gonna bust your ass into shape. You and me are gonna take this team to State."

"We're oh and three right now, Coach."

"We had tough games. Tough schools. That changes tomorrow night. You need one win, B. One win, and the rest of the season will fall into place. But we'll worry about that tomorrow."

I take a deep breath.

"So we're gonna find you a scholarship to some school. It won't matter which one. Any school that'll pay for you. There'll be plenty, trust me. It might not be Notre Dame, or Ohio, USC, any of those. But it'll be free. You're gonna go and keep your dick where it belongs and get a degree, and when that happens, you'll be all set. How does that sound?"

Don't answer. Might start crying. Fuck that.

"So you keep your shit together this year," Coach goes on. Must be pretending not to see what's happening on my face. "Keep your grades up. No drugs, no alcohol, no girl drama. There's not a single one of them worth risking the next four years. You hear me?"

I nod. Jaw's starting to cramp.

"Good. Now when you get to that school, wherever it is, you're gonna do the same thing there. No frat parties, no drinking and driving, none of that crap. You're gonna play. You're gonna play hard. You're gonna work hard. Maybe you play pro ball, maybe you don't. It won't matter, because you'll have the things you need to get out of here. You hear what I'm saying?"

"I think so, Coach."

"It's up to you, Brady. I just gave you the five-year plan to get everything you want. I wish I could promise you the NFL, but I can't. I will promise that if you do everything I just said, you can get out of that house, get out of this town, and you'll be set for life."

I nod again.

"All right," Coach says. "Hey. Maybe after the season, we

can take the team out camping. Fishing, hunting, all that. Just varsity, just the A-team. Whaddya think?"

"That'd be cool, yeah."

"You ready for dessert?"

"Yeah."

"Good man."

We get up. He slaps my shoulder and we head into the kitchen.

I'd take a bullet for this man.

# DANNY

The pain dims, but it doesn't go away. But it gets so I can ignore it. It's not for real, anyway; not physical. I don't think. No—this is something else.

A burst of music from the garage makes me glance up from my last bite of quesadilla. Cadence and her family don't seem to notice, or mind.

"What's that?" I ask her.

"My brother Johnny. He's making videos."

Another burst of music. It goes off, comes back on. Goes off.

"What kind?" I ask.

"You'd have to come see it," Cadence says. "Want to? Come on!"

"She gets distracted easily," Chuck says, and Audry laughs and says, "Squirrel!" Must be a family joke.

Cadence leads me out the front door to the small detached garage. Music is playing again, but not quite as loudly as before. She peeks in a side door, half of which is taken up by a two-paned window, then opens it as she knocks with her other hand.

"Hey, dorks!" she calls, and we walk in.

The garage is set up like a concert held at a trailer park. Five or six guys wander around, adjusting white sheets hanging from the ceiling as backdrops or checking a snake pit of extension cords piled on the floor. Suspended about a foot away from the sheets, attached to a ceiling beam, is a row of aluminum scoop floodlights, which currently wash the sheets with blue. Stools and milk crates are scattered around, and one of the guys is adjusting a black microphone in what looks like a stand made from PVC pipe. Against the opposite wall, there's one real guitar—and three wooden ones. Totally fake. I also spot a chipped violin and an acoustic guitar with no strings.

By the garage door, which flips up as a solid unit rather than rolls like ours, another guy from the group is filming everything with a tiny HD cam. He turns the lens toward us as soon as we walk in. If one of these guys is her brother, I can't tell which. They all look alike.

A big stereo in one corner plays Slipknot. One of the guys, with long hair draped across his shoulders, picks up one of the wooden guitars and mimes playing it.

What the green hell *is* this?

"Hey, Cadence," the camera guy says. "You want to do one?"

"Maybe. What you got?"

"Check out Brandon's phone," the camera guy says. To me, he says, "Hey."

I nod, but keep my mouth shut. I can*not* figure out what's happening here.

I shrink back against one unfinished wooden wall, while Cadence goes over to the stereo and hunkers down. She scrolls through someone's phone, then gives a shout. The music changes to something slow and acoustic that I don't recognize.

"Hey!" one of the guys shouts. "I had first!"

"Oh, shut up," the camera guy says. I decide he must be Johnny. "It's just Cadence. It doesn't count. We'll use it as a warm-up."

The guy who shouted lets it go with a shrug. Cadence grabs one of the stools and puts it . . . well, I guess "center stage," for lack of a better term.

"Anyone know this one?" she says. "I need a guitarist."

"I'll do it," someone says. He must be Brandon, because he adds, "It's my phone."

"Sweet!" Cadence turns to me, shading her eyes against the floodlights shining down on her. "Danny? You want to play something?"

Not knowing what to do, I shake my head.

"Who do you want to film and do lights?" Johnny asks her.

"You can shoot," Cadence says. "But I want Joel on lights."

One of the guys gives a thumbs-up and walks over to a black rectangular box with cords jutting out of it. A second later, the lights change. It must be a control board.

"Shouldn't you be doing the Ramones?" Brandon asks as he pulls the stringless acoustic guitar over his shoulder.

"Later," Cadence says. "I feel mellow."

"Whoa," Brandon says. "There's a first!"

She kicks at him without leaving the stool.

"You ready?" Johnny says.

Cadence nods. I still don't know what to do, so I sink down and kneel on the floor with my arms crossed, afraid to touch anything. There's an awful lot of electricity in this room.

One of the other guys resets the song to the beginning. Joel mixes red and blue lights from the floods near the sheets to create a purple backdrop, while all-blue lights wash across Cadence and Brandon, who stands a foot or so behind her and to one side, his hands positioned like he's actually going to play the fake guitar.

"Cue in five," Johnny says. "Four, three."

The music starts. Cadence closes her eyes and sways on the stool, her arms straight as she clutches the edge of the stool between her knees like a bird.

When the singing begins, Cadence starts lip-synching the lyrics. She's spot on, near as I can tell, and the song is pretty cool; very slow, very melodic. Sort of haunting. Johnny carefully films her "singing," while Brandon pretends to be playing the guitar. The view screen is flipped open on the camera, and as Johnny sidesteps in my direction, I can see the performance through the camera's eye. It actually does look like a real music video.

I focus on Cadence again as Joel manipulates the lights to wash the makeshift stage with red, and dims the backdrop to a low green. Brandon dutifully pretends to play a solo. Cadence's eyes are still closed, and her body drifts lazily back and forth.

She's beautiful.

The song ends. Cadence and Brandon hold their places for a moment—staying in character, I guess—until Johnny calls out, "Cut! Nice."

"Cool!" Cadence says, and bounds off the stool with her usual enthusiasm. "Send it to me."

"Will do," Johnny says. "And, hey, who *is* this guy?"

"Yeah!" Brandon says, scowling. He rips the guitar off his shoulder and lunges for me.

They *all* head for me, forming a tight semicircle, eyes narrow, teeth bared. I'm going to get eaten alive by dorks. Dorks who are a lot bigger and older than me.

Cadence only laughs. And when the semicircle of guys gets within about three feet of me, they laugh, too, smacking each other on the shoulders and saying things to me like, "What's up," and "Just kidding," and "Only messin' with ya, man."

"He's Danny," Cadence says. "He was just over for dinner."

Despite them all being at least seniors, or maybe even in college, they all go, "Ooooo!" like middle school girls. They also seem to think this is really, really funny.

"Whatever," Cadence says. "See ya."

The guys all say goodbye to her, like she's their own adopted sister. Slipknot starts playing again as she leads me back outside.

"What did you think?" she says.

"That was weird," I say, except, even thought that's true, it's not all that's true. What's true is that her face, framed by sharp, dark bangs, shadowed by blue light overhead . . . her face had hung like an oval moon, a goddess of dark happiness. I feel myself shifting around for about the fifth time that night, and struggle with the need to readjust my jeans.

"Yeah, but in a cool way, huh?" she says, reaching the porch.

"Sure. Yes."

She climbs up the two steps and stops, swinging around on one of the posts holding up the roof.

"Who was the band?" I ask. "The singer in there."

"Mazzy Star is the band. Hope Sandoval's the singer. You like it?"

"Yeah. You looked—"

I stop short and Cadence lifts her eyebrows.

"Like you were having fun." Not what I *wanted* to say, but it's what I can.

"It's this thing they do every so often," Cadence says. "Better than getting hammered, I guess. Or, you know, *high*."

I want to look away when she says it. Except I can't. I keep staring into her eyes. They are so big, and so dark.

"Did you have a good time?" she says.

"Yeah. I guess."

"You guess? Gee, thanks!"

"I just—"

"I'm kidding, Danny. You never smile, you know that?"

I guess I do. Know that, I mean. "Why did you invite me over?"

It surprises me that she doesn't answer right away. Cadence isn't one to stop and think, but that's what she's doing now. Like she's deciding how much to tell me.

She keeps swinging from the post with one hand, back and forth, like a gate. "Because my family's cool," she says finally. "Don't you think?"

"Yeah . . ."

"My dad, my brother. His friends. They're good guys. *You* could be a good guy."

"So now I'm a bad guy?"

"Not like that. I just mean that you could talk about whatever's bumming you out all the time. Or just choose not to let it bug you as much. I don't know."

"Easy for you to say."

"Yes. It must be that sunny disposition of mine."

The front door opens, backlighting her. Her dad steps out, stretches, then drops his arms.

"Oh, sorry," he says. "Didn't know you were out here."

The way he says it makes it clear that he absolutely knew we were. He's checking up on her. On us. Like I might be doing something to her. Okay, well, I would if I had half a chance. If she'd let me.

"Hey, Dad," she says.

Mr. Fuller—*Lieutenant* Fuller, it turns out; I got that much from Audry during dinner—comes over and hugs her with one beefy arm. She clings to his side, wrapping her arms around his middle.

"Did you make a song or whatever it is they do in there?" he asks me, keeping an arm around Cadence.

"No. Cadence did."

"Yeah?"

"Mm-hmm," Cadence says. "I think it'll be cool. Johnny probably already posted it, wanna see it?"

"Of course," Mr. Fuller says.

"Sweet!" Cadence pulls away from him and says to me, "You want a ride home?"

"I'm just going to text Pete to come get me. Thanks."

Cadence gives me a look that I can't quite interpret. "Okay. I'm going to go look up my video. Can I send you the link?"

"Totally." Footage of her in that blue light, to replay over and over? Hell yes.

"Cool. See you later. Thanks for coming!"

I wave, and she bounds into the house. I try to figure out how to say good night to her dad, but he clomps down the steps in bare feet. He comes over to me and crosses his arms.

"Nice having you over," he says.

"Thank you, sir."

"You don't gotta 'sir' me," Mr. Fuller says. "You all right, son? You were pretty quiet all night."

"It's nothing. Um . . . you have a nice family."

"That I do."

"And I don't think you have to worry about me and Cadence. Um. If you were."

"Oh, so that's it. Well. Hang in there. You got a couple years yet of school. You never know."

"Right. You never know."

"Just remember what I told you."

"Anything I do to her, you'll do to me."

"That's right. Take care, Danny."

Mr. Fuller goes inside. From the garage, I hear a metal

song start up. Multicolored lights flash in the space between the garage door and the concrete. I wonder how late they'll be doing this. If the neighbors get pissed.

What song I'd choose to do.

I walk out of Cadence's yard and stop. I face her house, and light a cigarette.

If we got married someday, her dad would be my father-in-law. Johnny would be my brother-in-law. We'd have Thanksgiving here, maybe. I'm suddenly seized with a burning need to see her room, see what she chooses to put on her walls, on her bed, in her closet. Rooms tell everything. There are no secrets, even if that's where we try to hide them most. Pieces of us slip out.

So that's what it's like to eat together without talking about grades or being in trouble. That's what it's like to have an older brother or sister that you actually like, who you can actually hang out with sometimes, even if their friends are around.

So that's what it's like.

The pain in my chest, which started before I even took a bite of dinner, is getting worse. It's like an emotional heart attack. Or maybe a real one, but I doubt it. Something about the food, or maybe the way they served it, or just the atmosphere of the house . . .

Everything that is wrong with my life is right with theirs.

I stand and smoke and watch Cadence's house for two cigarettes before Pete comes to pick me up.

# DREA

I gesture for Kelly to come inside. We pay no attention to my mom still weeping at the kitchen table. I can tell it weirds Kelly out, but what am I supposed to do, you know?

We get to my room, and Kelly jumps right to it again. "*What* is happening, what's going on? Why is your mom crying like that?"

"I just, can we go?" I say. "Just drive someplace? Please?"

Kelly's concerned/angry face relaxes, like she suddenly understands. "Sure."

Except then Dad shows up. He doesn't actually step into my room, he just hangs around the doorway.

"Hey," he says, and looks surprised to see Kelly. He must not've heard her come in.

"What's up," Kelly scowls at him, folding her arms.

Dad dismisses her with a half smile like he's so not impressed. "You out for the night, Andi?"

"Probably." I start stuffing things into my bag. Almost at random, honestly. A paperback, a notebook, a sweater, a couple of markers. None of it makes sense, I just have to be *moving*.

"Going to Kelly's?"

"No, she's driving me to the airport."

This takes him a second to digest. Am I just being a smartass? He screws his eyebrows together and squints one eye.

"You *are* kidding, right?"

"Whatever." I can't even look at him anymore.

"Right. You need any money, or . . . ?"

"Nope. Just solitude."

He looks confused.

"*Bye*, Dad," I say.

He takes the hint and goes away. Kelly closes the door behind him. "Will you please tell me what's going on, Drea?"

I zip my bag shut. "My mom said she screwed some guy. Can we just go?"

"*Seriously?* Well . . . *did* she, or?"

"I don't know. Doubt it. I don't care. I don't think my dad does either. Whatever."

"That's some seriously nasty stuff. You sure you're okay?"

"I *am*." I can tell my face says differently. "Can we go?"

We stalk out of my bedroom as fast as possible. No one stops us. We almost run from the house to Kelly's truck.

"I hate them," I say as Kelly pulls out of my neighborhood.

"I know. That's okay."

"I wish they hadn't ever had me."

"But then I'd be all lonely, so shut up."

That makes me laugh, suddenly. I didn't expect it. I cover my mouth, like it's not allowed. Then at a stoplight, Kelly whips out her phone and snaps a selfie of the two of us. I laugh again when she shows me the result. She's making a face, and I look stoned or something. She takes another while I'm laughing. It looks much better. I look human.

"You need ice cream," Kelly decides, and she drives toward

Sugar Bowl, which is this great ice cream shop near school, next to an indie coffee place called Jamaican Blue.

Kelly plays her music loud on the way and sings along. After a minute of listening to her, I turn the stereo off.

"Why is it okay? That I hate them?"

"Well, I guess it's sort of not, really, but I understand."

"You hate your parents, too?"

"I . . . *understand*, is all. No, I don't hate them. They're just busy. I mean, they have five kids, I get that, they can't make it to stuff, it happens."

Something clicks in my mind right then. I drop my eyes to the stereo for a second while I figure it out. Then I look at Kelly again.

"Did you ever try out for choir?"

"Uh, no."

"Why? Because they would have taken you. You know that, right?"

Kelly laughs, but it's forced, I can tell. "What? God, Drea, what are you even talking about? That makes . . ."

She stops and thumps the steering wheel with her thumb a few times, staring out the window.

". . . way too much sense," Kelly finishes a second later. "Look, they can't come, all right? They just—they couldn't. Not to a choir performance or a play or a band concert or a game. So, yeah, I try out for the stuff I suck at . . . because my parents don't need me all pressuring them to try and force one more thing into their schedule. So I just do what they tell me. I just babysit. It's all I know."

"Um . . . babysit *who*?" I say, because right now, she and I are hanging out, and that's not school *or* babysitting.

"My little brothers and sisters," Kelly says.

"Oh. For a second I thought you meant me."

And Kelly says, "Well, sometimes."

My eyes harden. "That's what you . . . ? Oh, okay. Great."

I throw open the door and stomp down the red brick sidewalk of Third Avenue. I don't look back, but I hear Kelly scrambling out after me. "Dre, wait, that's not what I meant!"

"Yes it is! I'm not a kid," I say over her shoulder, still stalking away from her. There aren't many people out, but the few who are take notice. I don't care.

"Yes you are," Kelly says, taking long strides to catch up. It's pretty easy with those long legs of hers.

Her words stop me cold. I spin around. "Oh, I am? Well then so are you!"

Kelly reaches me. "Okay, *fine*, I am, but Dre, I'm trying to help you."

"I don't *need* help, Kelly."

"I'm trying to save your life!"

"It doesn't need saving!" I yell at her. I cross my arms and add, "Maybe *you* just need it to *need* saving."

That stops her in her tracks. Slowly, Kelly walks sort of backwards to a bench and sits down, hands in her lap. She looks like I slapped her across the face.

Even though it's sort of what I meant, it's also not. I sit down beside her. "Sorry."

Kelly sighs. "Don't be. You might be right."

"I didn't mean to—"

"Yeah you did. It's okay." Kelly faces me. "But, Dre, I don't cut myself with knives. That's messed up, there's no other way to put it. It is not okay. Ever. Maybe I'm not the most sane person on the planet, but I don't hurt myself. Why do you do that?"

I do not want to get into this. Maybe I should have thought of that ten minutes ago.

"It's them, right? Your mom and dad? Because I get it. I do. I can *see* it when I'm over there. But what you're doing doesn't help. Prove me wrong."

I still say nothing. Because she's right.

Kelly scoots a little closer. "What do you want, Dre? Really."

"I just want to tell them," I say, staring at the sidewalk and not moving. "That'd be kind of nice. Just tell them what it's like for once. And I want Dad to tell Mom he loves her."

"So tell *him* that."

"He won't hear me. They won't hear me."

"Have you ever tried?"

"No . . ."

"Okay, so, that's something to think about then. It's better than making yourself bleed. And I mean, what's the worst that could happen?"

"They could have cataclysmic heart failure."

Kelly put an arm over my shoulders. "In which case, every-one wins."

I try holding back a laugh, but fail. Then I hug her, feeling like this awkward senior girl is more like a sister to me than either of my parents is an actual parent. If that makes sense.

We go have ice cream, and it is awesome.

# DANNY

"So?" Pete says the instant we pull away from Cadence's house. "Did you get any?"

"If I was five percent more masculine, I would knock you out right now."

"Whoa, man. Just kidding. Jesus. But no, did you?"

"We were having dinner with her mom and dad. So, no. Plus her dad would have me assassinated if I tried anything."

"Bummer."

We drive in silence for bit—silence except for Pink Floyd, of course. Just before reaching my neighborhood, Pete says, "What's the matter with you, man?"

"What."

"I dunno, you seem . . . unplugged."

"Yeah, well."

"Dude, so you like, you really like her."

"I guess."

"'I guess,' yeah, okay. Just own it, man."

"Fine, I own it. She's hot."

"Naw, that's not it. She is cute, I'll give you that. But that's not enough. If you just wanted to sleep with her, *then* that might be enough. But you want something else. Yeah?"

"Yeah."

"So what do you like about her?"

"She's a crazy person."

"Ha! That's sure true."

"But I mean, *I'm* a crazy person. I'm legit crazy. What do you think I got all those pills for? It's for being crazy. That's why they give them to me. But she's crazy the other way. Like shit just doesn't get to her. And when she's talking, which of course is all the god damn time . . . I don't feel pissed, I don't feel like a psycho. I guess that's why."

Pete pretends to look at me suspiciously. "*Are* you a psycho?"

I light a cigarette. "I guess we'll see."

"Welp, if that's how you feel about ol' Cadence, you may as well tell her. What's the worst that could happen?"

"Pretty sure I don't need to answer that."

Pete laughs. But I wasn't kidding.

We pull up in front of my house. I put my smoke out in his ashtray and get out of the car, ready to slam the door and walk away, but the kitchen curtains are open and I can see inside. The pain in my chest blazes to life again. A heart attack would be great right about now.

"You know what you're going to be for Halloween?" I say.

"That's like a month away, dude."

"Yeah, but it's coming. It's even starting to cool off at night."

"I don't really do Halloween. Except for candy corn. I love that shit. Hey, maybe I'll be a drug dealer."

"Clever. Thanks for the rides."

"You know what *you* wanna be?"

"Yeah. Pretty sure. Later."

I shut the car door and go inside the house. I get to my

room as fast as I can so I won't have to talk to anyone in the kitchen. Unsurprisingly, no one seems to notice or care.

In my room, I do a search for Mazzy Star, and download every single song I can find.

Meeting Cadence's family has set a vat of acid on low boil in my stomach. Not angry. Not at them, anyway. Jealous, I guess. That's not a word I normally use to describe myself. But after thinking about it for an hour and half, it's the only one that fits.

She's never going to care about me.

Not like that. We'll be BFFs for the next three years and that's it. She'll end up banging that Zach guy, sooner or later, if she hasn't already—

No. Shut up. That's not fair, thinking about her like that. She's not that way.

Cadence is the only thing that makes any sense in that place. In any place. Pete's cool and whatever. But Cadence . . . she's such . . .

Such perfection.

There are two possible solutions here. It's only fair to everyone to try both.

So I pull myself up and go into the living room. Mom's already gone to bed. Dad's watching an eighties horror movie on a network channel, holding his head up with the thumb and index finger of his left hand.

I stand in the doorway.

"Dad?"

"Mmm."

I keep my voice level. No peaks or valleys. Man to man. "Can I ask you about school?"

"What about it."

Take a breath. Take your time. Say it right the first time. Give him the chance.

"It's been a month, and I'd like to seriously talk about going back to the Academy. Please."

"No."

Don't lose it. Don't.

"How come?"

"It's late, Danny. I'm tired."

"Okay. Maybe tomorrow morning, we could talk about it. I've been going to see the counselor chick at school, my grades—"

"I don't think you'll do well back there. That's it."

"I'm not doing well *here*." My voice breaks on the words. God damn.

"Well, keep working. Go to class. Stay out of trouble. Maybe this summer we can discuss it."

My words come out thin and fragile. "I can't wait that long."

"Go to bed, all right?"

"... *Please*."

"Good night, Danny."

I don't move for a few seconds.

Then I do.

# CADENCE

About midnight, Johnny knocks on my doorframe. My door is open and I'm reading *A Wrinkle in Time.*

"Hey," he says, leaning against the jamb. "So who was that cat?"

"Danny? He's just a friend."

"Uh, does he know that?"

"Sure."

My brother grins. "No, I don't think so, Nutcase. He's crushing pretty hard."

I put my book down and blow my bangs out of my face. "Dang."

"You didn't know?"

"I wondered. I hoped not."

This is the truth. Like, I consider Pete a good friend, someone who despite all the things he does that I'm not on board with, would still stick by me. And he does make me laugh, like it or not. But he doesn't give off the same vibe as Danny, that there was always something right under the surface that he's hiding, but not trying *too* hard to hide, like he's hoping someone will figure it out.

"So why'd you have him over then?"

"I dunno. To meet you and Mom and Dad and the guys. Because you're cool. And he needs some cool people in his life. Pete's cool, but like different cool. You guys are for real."

"Oh, sis. You're not trying to save him, are you?"

"From what, do you mean?"

"Well, your boy Danny's got his whole bad-guy thing going on, and I respect that, whatever. No big deal. But if he's already decided that's who he wants to be, you can't change that."

"I don't believe that. Why not? Why can't people just choose to be happy? Just pick it. I do it all the time! Even when I don't want to. It just makes things easier, doesn't it?"

Johnny laughs and comes into my room. "I know you choose to look at the sunny side, Nutcase. That's why I love ya."

"Why do you think he's bothering?" I say. "I mean, there's lots of other girls."

"Because you, my friend, are a bona fide, authentic freak. And so you're going to attract other bona fide, authentic freaks. That can be good thing. I mean, look at the guys. Freaks! But I'd die for 'em."

"Yeah . . . I can see that."

But somehow, it doesn't make me feel a lot better. I don't want to hurt Danny. I think he's a good person inside. I really do. He and Pete make dumb choices sometimes, but okay. So did Johnny, so did a lot of his friends, so did Dad. They're turning out okay. But I don't want to be the person that makes it take longer for Danny to see that life doesn't always suck. If that makes sense. I'm not sure it does.

"If he makes a move," Johnny says, "let him down easy. That stuff can hurt no matter how you end up phrasing it, but just try to be gentle, okay?"

"Of course. I hope it doesn't come to that, though."

"Oh, it will, young one. It will. And then afterward, keep your radar up."

"What radar?"

Johnny shrugs. "Maybe nothing, maybe something. If it comes down to you having to say no to him, he might not take it so well. He might change how he talks to you, or stop talking to you at all."

"That's dumb!"

"That's how it is," Johnny says. "I wish I could say *I* never did it, but. Well, there it is."

"High school is starting to suck, Johnny."

He smiles. "Had to happen sometime. Don't worry, you'll survive." Johnny snaps his fingers. "Oh, one more thing . . ."

Then he grabs my book and runs off, forcing me to chase him around until Mom shouts at us to stop and go to bed. We say good night and go back to our rooms, and I drift toward sleep practicing different ways to be gentle with Danny, just in case. I really hope I won't have to, though. No matter what I say, it sounds wrong, sounds like I'm being mean.

Sad face. For real.

*FINAL SCORE*

SPARTANS     53

Bulldogs     12

## FINAL SCORE

SPARTANS          36

Titans            28

# FINAL SCORE

| Matadors | 11 |
| SPARTANS | 23 |

# FINAL SCORE

| | |
|---|---|
| Dons | 51 |
| SPARTANS | 00 |

*Here Today, Gone Tomorrow*

# DANNY

The football team got

REAMED

last night. It was maybe the best night of my whole entire life, just hearing about it from Pete, who was busy working the bleachers. Short of making out with Cadence or going back to my old school, it's about the best thing that could have happened to me.

THIS! IS! SPARTA!

GETTING! ITS! ASS! KICKED!

I want to celebrate, so Saturday night, Cadence and Pete and I go to a playground. We choose that location because: Cadence. Because that's what you do when you're Young And Have Your Whole Life To Look Forward To.

Cadence beelines to the swings, and I'm unsurprised. She leaps onto the black rubber seat and whirls around to look at me.

"Push me!" she shouts.

Something about her face, or maybe voice, or maybe the way the seat wraps around her butt—or maybe all three—immediately pops me up.

I don't answer her, but I dutifully march through the sand, which is not easy in my boots. I take care to touch the seat and chains, not her. I'd like to think she's giving me the chance to cop a feel—if that's a real phrase people actually use, which

I doubt—but I'm not sure, and so I don't risk touching her. I want to. Oh, I want to. But it's not worth making her mad.

Pete hops onto one of those bouncy toys with the big spring in the ground and rocks back and forth on it. He shouts, "Woohoo! Yippee ki yay mother truckers!"

Cadence laughs out loud, and I don't know if it's at Pete or the fact that she's reached Mach 2 in the swing.

"Oh, shit!" Pete cries, digging his feet into the sand. "Gotta smoke," he announces, and lights up a Marlboro. He keeps his seat on the dinosaur spring toy.

"*Wheeeee!*" Cadence squeals. I can't tell if she's trying to be funny or if she's really that weird. Either way: I love it.

"What're you guys gonna be for Halloween?" Pete says as he rocks slowly on the dinosaur.

"A pumpkin!" Cadence says. "But maybe not, I don't know. What about you?"

Pete blows out smoke. "An addiction counselor, what do you think?"

This makes them both laugh for some reason.

"What about you, Danny?" Cadence says.

I give her another push. My thumbs touch her hips, right below the waistband of her shorts. Rock Jack is pleased.

"Homicidal maniac," I say. "Isn't it obvious?"

She blows her tongue out, *pppppth*. It makes me smile, but she can't see it.

"Hey, you know what?" Pete says.

"You need another smoke," I say.

"No. I never had any friends."

The chilly autumn breeze seems to stop moving around us. I take a step back, and Cadence quits pumping her legs, drifting slowly to a stop on her swing. I don't know what to say, and I assume she doesn't, either. That was kind of a weird bomb to just lob out there at the top of the evening. Maybe it's the playground. Maybe it's tripped some memory or regressed him to a past life.

"Nah, I mean it," Pete says, as though we'd responded. He's looking off into the distance, contemplatively smoking his cigarette. "I sell people stuff, I been selling stuff for a while. That's just business. I like knowing the kings of the school are just plain old potheads like me. But you guys aren't like that."

He blows out smoke, shaking his head a little.

"I dunno. Screw it. Never mind. I gotta leak."

He climbs off the bouncy toy and walks into the darkness. Cadence and I watch, saying nothing until we can't see him anymore.

"I hope he's okay," she says.

"Yeah."

"I wonder what brought that up."

"No clue." I step to one side so I can better see her face. "You don't hang out with a lot of different people."

"No. Neither do you. But I've met some cool girls at Sat School. We have lunch together sometimes and stuff."

"So what is it about us? Me and Pete, I mean."

"Hmm . . . you ever lie to me?"

"No."

"Would you?"

"I doubt it. No."

"Well," Cadence says, and pushes off the ground with her feet to start swinging again. "That's a good start."

I get out of her way. Since we're being all philosophical and shit, I say, "Are you seeing anybody? Like, dating?"

She bursts out laughing. How such a big sound comes from such a small body, I do not know.

"No!" she says. "I think you two would be the first to know. Jeez." Then, still swinging, she says, "*Man* I love being up high! I think I'll be a pilot."

Pete appears from the darkness, walking into the orange overhead lights of the playground.

"I'm high as a pilot," he says, grinning around a freshly lit cigarette. He resumes his ride on the bouncy dinosaur. It's a joke, I think. He hasn't smoked anything but cigarettes tonight.

I watch him sitting there for a sec while we all ignore the fact that he just brought up some real shit. Then he belches and asks if we've ever seen this overweight kid at school who draws some amazing artwork on his own arms. And just like that, it's like the conversation never happened.

Except of course it did. Only half listening, I think about how high up I can get Cadence within my limited means. Because now I have a plan.

# DONTE

It's close to three thirty in the morning by the time I get up my courage. I didn't drink much, because I didn't want to sound stupid when the time came. I kept an eye on Amy. She didn't drink much, either. Does that mean she knows? Has she figured it out?

Tonight was the first time I've ever been mercy ruled. Might be the first time in school history, I don't know. After three straight wins, to get knocked down like that . . . man, thinking about Amy is the only thing keeping me from just sitting at home reliving it over and over.

At last I spot Amy alone, in the backyard. She's sitting on a long, poolside lounge chair and holding a red cup, and yawning.

There're some people in the hot tub, and some people making out in the shadows under a tree on a landscaped little hill. But that's pretty much it. Most everyone inside is losing steam. I saw Brady go after Brianna Montaro a while ago, but haven't seen him since. That brother was one depressed QB. I can't blame him. Hopefully Brianna can help him feel better, at least for a little while.

"Let's go," I whisper to myself, even though probably no one could hear over the music anyway. "Come on. Head in the game."

I step outside through the sliding glass doors, and shut them quietly behind me. Halfway to the chair, Amy looks up and sees me. She smiles, but she looks tired.

"Hey, what's up," I say, sitting next to her. The lounge chair squeaks under me.

"Hey, D. You drunk or what?"

"No." I show her my bottle. "This is like, my third. Since we got here."

"Mmm," she says, nodding. "Me, too. I mean, me neither. I promised Brianna and some of the other girls rides home. Been sipping peach schnapps for like five hours."

"That's cool, that's cool."

I lean back on my hands a bit, and scan the yard. There's no one who can hear us, as far as I can tell.

"Something on your mind?" Amy says, bumping her shoulder into mine.

The brief, platonic contact sends blood rushing through my arms and legs, like the shiver of excitement I get before every game.

"Yeah, maybe." My heart beats like I'm running forties on the track. Except forties feel good, ultimately. This feels . . . well, good, too, but different. Scary.

"What's up?" she says.

"I don't know, I was kind of like . . . damn."

"You okay? What's going on?"

I can't look at her all of a sudden. I roll the bottle between my palms, staring at the little round mouth, and chew my lip.

"Man, Coach would have my ass," I say finally.

She doesn't get it. "For what, how come?"

I don't answer. But when that non-answer stretches out for a full minute, she sighs and whispers my name; like, understanding. I peek over at her. Her face is sympathetic. Maybe sad.

"Guess I don't got to say it, huh?"

"No," Amy says, quiet. She reaches out and puts a hand on my forearm. Her fingers are cold from whatever's in her red cup. "He'd have *both* our asses. It's not just you."

"So if it wasn't for that?"

"Yeah, if it wasn't for that. God, Donte. I'm so sorry. It sucks."

"Yeah."

I'm half-excited and half-pissed. This isn't fair, at all. I *get* it, but it's bullshit. What's Coach care, right? What's it matter? Season's half over, anyway.

Amy looks around the backyard before scooting around a bit on the chair to face me. "Do me a favor?"

"Yeah, 'course."

"Sit on your hands."

I set the bottle down and shove my hands under my thighs.

Amy touches the back of my neck, her fingers just grazing my skin. She might as well have flipped on a light switch. Everything inside me lights up like neon. She puts the other hand on my cheek, and pulls me toward her.

I've been in love with this girl since meeting her freshman year at the end-of-year banquet Coach throws. We've never done *this*. Not once. As far as I know, none of the guys have.

It takes less than a minute to understand why she told me to sit on my hands. I want to touch her everywhere.

The kiss starts soft, kind of quiet, but a minute later we are locked in tight. She tastes like peaches. I worry distantly about my own breath, but she doesn't seem to care.

Three years, and I'm finally kissing Amy.

Coach would have my ass.

And I do not care.

After a long time, she pulls away, almost taking my lip with her. She runs the back of her hand across her chin, and laughs a bit. I do, too.

"Okay," she says, soft. "So, maybe I'll talk to Coach."

"Yeah?"

"Can't hurt. You want me to?"

I'm about to say yes, except—

Damn. I can't. It would be better coming from her, yes. But I'm the one Coach would take it out on. Not that he'd do anything real bad, he takes care of his boys. But still. We have the rest of the season ahead of us. Got to make up for last night's game. I can't afford to have things be weird on the team right now. I spent so much of the night planning how to talk to Amy, I didn't ever stop to think what might happen after.

"Maybe don't talk to him quite yet," I say, not hiding my regret. "I can't believe I'm saying this. But—"

"No no," Amy says, real fast. "You're right. Maybe when the season's over. You know. When you know what school you're going to and stuff."

School. College. It hadn't crossed my mind tonight. Kissing Amy, wanting to be doing it, and now having done it after so long . . . going to school was the last thing I was thinking of. Man, how stupid. Even if Coach didn't care if we got together, now *or* postseason, we both have college to worry about. Probably going different places. Damn, I'm dumb.

On the other hand, we'd have a little while. Some time. Who knows?

"Okay," I say. "After the last game? You could talk to him then?"

"Totally," Amy says. "Something to look forward to."

"What about Brady?"

"What about him?"

"I just mean, there's not like . . . you know. Anything?"

"Me and *Brady*? No! He comes over a lot, but that's because—well, you know."

"Yeah . . ."

"No," Amy says again, like she can't believe I even asked. "Brady's like my brother. Well, okay, not like my brother-brother, he's a total loser. But you know what I mean."

"Yeah. Okay. I just, I don't want him to be all, you know."

She tilts her head. "You're a good friend."

"Yeah?"

"Yeah." She kisses me again, but just a bit, then shivers. "*When's* the last game of the season?"

We both laugh, and she leans her body into mine. I put an arm around her shoulders, and she lets me.

All things considered? It's the best party I've ever been to.

# BRADY

Close to three thirty in the morning by the time I get Brianna Montaro into Martin's bedroom.

Saturday night. Party at Martin's house. Planned it after we beat the Titans couple weeks ago. Knew Martin's parents would be out of town. But then the Dons game happened.

They mercy ruled us. Me.

Biggest party so far this year. Everyone knew about it. Coach probably even knows about it. Place is packed. But everybody's pissed. Can feel it underneath the music.

Martin paid a few freshmen to stand guard up and down the block to call in if the cops show up. Early warning system. Paid a JV basketball kid to be in charge of keys and Ubers. Nobody's driving drunk. Probably a lot of us will sleep here, anyway. Martin thought of everything. Except how to win last night's game.

I can barely move. Lost track of beers hours ago. Brianna's sexy look has fallen apart. Some kind of hair tie thing is halfway down what used to be a ponytail. Her eyes are half-closed. Maybe it just looks that way because mine are, too.

We fall onto Martin's mattress. Brianna says something. I say something back. I don't think either one of us knows what.

Try to get my fingers under her shirt. They feel twice as big as normal. Can't make them work. She reaches down and grabs the edge. Tries pulling up. No luck.

This isn't how I imagined things going.

"Waitwait*wait!*" Brianna shouts suddenly. Gets up off the bed.

"Wha?" Can't figure what I did wrong.

"I gotta go home," Brianna says. "I gotta paper."

"Paper?" I sound stupid. Maybe I am.

"For history, I gotta paper I gotta do, I only got a ninety-one in there . . ."

She's looking around the room for something. Don't know what.

"School?" I say. "Babe, come on, come here."

Brianna stops looking around. Stares at me.

"I have to win," she says.

"Naw, come on, you need to relax," I say. Try to smile. "Bree, you'll be fine. I wish I was half as smart as you."

"*Smart doesn't matter if I don't ace the class!*"

Yells it. Makes me wince. I force myself to sit up. It's not easy.

"Come on, what's up with you?"

"Have you not heard of my brother and sister?" Brianna shouts. I don't think she's that drunk after all. "He was valedictorian and went to Swarthmore, my sister was salutatorian and goes to Brown—"

"I don't care about report cards right now."

Brianna keeps going. She's not listening at all. "I have to do better, and it's got to be this year because next year barely matters—"

I reach for her. She pulls away. Makes me mad. But then I'm

facedown in Martin's pillow and I don't know what happens to Brianna after that.

I just know that I lost.

Everything.

# CADENCE

Friday after school, Danny asks me to meet him at a church that night. Not to actually go to a service or anything, just to meet him there. It's kind of suspicious, but he won't tell me what it is we're going to do.

So of course I go. Curiosity and all that. I hope it doesn't make God mad. I take a trolley to the church, a big Baptist place with a square tower on the roof and a cross on top of that. Danny's waiting for me, sitting on a short wall that runs along one sidewalk.

"Hey," he says, standing up and rubbing his palms on his jeans.

"Hi! Doesn't *Hamlet* open up tonight?"

He snorts. "Yeah, I guess, I don't know. I'm not going. Come on, follow me."

"Famous last words." But of course, I follow him. "Where's Pete?"

"This is just an us thing."

Uh-oh. I'm not sure this is a good idea. I hear Johnny's voice in my head, something about Danny "making a move." But because I'm a wee little freshman who doesn't think things through, I follow Danny up a decorative brick wall that has lots of holes and stuff. It's an easy climb, though it's high. A few seconds later, I'm on top of the roof with him. I brush my hands off, and Danny walks casually to where a ladder has been bolted to a sloped roof that goes even higher than where we are now, like a steeple I guess.

"You're kidding," I say.

"I never kid. Didn't you know that about me?"

He starts climbing up. I wait till he gets to the top of the slope, which levels off into a little plateau where a simple, slender cross is fixed, looking out over the city.

"Well?" Danny calls.

"You're seriously going to break into a church? Are you in that big a hurry to go to Hell?"

"I'm not breaking in," Danny says, sounding hurt. "Jesus, why would you say that?"

"Don't swear," I say, eyeing the cross warily and waiting for lightning to smite us or something.

"Would you just get up here?"

So I just get up there. Danny sits down crisscross applesauce beneath the cross, and I turn around three times like a dog before doing the same. Then I take in a breath.

"Wow."

"I was hoping you'd like the view. Me and a friend of mine from school used to come up here to smoke. My real school, I mean."

The church tower looms high. There are taller buildings within a few blocks of here, but this is the highest point for a ways around. All around us, orange and white lights cast glows on the streets. Traffic seems to be moving smoothly, no horns. There's even a little breeze up here that teases my bangs around my chin.

"Dude, this is cool," I say. "Sorry about the 'breaking in' thing."

"It's cool," Danny says, but he sounds nervous. His hands can't keep still.

"What's going on?" I say, feeling like I shouldn't ask. I don't know if it's like instinct or just what, but I have this terrible idea of what he's about to do.

Danny looks at me. He looks *so* tired. I look at him. He looks at me. I look at—

—him moving toward me, closing his eyes and opening his mouth!

I lean back. "Dude!" Dang it, I *knew* it.

His eyes go wide. "What?"

"What are you doing?"

Danny resets himself. He gestures wildly at the city below us, like that's supposed to make everything clear. "I was . . . I mean, I just wanted to kiss you."

I cover my eyes. "Danny . . ."

He faces out. "You don't want to."

"No." I say this as gently as I can.

"Shoulda known. Who is it? That Zach guy?"

"No. I mean, I hope so someday, but no, it's not that."

"Yeah yeah yeah," Danny says, and clenches his mouth shut.

Part of me wants to leave, because dealing with Danny gives me headaches sometimes. But I can't, because the truth is, I like him, and regardless of why, he's hurt. I don't like him in a boyfriend way, or a kissing way. Just in a friend way. But a good friend. Someone I know I could call at three in the morning if I needed to. And like I worried about, now I'm sure I hurt him even though I didn't want to, and walking away right now doesn't seem like a friend thing to do.

Danny says, "Did I ever have a chance?"

"Oh, Danny . . ."

"Stop, no! No 'Oh, Danny' shit. Just tell me."

I sit up straight. "No. You never had a chance. There. Does that make you feel better? Because it doesn't make me feel better. It makes me feel like a bitch."

Danny's quiet for a long time before saying, "You're not. I get it. But we are friends, right?"

"I sure hope so."

"Then, as a friend, can I ask you . . . look, it's just really important to me right now if I could . . . if I could just kiss you."

"I don't think that's something that friends do."

He's not looking at me. "Cadence. Please. You don't understand how much this means to me right now."

"I'm sorry, no. It's not okay. Nothing good's coming out of that."

"Even if it's a mercy rule?"

"A what?"

Danny sits there for a long time before standing up and staring at the traffic. I don't think he sees it.

"In football . . . in high school football, I mean . . . they've got this thing called the mercy rule. It means that if one team is kicking the hell out of another team, then the clock doesn't stop running anymore, so that the losing team won't be any more embarrassed than they already are. In fact it just happened to us last week. To our school. *Football.* It's a football rule. Sounds nice, doesn't it? Civilized? Yeah."

He pauses for a sec before whispering it again, like to himself: "Yeah."

Then he goes on. "Except there's no mercy rule the rest of the time. Not in real life. I don't get one. You don't get one. It's not like once you've been beat down to a certain level, they leave you alone. Nope. They just keep going. Harder and harder. I suppose they're playing by professional rules at that point. Well, I guess that's okay. Because the clock still runs out. This clock has run out, too."

"Danny?"

No answer.

"I'm sorry."

"Yep," he says. "Gotta go."

He moves to the ladder and hikes down it. I stay put. When he gets to the ground, Danny shoves his hands into his pockets and walks on down the sidewalk.

What I really want to do is get up and go after him and hug him. But I can't do it. Because for one thing, he looks like he doesn't want anyone bugging him. And for another . . . well, dang it! Why does contact always have to be something sexual? Why can't I hug him without it turning into a sex thing? It's not fair.

Boys are dumb.

I wait until he's out of sight before climbing down myself and taking a trolley home.

*FINAL SCORE*

SPARTANS      03
Trojans      27

*Too Tough to Die*

# BRADY

We always review the game Saturday mornings. Can't even look at the screen. Not even when Coach tells me to five different times.

"Brady!" he says. "Your head in the game?"

"No, Coach."

"Damn skippy!" Coach says. "Damn it, son, the season's not over. This is for life, not for points! We lose the rest of these games, that's how it goes. We lose the rest of the games because you all didn't put out, that is unacceptable! You get me?"

"Yes, Coach."

"Good! You want to win those games?"

"Yes, Coach."

"I can't hear you! All of you, you want to win those games?"

Everyone but me screams, "*Yes, Coach!*"

Can feel the whole team looking at me when they do it. Can feel my backup QB shifting around. Wanting to take my spot.

I don't say anything else the rest of review. When it's over I walk out fast. Kinda expect someone to call me back. Like Donte. Or Coach. But they don't. They let me go.

I walk all the way home. Thinking. Choosing.

Decide I know what I got to do.

Turn left and head for Starbucks.

Not the first time I've had to spare for change. I'm good at it. And this isn't sparing. Not really.

It's leveraging my resources.

I say *Hi* to a hefty brunette in office clothes. Wonder what she does that she has to be dressed up on a Saturday morning.

"Sorry to bug you. I have this Starbucks card, but I'm short on cash—if you were going to pay with cash, would you mind giving that to me and I'll charge your drink to my card? I'll even throw in a muffin or something, so you know I'm on the level."

She says no. Lotta people say no. I can tell it's because they think it must be a scam. But a few say yes. Doesn't take many Frappuccinos to get the money I need. I feel bad about charging so much on the card.

Won't matter a few hours from now. I'll write Coach a note or something. Apologizing. For losing again last night. For getting mercy ruled last week. For taking the team down. For everything. He gave me a plan, and I blew it already.

Head to Walgreens. Buy a bottle of Tylenol. Go across the street to a grocery store and buy another one. On the way home I hit a convenience store for one more.

That should do it. Should be enough to make shit stop hurting.

# DONTE

My cell phone rings with a Linje Knife ringtone. Man, I'm tired. Just want to stare at TV all day. I grunt as I lean over my outstretched legs to pick the phone up off the table. The ID shows it's Brady.

"'Sup," I say, lazily scrolling with the TV remote. Nothing's ever on on Saturdays.

"D?"

"Hey, man." I sit up a bit. Brady looked so damn tired and just *done* that no one tried to stop him when he left review this morning. He really didn't look like someone who wanted to do any talking, so I let him go.

Now he sounds like he sure as hell needs someone to talk to.

"Need your . . . help."

"Sure, yeah, what's going on?" I say. "Where you at?"

". . . Home."

"You don't sound good, man."

Silence.

"Brady? Hey, man, what's up? Brady. Brady!"

"Help."

The remote falls from my hand as I race for the new-old car. "Tell me what's up," I say, fumbling for my keys. "B? Come on, man. Tell me."

But the line is quiet. The clock on my cell phone screen still ticks off seconds, though. Brady hasn't hung up. He's just not making any noise.

Cursing, I peel out in the rush to get to Brady's apartment. I wonder if I should call 911. But what if Brady's just hammered? Just had too much to drink? B doesn't need the cops coming to that address, not when they're there so much as it is.

I choose the hard thing, and turn off the phone. This way, I can focus on the drive.

Saturday—not much traffic. I make it in less than ten minutes. They feel like hours.

Not bothering with being polite, I throw open the flimsy front door of the apartment and rush in. Brady's in the living room, wearing nothing but paper-thin white boxers.

There's a row of Tylenol bottles lined up on the coffee table. Guarding them is a half-empty bottle of Vodka. His mom's brand, called something like "Cheap-Ass Shit."

"You get hurt, B? What kind of . . ."

Then it hits me. B's breathing is shallow, his skin yellow.

"Oh no . . ." I run over to my friend. "Get up, come on, man, get up, ah shit, what did you do? Huh? What'd you do? Shit, man, get up."

I haul Brady to his feet.

"Nooooo," Brady groans, only half-conscious. "S'okay, I'll throw it up, I'll throw it up, see?"

He lifts his right hand toward his mouth as if to shove the fingers down his throat, but the hand only travels halfway.

I swear again and somehow manhandle Brady out of the living room and shove him into the new-old Accord.

"Damn, damn, *damn*," I hear myself chant, fumbling for my keys again. They drop on the pavement. I pick them up, drop them again, hit my head on the mirror—

*Stop*, I tell myself, possibly out loud, but I'm not sure. *Get your head in the game. This a man's game. This a man's game now. Don't be afraid, just get in the game.*

Carefully, I slide into the driver's seat, start the car, and accelerate out of the neighborhood. Brady is motionless in the passenger seat, head thunking against the window.

Instinctively, I punch Brady on the arm. It's like hitting a plastic sack of meat.

"Wake up, man," I say. "C'mon, B, you got to stay up. Come on. Head in the game."

Brady lifts his head, eyes bleary.

"Sorry, man," he says, gazing but not seeing out the front window. "I din mean . . . sorry."

"Just stay awake with me, all right?" My tires squeal around a corner. Why's the hospital so far away? "Just stay up, man. How many'd you take, huh? Do you know how many you took?"

"Bottle," Brady says after a pause. "Or two . . ."

"*Two bottles?*" My voice hits the same pitch as the tires did around the last turn. "You took two whole bottles, B? When? How long ago?"

"Dunno. Hour. Coupla hours. Maybe more. D, I'm sorry, man. Couldn't'a find a gun . . . had to use the pussy way . . ."

I focus on the road, on the hospital so far away.

BRADY

# DREA

Best costume idea ever! Kelly texts me the Saturday before Halloween. Have you seen Nightmare Before Christmas?

No, I send back. I'm lying on my bed, trying hard not to listen to Mom sobbing in the kitchen at the moment, my earbuds in deep and music turned up, but it's not enough. It's one of the songs Kelly sings in her truck all the time.

Google Sally Nightmare Before Christmas, Kelly writes. Look at her hair! Oh my god you would be perfect! Please please please!

Grateful for the distraction, I do what she says, the entire time wishing Dad would just do something about Mom.

I guess I'm not as distracted as I thought.

I search Google Images and look at a thin, pale doll with hair very close to my color red, her skin stitched together like she's been broken over and over again.

Kind of cool, I write.

Go watch the movie, Kelly orders. Or you can come over here if you want to but I am covered in two different shades of baby poop at the moment.

Smiling despite the sounds that sink through my closed door from the kitchen, I write, Okay I'll find it online.

Awesome! Kelly writes. Let me know as soon as you're done what you think!

I will, I write back, and get up.

Mom's in her spot at the kitchen table, draped over it and

moaning. I don't know where Dad is. I start to walk past like always, then stop and peek back in.

"I'm going to watch a movie," I say. "I think it's like a cartoon, sort of. Kelly said to watch it. Do you want to watch with me? I can make popcorn."

Mom lifts her head and looks at me like she has no idea who I am. I don't know what else to add, so I just stand there feeling stupid for a long time.

Just when I'm about to roll my eyes and keep walking, Mom croaks, "Sure."

I nod, and go to the cabinet where we keep the microwavable popcorn. Mom shuffles past me, down the hall to use the bathroom. By the time she's done, I have the popcorn ready and in a ceramic bowl, and have found *Nightmare Before Christmas* online and plugged my laptop into our TV.

We sit on the couch, not too close but not too far apart. She looks better, like maybe she washed her face. Neither of us says anything as the movie starts, and in less than a minute I can see why Kelly loves it so much: it's a musical, for one, and it's Tim Burton.

Mom and I watch the whole movie together, our fingers touching sometimes in the popcorn bowl. When it's over, Mom looks over at me.

"Thank you, Andi," she says.

It makes me want to cry. But I don't want to do that, so I nod real quick and get up and run for my room.

I text Kelly. It was great.

She replies right away. I knew it! So you'll be Sally if I make your costume?

Yes, I write back. Then, after thinking for about a second, I add, I like how she stitched herself back together.

# VIVI

I put on a new blouse Sunday morning. It's green, a dazzling green that Sam says brings out the hazel in my eyes. Until Sam, I didn't know I had hazel in my eyes.

Dad shuffles into the kitchen with his walker. He's still living in the guest bedroom downstairs instead of his suite upstairs.

"Ah, *mija*," he says, smiling. "You're looking good today."

I grin like an idiot. "Gracias."

"How is the car?" He groans as he tries to drop into a padded chair at the table.

I ease him down into the chair a little at a time. It's going to be months before his back is better. If it does get better.

"The car's great," I say.

"Good, good."

"You want me to fix you breakfast?"

"Oh, I can still manage to feed myself."

"It's okay," I tell him. "I've got it."

Dad smiles at me and sighs as he opens up the newspaper I brought inside earlier. We could never afford to get the paper before we moved here, and Dad loves going through the whole thing on Sunday mornings.

"We should get a housekeeper," he says, flipping through the sports page. "Maybe someone live-in, who can take care of the cooking and cleaning so you don't have to do it."

I mix eggs and milk together in a stainless steel bowl.

"Marlene could do all that. She's your sister, she'll probably work cheap."

That makes us both laugh as I fix him scrambled eggs the way he likes, sausage links, and toast. This would have been a huge meal a few months ago. Now it's just the things I knew to buy and make.

Not everything has gotten fancy as suddenly as my new clothes. Not yet.

Once Dad is all set up with his breakfast, I kiss him on the cheek and head out to the Camaro. I cruise fast to Jamaican Blue, and find Sam sitting on the grassy corner of Fifty-Third Street and Third Avenue. He meets me at my car and kisses me.

"That shirt looks great on you," he says.

I twine my fingers into his. "Thank you. Let's eat."

It's a good start to the day.

# CADENCE

"Danny's not talking to me," I tell Pete on Sunday afternoon. I can't get Danny out of my head, and he's not returning any messages or calls, so Pete seems like the best person to talk to about it.

"Me, either," Pete says. "Not since like Friday."

"But I didn't *do* anything. This is bogus."

"Dude, it doesn't matter," Pete says, pulling into Taco Bell. "You're trying to be logical. A guy with a hard-on for a chick ain't gonna be logical."

"Okay, could we please call it something else, please?" I hate when he talks like that. Like he's not smart. He is.

"Sorry. Uh . . . boner? Stiffy?"

"I was thinking crush. It *is* a crush, right? I mean, that's what this is with him."

"Definitely. Pretty bad, too."

"Has he talked about me at all?"

"Before you tore out his still-beating heart and feasted on it with Tabasco? Yes. But not since."

"Whoa!" I shout. "Hang on, back up."

"May I take your order?" Taco Bell asks.

"Hold that thought," Pete says to me. Then out the window he says, "I'll take a—"

"I will not hold that thought!" I say. "That's crap! It's not my fault he likes me, and it's not like I said I hated him. All I said was that I wasn't going to kiss him, and that's my *right*, Pete! I don't need to get called a bitch because I don't like him back the same way, or because I wouldn't go down on him in the art supply closet or whatever!"

". . . You want hot sauce with that?" the Taco Bell person says through the mic. It sounds like someone's laughing in the background.

Shocked, but also at least a little amused, which pisses me off, Pete says, "I'm gonna go ahead and order now. I can't think on an empty stomach."

I fold my arms and stew while he orders. The people at the window are clearly enjoying themselves as they pass Pete his sack of food. One of the workers shouts at me as Pete drives off, "You *go*, girl!" followed by a bunch of laughs.

"But you know what I mean," I say to Pete when we're away.

"I do. No argument here. I was kidding about the Tabasco thing. What I'm saying is you're not looking at it from his perspective. Guys are dumb. Start there."

"I know *that*."

"So, let him chill out," Pete says. "Either he'll be friends with you, or he won't. Maybe it's best if he isn't, at least right now. He'll get over it. Then you guys can be all buddies again."

"Is that what you're going to do?"

"Well, he and I still have business to conduct," Pete says.

"I really wish you'd stop doing that."

"Relax. They'll get it somewhere if they don't get it from me. You know that."

"Then *let* them."

"Ah, you're precious. Soft taco?"

I take it. "So what do I do tomorrow when I see him?"

"Say hi," Pete says around a mouthful of taco. "If he doesn't say anything back, let it go. He'll get his shit together, or he won't. It's sort of that hard and that simple at the same time."

"Well I don't like it."

"Me, either. But just give him time. He'll work it out."

I take a big bite of my soft taco and think, *I hope so.*

# DONTE

I go back Sunday morning. So far, I haven't told anyone about B.
Not my mom, not Amy, not Coach. I walk cautiously into Brady's
hospital room, not sure if Brady will be asleep or what. But he isn't.
He's propped up on a couple pillows holding the wired remote
control for the TV in one hand. A piss-yellow plastic pitcher of
water stands guard on a tray nearby.

He looks thin.

"Hey," I say.

Brady's eyes flick toward me, then his head moves.

"Hey," Brady says. He sounds tired. But . . .

Alive.

"So how's it going?" I approach the right side of the bed. I
keep my hands buried deep in my orange Spartan hoodie, fists
clenched.

Brady turns the TV off.

"Whatever," he growls. Then he sort of rolls his eyes at himself, and amends, "Not bad."

"So how long you in for?"

"Dunno. Prolly get home tonight. Gotta see a shrink or
whatever."

"That's cool," I say, for lack of anything better. I feel dumb
saying it, but the feeling passes quickly. I feel a *lot* more than
dumb.

My fists clench tighter.

Brady shrugs against the starchy white sheets. "Mighta jacked up my liver. But prolly not. I got here quick enough."

His eyes dart to mine, spiral-fast. What we both know he should have said is, "*You* got me here quick enough."

"So you're okay?" I say, starting to chew on my lips.

"Yeah."

"You're sure?"

Brady smiles. It's kind of weird. Like, gentle or something. "Yeah, man. It's all good."

"Yeah? Good. That's good."

Then my hands fly out of my pockets and grip the railing of Brady's bed. I lean close to his face. Brady flattens himself back into the pillows.

"That's real good," I say between gritted teeth. "Because if there's a next time, make sure you do it right. 'Cause I'm not going through this shit again. I'm *not*. You can't do that to people, man. You *can't*. You can't steal from me like that. Got it?"

I don't even wait. I spin on one heel, headed for the exit. I'm too close to taking a swing at my best friend. I've never been so scared and pissed in my life.

Just as I hit the doorway, I hear him say, "She ain't been here."

I stop. I'm still shaking.

"*Brianna*?" I say, not turning around. "That's who you're worried about right now? Are you shitting me, man? That's who—"

"Brianna, shit," Brady snorts. "Come on, man."

It sinks in. Not Brianna. Not Amy, either. Not someone from school.

I slowly turn back to face Brady. But he's already thumbed the TV on again. Disgust changes his face into some kind of wicked mask.

"I'm sorry, man," I say.

Brady gives his head one solitary shake to the side.

"You talk to her?" I ask. "At all?"

"Called. Couple times. A *few* times."

"Tell her where you were?"

"Yeah. 'Course."

My fists aren't clenched anymore.

Brady waves, half-heartedly, his arm barely coming off the mattress. "Whatever. Don't matter. Thanks for comin', D. Sorry to . . . put you through shit. You bailed me out. Thanks."

The channel changes. I stand there fidgeting for a second.

"I could stick around, I guess. If you want. Game'll be on soon."

"Yeah. Bears-Packers and Niners-Cards."

"Butler's probably freaking out."

"Yeah, right?"

I drift into the room and sit in a pleather chair close to the bed.

"I mean it," I say. "Not ever again, B."

"Naw, man," Brady says. "Swear to God. Never again."

"All right."

The Bears win and the Niners win. English will probably be a good class tomorrow, we both agree. Watch the next game after that, too, talking about the players and whatever. Nothing more needs to be said. Including the fact that nobody else is going to know this ever happened.

# CADENCE

When I get to school Monday morning, I spot Danny right away, sitting on the sidewalk leading up to the school entrance. He's got a notebook and keeps looking up at people, writing stuff down, looking up, writing.

I remember Pete's advice and march straight up to Danny. "Hi."

"Hello." He tilts his body to one side to look around me.

I sidestep into his line of vision. "Are you going to keep ignoring me?"

"You should probably hope so."

"What's that even mean?"

He finally looks up at me. "What are you going to be for Halloween?"

"I don't know. Nothing. I'll just be me. I don't know. Why?"

"If you're not going to get into the spirit of things, maybe you should stay home. Blow some bubbles or something."

I fling my arms up in the air. "All right, Danny. Fine. I tried. You have my number."

"I do."

"If you decide we can be friends, text me. Till then, I'll just leave you alone. That's what you want, right?"

"Gee, Cadence. It's not always about you."

That's it. I'm done. I stomp past Danny and go inside school. The hall is jammed with people. I feel like punching my way through them, but just then, someone steps in front of me and creates a bit of breathing room.

"I got ya," Zach says. "Follow me."

Grateful for both the space and a friendly face right now, I keep in step behind Zach as he uses his tremendous height to pick the easiest way through the crowd. A few seconds later, we're in another hallway. Not exactly where I need to go, but at least there's space.

"Thanks," I say to Zach.

He smiles at me. "No problem. I—"

"Zach!" a girl calls.

THE Brianna Montaro comes bouncing up to him, ponytail flopping. She looks hungry and she looks tired and she looks way, way too stressed for high school.

"Please tell me you took good notes for Garcia's class," she says to Zach. "Oh please God, tell me you did."

"I took them," Zach agrees. "How good they are, I don't know."

"Can you please send them to me? I'll do anything."

"Sure, no problem. But you might want to ask Vivian. Hers are always better."

"Who's Vivian?"

Zach looks confused and amused at the same time. Camused!

"The girl you sit next to in English?" he says.

"Oh, is that her name?" Brianna says, but like, reflexively. She obviously doesn't care about Vivi, and she hasn't even looked at me yet. She shakes her head fast. "I can't ask her. She's a bitch."

"How do you figure?"

"She's acing Garcia."

THE Brianna Montaro says this like it should be obvious. At first I figure she's being sarcastic, but she doesn't laugh and doesn't smile. No, she really wants Vivi's head on a pike for the great crime of succeeding in school. Sad face! Thinking back to Vivi and Brianna in the girls' room a few months ago, Vivi doesn't strike me as the bitch in that equation.

Second-to-last bell goes off. "I'll send them to you tonight," Zach promises. "Okay?"

"Thank you!" Brianna says, and bolts into foot traffic.

Zach watches her, and I say, "She's nice to you."

"Hmm? Oh, Bree? Yeah. She's okay."

I don't have time to disagree. Class is about to start. "Well, thanks, for escorting me. You want to have lunch sometime?"

I figure the worst he can do is say no. Anyway, with Danny being all weirdo, I don't want to have to eat lunch by myself every day, although maybe I could ask Vivi, or Kelly. But they both have cars and I bet they go off campus for lunch like Zach and Pete.

"Sure, okay," Zach says. "Um . . . how about Friday?"

*Whoa!* Forget Danny, my day just went supernova!

"Awesome!" I say. "Yeah, cool!"

Zach laughs a bit, like I just tickled him or something. "All right, we'll work it out. See ya, Cadie."

"Bye!"

He pushes himself into the flow of students while I dart and bob and weave through the halls, absolutely thrilled to freaking death!

# BRADY

Brianna comes up to me while me and Donte are at my locker before Butler's class on Monday morning. She looks good. Put together. We haven't talked much since the party.

Other stuff on my mind.

"Hey," she says.

"Hey." I shut the locker.

Donte is standing behind her. She can't see him when he wiggles his eyebrows at me. He walks away so we're alone.

"I'm sorry about the party," Brianna says.

"Don't say that. You didn't do anything."

"I just feel like we were having a—like, a *moment* together . . ."

"We were. We definitely were."

"So, was it just the alcohol?"

The bell rings. Neither one of us move. Lots of other people run.

"You mean, like, is that the only reason we . . . ?"

"Yeah."

"No."

Don't know if that's a hundred percent true. Maybe it is. Maybe it isn't. I'm a dumb jock. But not dumb enough to tell a girl I hooked up with her because of being drunk.

"Okay," Brianna says.

We stand there for a minute. Don't know what I'm supposed

to do. Then she says, "Have you started on your school applications yet?"

"No."

"Brady! You have to."

"Yeah, I know."

"No, you don't. You think you do. Okay, forget it, I'm going to help you."

"I don't need—"

"Yes, you do. You want to get into a good school, don't you?"

Oh, hell yes. What I say is, "I guess."

"So we'll work together on it. I need to keep working on mine anyway."

"You're a junior."

"Oh my God, are you kidding me? That's the best time to start. Look, you've got Butler for English, right? This period?"

"Yeah."

"Okay, I've got Mrs. Black for health. It's a blow-off. She'll let *me* out, he'll let *you* out, and we'll go to the library instead. At least once a week, like on Fridays. They'll totally let us do that if we tell them it's for college. Okay?"

"Um. Okay."

"See?" Brianna says. "This is great. We get to see each other, you'll get into a great school on a scholarship, and I'll go to . . . to whatever school my dad tells me to, and that's it."

"We can go out," I say. "Go hang somewhere. Not just school."

Brianna smiles. It's not a real one.

"I'm still busted for the party," she says. "The one time I take a night off to be a regular person, and . . . anyway. I don't have any time outside of school, really. I'm not blowing you off, I swear. It's just true."

"You got grounded?"

"For the party? No. I just have to keep to my old schedule, which is school, school, dance, and more school."

"That sucks."

"Yeah. But now we'll have Fridays. *Right?*" She pokes me in the chest.

"Right. Fridays during first."

"Cool. Hey, we're late. Let's go."

I grab her arm. "Wait a sec."

She turns. I pull her close. Kiss her. It's much better than when we were both drunk.

After a minute we split up. Now she really is smiling.

"See you later," she says. Runs down the hall.

Laughing.

Never heard her laugh before.

# VIVI

Thursday afternoon, Mrs. Garcia hands back our latest assignment one minute before the bell. There's a big fat A on my essay about Mary Shelley's *Frankenstein*. Brianna Montaro gets a B.

"Shit!" she shouts, pounding both hands on her desk. It makes me jump.

Mrs. Garcia arches an eyebrow and says, "Brianna? It's an eighty-nine. Not a big deal."

But THE Brianna Montaro looks like she's going to hyperventilate. She swings her head toward my desk. I don't cover my grade. THE Brianna Montaro fixes me in her crosshair gaze.

I smirk.

The bell rings. Everyone gets up and heads for the door. Sam waits for me. I squeeze past Zach Pearson as he heads down my row and slow my walk toward Sam, watching Zach sit at my desk and say something low to Brianna. Brianna throws her essay into the air and shouts at him, "It doesn't matter, I can't win! I can't *win* in this place!"

There're only a few of us left in the room. Sam and I see it, Mrs. Garcia sees it, a couple other slowpokes see it. Brianna doesn't care. She tries to grab the straps to her Merona bag but it gets snagged on her seat.

"Brianna?" Mrs. Garcia asks gently, coming from around her desk. "Do you have a question about the essay? I'd be happy to—"

"*No!*" Brianna shouts, finally unsnagging her bag and standing up. "It's not your fault, I did it wrong, that's all that matters, right? *Right?*"

I pull close to Sam as she shoots through the doorway and into the hall. She's got *kanji* lettering written across the backside of her yoga pants. She has to stick out her butt in that awkward way too-skinny girls do to make it look like their butts aren't flat.

Before anyone can speak, I hear two people colliding in the hall. I hear Brianna wailing, "Look out, you vamp freak!"

Sam and I peer out the door. Brianna stalks down the middle of the hallway, her rage forcing people to the sides like the tip of a spear. Across from the doorway, Cadence's friend Danny, the weird kid we met at the coffee shop a couple of months ago, stares after her for a second before calling, "Looking lovely today! Your bitch is extra shiny!"

And right after that, a cluster of basketball players jostles him aside, calling him a number of names. Danny regains his balance, nods, and walks down the hall with an odd, deliberate smile on his face.

"I always thought the Dez sucked," I say to Sam. "But all we had to worry about there was getting shot or stabbed. It's way worse here."

He raises his eyebrows in agreement. He and I move into the hall, and Zach Pearson pulls up alongside Sam.

"Hey," he says. "What'd you guys get?"

"Ninety-eight."

"Eighty-seven," Sam says. "You?"

"Seventy-nine," Zach says. "I don't think I'm allowed to speak English anymore."

"It's a hard class," I say.

"Not for you," he says, but grins. He holds up Brianna's essay. "Did Brianna go this way?"

"Yep," Sam says. "Just follow the line of bodies."

"She *does* get a little intense," Zach says, then nods at us and jogs off down the hall.

"That's not the word I'd use," I tell Sam.

"Well, whisper it real sexy to me," Sam says, and kisses my hair just above my ear. I can barely feel the kiss up there—but I also feel it everywhere.

"Did you see her butt?" I ask Sam.

"Oh, man, is this one of those girl tests?"

"Not this time. She had *kanji* on her pants."

"Oh, that. Yes. Hard to miss. I don't think there's a lot of 'Montaros' in Japan."

"What do you think the translation is? I bet it's 'Juicy.'"

"Yummy?" Sam says.

"Spank This."

"Slutty McOpenlegs."

I'm giggling by then. And it's no longer an entirely foreign sensation. "Maybe I should ask her."

"I'll give you a dollar if you do."

"Maybe I don't want a *dollar*."

I try to say this in some kind of sexy way. I'm not sure it works at first, not until Sam eyes me and says, "*God* you're hot."

So that helps.

"*Muy caliente*," I say, and squeeze him closer to me as we walk. It's hard to sync up our steps, but I don't care. People are watching. And I like it. It gives me an idea, and not a new one. This is Thursday, which means Marlene will be taking Daddy to rehab this afternoon.

"Let's ditch seventh, go to my house," I say to Sam. I haven't actually taken him inside before.

"Well—sure, yeah. You're so daring."

"I know, right?"

I take his hand and we head for the parking lot. Nobody stops us, because a lot of seniors don't have seventh hours, and we blend right in with them.

I drive us to my house and park in the garage, letting us in through the garage door connected to our kitchen. Sam follows me in, past the kitchen and toward the foyer where the staircase begins. His eyes are enormous.

"This is your house," he says. Like he can't believe it.

I look at the bare, beige walls. The polished marble entry floor. New carpet. Chandelier shining down above us. Double front door. Suddenly everything I'd planned in the last hour blows right through my head, and all I can feel is embarrassed.

"I'm sorry," I say.

Sam turns. "For what?"

I can't answer.

"Oh, hey," Sam says, touching my shoulder. "Viv . . . jeez, what's the matter? I didn't mean to be a jerk or anything, I'm just not used to it is all. Viv?"

"It's not *us*," I whisper. God, I sound like it's the first day of school again. What was I thinking, bringing him in here?

"Not who?" Sam asks.

"My dad and me." I count flecks of gold in the floor. Is it real gold? It can't be. Can it?

"What do you mean?" He sits on the step leading down into our front room. It might have another name. Something proper. I don't know. I could ask a neighbor, except they don't like us.

I want to tell Sam that.

I want to make him see what it's like. That our old house would practically fit into Dad's new bedroom, but that it was us, it was where we belonged. That I belonged at Southside High near the Dez, not here.

That this is a dream, or a nightmare, and eventually it's going to end.

And it won't bring Mom back. Even though it should.

What I do instead is sit next to him and say, "Nothing."

Sam smiles at me. "You're a very strange person. Anyone ever tell you that?"

I nod. It's not the only word they've used.

"Who?" Sam asks.

His question surprises me. Did he read my mind? No—he's replying to my nod, that's all.

Sam fakes some kind of Mafia-movie voice. "You want I should whack 'em? Take 'em out? I can do dat. I do it for you. Don't worry about it. Fugget about it, I'm *known*. In all da five boroughs."

No one but Dad has ever been able to make me laugh like Sam does. It's not even that funny. But the way he says it, I can't help it.

"Are we dating?" I ask when we're not laughing anymore.

Sam raises his eyebrows. "Um—I don't know, are we? I mean, that would be cool. Totally."

"Really?"

"Yeah. Really."

I've never met anyone like Sam. Maybe we can get married someday. I guess that's a long time from now. But it would be nice.

And we could afford a huge wedding.

Maybe the money isn't all bad. I wouldn't have met Sam if Daddy hadn't been hurt.

"You want to see my room?" I say.

"Sure."

"There's no furniture. My clothes are still in boxes."

"How come?"

Sam is smart. I want him to figure it out so I don't have to say it. But he doesn't. He just watches me, eyebrows still raised, waiting.

"Because," I say finally, "I didn't think it would last."

"But it has. And probably will."

"Probably."

Sam puts an arm around my shoulder and squeezes. "I like boxes."

I take his hand from my shoulder, kiss the top of it, and then guide him up the staircase. I'm still not used to it. The carpet is too thick under my feet. I want to creep along the edge where it's just bare wood.

"Where is your dad, anyway?"

"Rehab. He goes all the time."

We reach my room and I open the door. I could park a couple of school buses inside. Until we moved here, I'd never seen a house with rooms this size. And this isn't the biggest house on our block.

The three boxes I packed look small and insignificant. Daddy says not to worry, we're going to fill my room with everything I want. I don't even *know* what I want. I don't think Daddy cares.

"Okay, so, this is nice," Sam says, walking in.

There's not much to see. The walls and ceiling are white. A dark wood ceiling fan sits in the middle. I've got a walk-in closet at one end. I have two windows, both looking out over our swimming pool.

I have a swimming pool.

I close the door as Sam walks silently over to a window and looks out. "That's a great yard," he says. "If I was ten, I would totally play War down there."

"You played War?"

"Every day after school, and every weekend," Sam says, turning to face me.

His eyes flick toward the door, where I'm standing against it, hands tucked behind the small of my back. Then Sam's gaze meets mine. In that heartbeat, he knows. He knows I've already decided. I can see it in his face.

"Hey," he says softly.

I push my shoes off with my feet, shoving the heels off first. Sam sits against the windowsill and pulls off one shoe, then the other.

He shoves the white plantation shutters closed, *swish-clack, swish-clack*.

"Shit," he says.

My hands freeze at the hem of my shirt. "What?"

"I don't have any . . . you know."

"Oh." My hands are trembling.

He turns back around. "We could probably, you know, think of something, though. I mean, we don't have to . . . *actually* . . ."

"Okay," I whisper. It briefly—very briefly—crosses my mind that if we can't *say* it, we probably shouldn't *do* it.

But that leaves a lot up to interpretation. We'll think of something.

The carpet feels at least an inch thick under my feet. It's like wading through a soft stream to where I meet him, in the middle of my new bedroom without a bed.

It feels just as thick underneath me as we fall to the floor together.

# DANNY

My sister appears contrite for the first time in her pathetic life. She won't even look at me. Not that that's unusual.

"You," I say.

She nods, and finds something fascinating to study on my carpet.

"You. You stole my phone. On the first day of school."

"It was a joke, Danny. I was pissed about how you were dressed and the way you were talking, so I just grabbed it when I came to get my—"

"The police department is investigating me for child pornography," I say, pointing to the wall as if the SWAT team is right outside it. "And you're *just now* telling me?"

"I said I was sorry—I *am* sorry—I didn't know."

I start giggling. It scares even me. I haven't slept much lately.

"Didn't know? You didn't know someone used my phone to take a picture of a naked kid and I got blamed for it? You're—"

I choke. I can't stop giggling. And I'm not even high.

"You're trying to tell me that between Mom and Dad and the . . . what is it . . . ah yes, entire school, that you *didn't know*?"

"Danny—"

"Are you shitting me? Ha ha ha! You didn't know. That's great. That's, that's unreal. How dare you? How can you stand there and pretend you had no idea, dude?"

"I didn't want anyone . . . I didn't *mean* for anyone to get in trouble. It was supposed to be a prank, just a joke, okay? So, it's over."

"Oh, ain't *that* the truth, sis."

"Look, don't be all weird about it, okay? It was a mistake, it wasn't supposed to go this far. So just—"

Still laughing, because

I

CAN'T

STOP.

I hold up my index fingers. "Ohhhhh, hold on! *Now* I get it. Of *course*. You know who took the picture, don't you. You know who it is, and you didn't want to rat them out. You were afraid you might get—get *whacked* or something, huh? They'd rub you out? That's it, isn't it."

"Danny, it doesn't matter. It was just a joke, it got out of hand, and I'm totally sorry. Okay? Can we just forget it?"

"Yeah," I say, wiping my eyes. "Okay. It was a joke. You win. Ha ha. Get out."

"Hey, look, I—"

"Get the almighty shitballs out of my room. Pretty please."

When she's gone, I stare at my closet door for a while, considering my options. Halloween is tomorrow. My costume is all ready to go. Nobody's going to like it, but what have I got to lose now? If they'd just listened when I said to send me back to my old school, we wouldn't be in this mess.

Okay.

I'll give him

ONE

LAST

CHANCE.

But then that's it.

I figure Big Sis must've already told Mom and Dad that this whole cluster-schlong was her doing. She wouldn't want it to come from me. So now all I have to do is give them the opportunity to set the record straight with me. Easy. Then I can go back to my school, forget any of this ever happened. Maybe I'll even start taking my meds again. Why not.

I go into the living room and stand in the doorway. My head hurts. It takes three full minutes for Dad to look up.

"So?" I say politely.

"So, what."

"Is there anything you'd like to say to me?"

Dad says, "Okay . . . have you done your homework?"

He *must* be joking. Breaking the ice. "That's it? That's all you got?"

"Danny, I'm tired. Can we not screw around right now?"

I watch him for a few more seconds, waiting for a burst of insight, an epiphany.

"Sure thing," I say, friendly. "No more screwing around."

I start to go, but stop and peek back inside. "You know, I . . . I hope you have a great weekend. Really. I mean that."

Then I leave before he can respond, although I'm pretty sure he wasn't going to.

Tomorrow is Friday. There will be a game. *Friday Night*

*Lights* and all that. There's a rally after lunch. A costume contest. Strict rules, of course. But less strict, most likely, than the usual dress code. Everyone will be dressed up. Ten bucks says all the Athleaders will wear their jerseys as a costume, because that's how brilliant they are. Or maybe they'll do something cute like trade outfits with the cheerleaders—which is not at all *gay*, so long as they all do it. Kilts? Gay. Skinny jeans? Gay. Hypocritical motherfuckers.

Halloween. No one will think twice about someone wearing a mask.

So, that's it then. I take pills and play games, mostly, for the rest of the night. Think about Cadence. I should text her. She deserves that much.

Happy Halloween.

# CADENCE

Thursday night, I'm on the verge of passing out with a novel on my lap when my phone buzzes. I check it for a new text message.

**Do not go to school tomorrow.**

Danny. Nice. First time he's made contact since Monday after lunch. I almost don't respond, but then I do because I'm still a big dopey sucker.

How come? I write back. Are you ditching? Ditching is bad for you, you know ☺

I add a smiley and set the phone down, picking up my book again. Maybe I wasn't as sleepy as I thought, except then after, like, a paragraph, my head starts bobbing.

My phone goes off again.

The screen reads: **Just don't.**

"Oh, great," I say out loud, and start typing back.

What's he up to now? I can't even begin to consider all the pranks he must be waiting to pull tomorrow, since it's Halloween and all that. Rotten eggs in a water balloon launcher, maybe? Or isn't there some old gag with cherry bombs in the toilets? I'm not sure exactly what a cherry bomb is, but something tells me Danny does and that he wouldn't hesitate to blow up a couple heads—that's navy speak for toilets—just to make everyone jump. I even catch myself grinning at the idea. Maybe it would be kind of funny. And hey, at least he's trying to give me a heads up.

I write, What are you talking about?

Then I wait for his response, but it doesn't come. Great, he's probably being all cranky-boy, since he loves doing that so much. Still, I try again, anyway.

Hey man, what are you talking about?

Five more minutes go by.

What's up?

Then:

Dude come on

I yawn. It's so late already! I think about trying to find some kind of costume to put on tomorrow after all, but really, Halloween's not my thing. I don't exactly have a lot of costume pieces lying around. Maybe I'll wear a skirt. That would be enough of a departure for me for no one to recognize me!

Danny still hasn't answered. Well, fine. I'm tired, and I'm going to bed. I send one last message.

Text me back

And then I put my book away and climb into bed.

The only message waiting for me in the morning is a pic from Kelly, showing off her costume. I let her know it looks awesome, and I don't bother trying to reach Danny again. There are much more important things to worry about.

Things like: I'm going to lunch with Zach today! I need to find something really cool to wear. Something *fascinating*.

# DREA

Halloween.

The bell beginning classes rings. In the school parking lot, me and Dad have been sitting in his Jeep for five minutes in silence. Dad hasn't turned off the engine, though. It's chilly outside, but not cold, you know? He has the heat on. I wonder if my Sally makeup will run. Kelly did an amazing job on the costume, and because of Dad's job at the theater, I picked up few things about makeup, so that looks great, too. I look just like Sally, stitches and all.

Sally, who knits herself whole. Maybe Kelly was trying to tell me something.

The parking lot is emptying of students in various getups and costumes, eager to enjoy the regressive holiday and the Friday. Some teachers, it's rumored, will be handing out candy.

Dad lights a cigarette in his trademark way and leans back into the worn cloth upholstery. The Jeep is twenty years old. He rolls the window down and gazes out, blowing smoke, as if channeling James Dean.

*Poser*, I think.

He isn't looking at me. But this expression is his "thoughtful face." His head is tilted at a slight angle, a master gesture one of my many "uncles" pointed out to me years ago.

"Any time Frankie tilts his head like that," Uncle Joe told me, "he's thinking about something. Just sit tight. He'll say it eventually."

So I wait, scuffling my sneakers against a pile of CD cases on the floor. I can't believe Dad still uses CDs. How old. How stupid. I shouldn't even be in the Jeep, except Kelly had to come early and do college research in the library. I see her truck parked at the other end of the lot. Now instead, I'm here, with Dad, who rather than just rolling up to the sidewalk to let me hop out, pulled into a spot and put the Jeep in park, like he had something to say.

Or, maybe—just maybe—he knows *I* do.

And then it comes. Even if I wanted to stop, I don't think I can.

"Why don't you love Mom?"

Dad acts unsurprised by the question. "I never said that."

"Didn't have to," I mutter, and scratch my sleeve. My scabs are healing, itching like crazy.

But it's been awhile since I cut. Dad turns his head toward me, then away again. He takes another drag.

"What about me?" I say.

Dad's hand freezes, poised outside the window. We both watch as a late student rolls a huge silver truck into a handi-capped space. How rude.

Dad says, "What about you, what?"

The late student, dressed all in black for the holiday, strug-gles with a green duffel bag. It falls heavily to the blacktop, and he heaves it with both hands to get it up and over his shoulders. I watch him with only half-focused eyes. He's a movie playing in the background, nothing more.

I don't answer Dad.

"What's on your mind, kid?" he says softly, turning away from the kid with the bag, and tilting his head back to watch the trees wave gently overhead. It's a pretty day.

Some organ in my torso twists like a wringing rag as I say, "I hate you."

Dad looks over at me, studying. For the first time in years, I meet his gaze without looking away or blinking, even though it's not easy.

"I know that." His voice is still smooth, unemotional. But now there's an undercurrent of something else. "I could guess why you do. But will you tell me? I want to hear it."

I didn't plan on this. None of it. I'd rehearsed a thousand different scripts in my head a thousand times, knowing Kelly was right and that I needed to say something, you know?

But I hadn't expected to ever actually be saying it. None of this is like I imagined. I wanted, *needed*, a showdown with him, with both of them. Wanted to throw dishes like Mom, and hear them crash with great satisfaction against the kitchen tile, you know? Grab the steering wheel while driving someplace and veer us all into a light pole. Wait till a rare dinner out to cause a scene worthy of a Maxie—the local annual theater critics' award. Scream profanities and accuse them of all they'd done wrong.

Instead, this. He isn't taking his cues, isn't following my script. But at least I'm listening to Kelly's advice, telling him exactly what I'm thinking for once. At least I'm talking. There's a faint pride in that.

"I don't know why." I go back to work on my thumbnail. I'll have to switch hands soon. The kid in black has disappeared inside the building. Nothing now to distract us even a little bit.

"Sure you do, Sweet."

"Stop calling me 'Sweet.' I have I name."

"I know. I picked it."

I don't gasp, exactly, but I do feel my breath catch for a second. Dad gives me a sidelong glance.

"It's true. I always knew my first girl would be named Andrea. That happens to be you."

This news unwinds the solid organ that twisted earlier. "Why Andrea?"

"I just never met an Andrea I didn't like." He coughs a little laugh, which turns into a real cough, and he has to hack and spit out the window. "Do you like 'Drea' as a nickname?" he asks suddenly.

"Yeah."

"I thought I heard your friend Kelly use it once. See, I figured with a name like Andrea, you had lots of choices. Andrea, Andi, Drea, Dre. There're four right there."

He laughs a bit, but stops quickly.

I plunge in. "Did Mom really sleep with someone else? Dustin?"

"I doubt it." He takes a slow drag from his cigarette. "Your mom and I . . . we had the best time when we met. We laughed a lot. I mean, *a lot*. We had a blast. And over time, I think what happened is, we just assumed it meant we were in love. Andi, the reality is, I love your mom, and I've loved her for a long time. But I'm not *in* love with her, I never was *in* love with her, and she wasn't with me, either. We're terrible as a couple. If you haven't noticed."

"Kinda, yeah."

"Well, please believe me when I tell you that we both love you. That's never been a question, not once, not now, not ever."

"You resent me."

"No, I don't. Can you believe me?"

I consider that for a moment. Can I? "Okay," I say.

And it's true. I can believe him when he says that.

"But can we do something about it?" I go on. "About you guys? I hate it. Dad, I hate it, and it hurts me, and I hurt myself, and I want to stop, but living there, it's like—"

I stop. *Cut myself short*, so to speak, and the thought almost makes me laugh.

"What can I do for you, Andi? Give me an assignment. I'll do it."

"Do you love her?"

"Sometimes."

"Is 'sometimes' enough to be married?"

". . . Sometimes. Yeah."

"If it is—I mean, if it really is? Then look at her. Tell her you love her if you really do. And if you don't, then just call it off and get it over with because I can't deal with you."

Dad blinks. Frowns. Slowly nods. "All right. That's fair."

"Good. Thank you."

"What do you mean, you hurt yourself?"

I'm tempted right then to roll up my skintight white sleeves with the broken-doll stitching Kelly did on them, show my scars, and tell him the entire truth. But the last bell for first period rang a while back. I should go. I'm already running late.

"Nothing. I'm fine."

"Hey," Dad says. "I love you."

"I know. I love you."

"You still hate me, too?"

"Lil' bit."

"We'll work on it?"

"Okay."

He reaches over and pulls me awkwardly close in the front seats, kissing my head. "Have a good day."

"You, too."

"Your costume looks incredible, by the way."

"I know. Thanks."

I—Andrea-Andi-Drea-Dre—climb out of Dad's Jeep, pulling my backpack with me. I wave to him through the window after shutting the door, and he waves back. He pulls out of the parking lot while I meander casually toward the school, feeling better than I have in a long time.

I pull out my phone as I walk, sending Kelly a text. I did it. Talked to Dad. Thank you. ☺

Kelly will be happy for me. We'll catch up during lunch, and it will be the start of a good weekend. Maybe we can hang out, if Kelly isn't busy babysitting.

I open the front door of the school and head down the main hall. The kid from the silver truck stands a few yards away, playing with something black. The hallways are like a tomb, long and silent.

"Hi," I say, on a whim. It's one of the very few times I've said something to someone first. But it's that kind of day.

The kid looks up. He has no face. Or, more accurately, his face is covered by a matte-black mask with only eyeholes and some pinholes around the mouth. His Halloween costume consists of black, multi-pocketed pants, a long-sleeved black T-shirt, and some kind of black vest contraption that makes me think of a safari.

It takes a second for me to realize that he's pointing a gun at me.

He—it must be a *he*, right?—he holds it at his hip in both hands. For the barest of moments, I can see his eyes behind the dull black face mask.

"Sorry," he says. His voice is muffled.

*For what?*

I try to say this, but then I'm being pushed. My breath coughs out, and I feel my shoulders smack into the brick wall behind me. I slide down, my eyes never leaving the boy in black. Like an afterthought, I hear a loud and fast sputtering sound.

I try to say something, wanting to tell him to stop, to leave me alone, I haven't done anything wrong, haven't done anything to him, whoever he is. But I can't talk.

"Sorry," the kid says again

What is this stuff in my mouth? It's red. So red. Red like the blood when I'm cutting. But I stopped, I promise I did, I

*Death of Me*

# COACH

He bangs his toe against the bed first thing in the morning, so that's just god damn great. But at least it appears that his son is already up and out, and he fights against the guilt that rises in him when he realizes he's pleased by it. No—not pleased. Relieved. A quiet morning is a thing to be appreciated, that's all.

Got to do something about that kid, he tells himself. Got to, got to…take him outdoors, go fishing, hunting. Something.

"Daddy?" his daughter says as he limps crankily into the kitchen.

"Hey, Peach. What's up?" He ruffles her hair. She appears to be dressed in some kind of English schoolgirl outfit, and he's pleased to see it's not slutty. It might be from those Harry Potter books, but he's not sure.

"Um . . . listen, I know you're going to be mad, but I have to tell you something," she says.

"Tell me who you're dressed as first."

"Huh? Oh. Hermione."

"Should I know who that is?"

"She doesn't play for Green Bay, so, no."

That makes him laugh, and the throbbing in his toe fades. He starts making toast. "Aren't you running late for first period?"

"I have study hall, I can miss it. I have to tell you this thing."

*Pregnant*, he thinks. If it's one of his boys, oh, there will be god damn hell to pay. He's not an idiot; Donte's been making eyes at her for a long time. "Okay, so what am I going to be mad about?"

"So, you know the whole thing about that picture of the naked kid that was going around?"

"On your brother's phone." He resists a flare of anger at the reminder. "Yeah, I know all about it."

"Okay, but, Daddy? I don't . . . think it was his fault."

He gets out the butter. This doesn't sound like pregnancy. He's glad he didn't snap at her. "It's not, huh?"

"Um . . . I took his phone? And then someone took it from me. I don't know who. Might've been someone on the baseball team, I'm not sure."

Coach frowns as this news slowly works through his brain. "Danny really didn't have his phone? You're saying he did not have it when the picture was taken."

"No. He couldn't have. I'm sorry."

His throbbing toe and the early hour aren't making things as clear as he'd like, so he repeats, "He didn't take the picture."

"I don't see how it's possible. I'm really sorry, Daddy."

"Well, god damn," Coach sighs. The district attorney hasn't decided on a charge yet, so maybe this would change things. Maybe there's a way out of this, after all. "I need you to tell all that to our lawyer and probably to the police, okay?"

"Will *I* be charged or something?" Amy says, and the fear in her voice hurts him. "It was just a prank. I was just messing around with him for his first day at school. He was being such a little shit . . ."

"No no, sweetheart, I'm sure it won't come back on you. We just have to let them know so they'll back off Danny. You were right to tell me."

"Are you mad?"

"No. Your *brother* will be." And that, he has to admit to himself, might be somewhat amusing, if it doesn't cause the kid an angry fit. For a smart-ass, he's been pretty quiet the last couple weeks. It makes Coach think about volcanoes, or the calm before a storm.

The thought shoots a jet of acid into his stomach.

"I told him already," Amy says. "He's just giving me the silent treatment. Ooo, shocker."

Coach hugs her tightly, chuckling. Silent treatment, indeed. The kid hasn't said a word to *anyone* all week, as far as he knows. "You want me to give you a ride to school? I think I'll skip the gym."

"Sure."

Monica comes in, stretching. Coach notes she looks good, even in a robe and no makeup. He gives her a quick kiss and goes back to preparing his toast.

"Where's Danny?" he asks her.

"I thought I heard him leave early," Monica says, making bedroom eyes at him clandestinely so Amy won't see. "Something to do at school, I guess."

"Or to get high," Amy says, helpfully.

"Worry about yourself," Monica admonishes.

Coach grins. Once done with his food, he gives Monica another kiss, and tells Amy to hustle and get her backpack.

Now he realizes there's one small problem.

"Where're my keys?"

"Did you look on the peg?" Monica says.

"Of course I looked on the peg, I'm looking at the peg right now, where are my god damn keys?"

"Did Amy borrow them for something?"

"Don't look at me," Amy says, returning.

"I can drive you if it's a big thing," Monica says.

"My keys are a big thing," Coach says.

"Look, mine are right here," Monica says. "I can drop you off on my way."

Coach opens the door to the garage, as if perhaps the keys will be floating there, thinking perhaps he left them in the truck's ignition, the middle console, or hanging from the door lock.

"That's not the point," he rumbles. "The point is I need my keys for work, too, all the classroom keys are on it, so it's not just about the car, it's—"

He stops cold.

"Well I don't know what tell you," Monica says. "I'm pretty sure they were on the peg when we went to bed last night, so if they're not there now then one of the kids must've taken them. Look in the truck."

The truck is not, in fact, there. But that's not what's turned his blood into ice.

"Call the police," Coach whispers. He can't make his voice work.

Monica frowns. "If Danny took the truck—"

"*Call the police NOW!*"

His voice is high, like the wail of a wounded animal. Monica steps over to the open door as Coach runs to the tall gun safe kept in the garage. He holds the door to the safe open with his right hand and stares into it, like it's a refrigerator full of Super Bowl snacks. Coach's hand trembles as he reaches inside the safe and pulls out the only remaining weapon.

A pump-action pellet gun. The one he bought Danny over a year ago, the one that got him kicked out of school.

Monica steps into the garage. So does Amy.

"What is it?" Monica says.

Coach fights rising nausea. Rising certainty.

Monica touches his arm. "Dan? What is it?"

DREA

# DONTE

I check myself out in the mirror of the boys' restroom. The team decided to wear shirts and ties for Halloween. I'm looking good, and I know it. Looking good for Amy. Season's almost over. Not our best, but I know I'll have some offers coming in soon. Once the last game's over, Amy's going to talk to her dad. See what happens next. So yeah—I like looking good for her.

I double-check to make sure I've got the green hall pass in my pocket. Then I swagger out of the bathroom, heading back to Butler's class. Part of me is a little jealous that Brady got a pass to go to the library with Brianna, but Brianna's helping B look for schools and fill out the FAFSA form, all those sorts of things. It's good. It's a good thing to miss English for.

I think he'll be all right. Maybe none of us is going to Ohio or USC, but that's okay. I'm going to college, first one in the family. Brady, too. It'll work out. Maybe we'll all even go to the same place. Amy'll be hearing back from her schools soon. We can compare locations, see if we get into the same places, or even just nearby.

Turning a corner, I see some kid dressed all in black, like a ninja or a SWAT cop. The weapon in the kid's hands looks damn authentic. The tips of toy guns are supposed to be painted orange, like Ramon's are.

My phone starts buzzing in my pocket as we walk toward each other. I pull the phone out while addressing the kid.

DREA

"Damn, dude," I say. "Dr. Flores know you carrying that shit down the hall?"

The kid drops a massive duffel bag to the floor. It makes a clunking sound. He levels the rifle in his hands.

See, now's he going and making a thing of it. That's a bad idea. "Aw, come on, bitch," I say. "Don't be getting—"

I land on my back.

It feels like my body's trying to breathe through new holes in my lungs. There's a sound like wet asthma, and it fills the hall.

I somehow watch as the kid in black looks at my phone on the tile floor. My thumb must have tapped the answer key, because Amy's voice comes through. I hear it so clear, so fine and so nice . . .

"Donte, it's me. You have to get out of school. Okay? Are you there? Listen to me, get out of school, I—I think my brother Danny's—"

The kid in black brings a booted foot down on my phone, smashing it silent.

I think the kid picks up his bag and walks down the hall.

I got to get up, got to

# BETWEEN CLASSES

The girl dressed like a stitched-up doll wasn't a target, not necessarily. He knew someone would have to go first, that's all. Break the ice. If he could do one, he could do a hundred. Whoever happened to cross his path first, they had to go, that's all. That's it. Life sucks sometimes. You don't always get to decide things.

He's a little surprised he didn't throw up—or at least, not yet. In fact his heart feels like it's beating once per minute, in great slow waves, instead of the rapid pace he'd anticipated despite the pills he took to keep calm. There is a method to all this. There is a goal. The pills are working excellently.

The bell ending first period rings. The faceless gunman stops in the middle of the hall, drops his bag again, reloads, and holds the rifle at hip level.

Doors open. Students pile out. Shouts of eagerness, of delight over the Halloween holiday. Some people have really outdone themselves, with spot-on celebrity impersonations or outstanding visual effects. Seven people from the drama department have done themselves up like *Walking Dead* characters and attendant zombie walkers.

So when the real blood sprays from one of their torsos, it's no wonder most people think it's part of the day. A cool trick.

Then the sound hits. The rapid stutter of the semiautomatic rifle that is somehow not nearly as loud as most of them would think, but loud enough to identify itself, loud enough to make clear that this is not part of the day after all.

Screams rise at once, a chorus of fear and disbelief. People run for cover. They dive into classrooms, they run down the hall. A few get knocked over. A few can't move.

The gunman waits for the worst of the noise to settle before reloading again. A few students roll around on the ground, moaning. He paces by, looking for friends and enemies and seeing neither until he encounters an Athleader, a tall guy named Martin, he thinks, on the ground squeezing tight to the wall. Paralyzed, it seems, with fear and something like a refusal to believe this is happening.

The gunman lowers the point of the rifle toward Martin.

Martin waves his hands in front of him, scooting away fast, his paralysis gone. "C'mon, man, don't. Don't, all right? Come on, don't do this."

The gunman keeps the AR at his hip.

"Dude, bro, c'mon," Martin groans. He really says it. *Dude, bro.*

"Come on, what?" the gunman says. The voice is robotic, disassociated.

"Come on, don't kill me man, all right? Don't kill me, please . . ."

"Okay."

Martin stops sliding backward. Lowers his hands a bit. Like he's not sure he should believe it.

The gunman pulls the trigger, waving the AR back and forth. Martin's knees explode. Martin screams, high and hard and loud.

This is real, the gunman thinks. It's happening, people are really dying. Maybe I should stop. Maybe . . .

A door opens. It's Mr. Bladder. Or Ballsack. Whatever his name is. Apparently, he missed the opening anarchy, mistaking it for good clean Halloween fun.

"What in the world is—"

Loud flutters of lead poke into his chest. For one second, the pattern is like a smiley face. Have A Nice Day.

Butler/Bladder falls against the door and slides down it. People in the classroom scream. The gunman walks over to the door and peeks inside, working through a quick word problem: if one quarter of the class is on its feet and one quarter are already on the floor, how many are still frozen in their desks?

"Mmm," he says, scanning the crowd. "Nah. Have a nice day."

He moves on. He has other things to do, and the clock is ticking. He grabs his bag and moves further into the school.

"Attention, attention," Dr. Flores bellows over the intercom. "This is a lockdown. This is a lockdown. This is not a drill. The code word is red pen. The code word is *red pen.*"

*That's two words, Dr. Floor,* the shooter thinks, just as someone peeks through the windows in the library doors, then disappears as they meet his own gaze. He moves toward the library. There's no reason to go to the gym.

The freshmen will be safe there.

# VIVI

"The code word is *red pen,*" Dr. Flores bellows over the intercom, interrupting my chemistry teacher's lecture on titration curves. She keeps on talking right over it, and hardly anyone pays attention.

Our classroom door opens and Mr. Winters, my French teacher, pokes his head in.

"Shut it down," Mr. Winters says.

"Shut what—"

"Red pen," Mr. Winters says. His eyes are as wide as the windows.

It's like some invisible hand yanks my chem teacher's spine out from the base of her neck. Like she didn't hear Dr. Flores say it just five seconds ago. She stands up straight and walks briskly to the door with her keys in her hand. She pulls the door shut as Mr. Winters goes away down the hall. Our teacher locks the door, hits the lights, and the room goes dark.

She points to a wall where the American flag is hanging from a thin black stick.

"Against the wall," she says, her voice firm, face set in plaster. "Get down, no talking."

Which makes everyone start talking at once.

"Quiet!" our teacher says and it vibrates the bones in my arms.

We all shut up.

"Against the wall," she repeats. "Right now. Absolute silence. Get on the floor, stay low. This is not a drill."

But we don't move, not yet, maybe because we're still hoping that this is not a—

"Lockdown," she says. "This is a lockdown, get out of your seats, and move to the wall, now. There is an active . . . an active . . ."

She can't say the next word.

At last we listen. We all shuffle to our place under the American flag and don't say anything.

Then: shots.

Semiautomatic rifle shots. I recognize them from the Dez. Twenty-two caliber bullets. I used to go to sleep to them when I was little. What are they doing here? We're supposed to be safe here, me and Daddy, that's why we came all the way up here . . . to get away from all that down there . . .

We move in slow motion, trading wide-eyed stares of disbelief. It must be a joke. We're all thinking it. It must be some Halloween prank, and somebody is really going to get their ass beat when it's all over.

Down some nearby hallway is the sound of drums snapping; no, popcorn bursting; no, .22 caliber rounds being fired in rapid succession . . . it echoes throughout the entire school. People gasp. Fists get jammed into mouths. Our teacher's eyes are unblinking, her jaw tightly clenched.

"We should *do* something," a boy grunts.

"Shh!" the teacher says. And I'm glad. We should do nothing, we should sit and wait and someone will come get us, someone will come get us, someone will come.

And where is Sam? Is he okay? Oh, God, God, no, don't do this . . .

# DONTE

My eyes creep open. Not far away, a boy is splayed in the hallway, blood pooled beneath him. The kid groans. Moans. Weeps. Words.

I got no spit. No feeling in my left arm. But I got a mission. A job. A duty.

Drag myself toward the boy, using one arm. One-ninety never felt so heavy.

"Comin'," I say, or think I say.

The boy must be three, four, five football fields away. This crawl is taking so long.

"Comin'. Comin'."

"*I'm sorry!*" the kid screams.

Gotta get to the kid.

I reach him. Sit myself up against the wall. Need a break. Just a quick break. Where's the water girls? Need a drink.

Everything goes black.

Then red.

Then I can see again. It's been two seconds or two hours since I reached the bleeding kid.

I grab the boy's shirt and pull him close. Blood comes out from his mouth. Tears crease his face.

"Sorry," the boy mumbles.

He's a drama kid. Played in that show. *Hamlet.* That was years ago. Wasn't it? No. Last week. Maybe. It was before. Before the pain. Before the numb. My chest hurts, I think.

I pull the boy up into my lap. His head's below my chin.

"Doan wanna," the boy spits.

"Shh," I say. I kiss his hair. "Don't be afraid. Don't be afraid."

"Doan wanna die."

"Don't be afraid. I got you. Don't be afraid. Don't be afraid."

Shouting. Somewhere far off. Then an explosion of noise. And another. I think I should jump at the sound but my body won't respond. I feel the boy's chest on top of me, rising. Falling. Rising. Falling.

Falling.

Falling.

"Don't be afraid. I got you. This is a man's game now. Don't be afraid."

Everything goes black.

Then red.

Then

# DANNY

The warning bell for second period goes off. Maybe it's warning people about me. About today. Today is here. I am here. Today's the day.

I walk into the library. Carefully, but not slow.

The library is quiet except for the buzz of students desperately trying to be—

quiet.

The library isn't even a quarter full, and it must be my lucky day, because it's easy to find Brady Culliver and Brianna Montaro huddled behind a table, their backs to a bookshelf.

I stop in front of them and raise the rifle.

"Oh my God," Brianna Montaro says, like a sigh. Not a scream. I'd rather

SHE SCREAMED!

Brady Culliver says

*nothing.*

He wears a white button-down with a black-and-gold striped tie. His eyes cross momentarily on the barrel as I point it in his face.

It makes me

LAUGH!

But not out loud. Just inside. I whip off my mask because it's too fucking hot. And I want them to know who it is. They have to know. It's all part of the

PERFECT PLAN.

The tabletop is littered with college guides. There's no college in his future. There will be no future at all for these two.

"Any last words?"

"I'm sorry," Brianna says.

". . . What?"

"I'm so sorry," Brianna says—then erupts into tears. They seem to jet from her eyes and bathe the floor.

THE Brianna Montaro is wracked with sobs. Her entire body convulses. Her eyes disappear into her

SKULL,

pushed back by the force of her weeping.

Brady is still staring at the gun, frozen. But then his eyes dart to Brianna Montaro. He glances up at me.

"Don't do it," Brady whispers. "Come on, man. You don't want to."

"Oh, but I really, really do. Just like you really, really want to bang my sister. Move into

MY FUCKING HOUSE!

Be my dad's son. Don't tell me what I want."

Brianna is having trouble breathing now. Her inhalations are jagged and shallow, the cords of her neck straining, her cheeks awash with tears.

"Would you shut up?"

Brianna tries to answer. Takes rapid breaths, trying to get the air to respond. At last she manages to say, "I'm g-g-g-gonna die."

We're back on script. *How stale, flat, and useless are the things of this world!* Something like that. I forget the line now.

"That's right," I tell Brianna. "But I tell you what I'll do."

I set the AR on the table and take Dad's pine-green nine millimeter Glock from my bag. I'll use this instead. Less risk she'll get paralyzed or become a vegetable or something. It'll be quick, like turning out a light, no big deal. The round is bigger, so it should do the job.

Brianna keeps babbling. "I just p-p-pissed my pants and I'm scared and Jesus God I'm s-s-s-so sorry, Danny."

Never—

Never, even once, have any of them said my name.

Although Brady hasn't moved, there *is* movement in his eyes. But it's not a plot or a plan. Brady is not gearing up to try for one last jump, to try and get the gun away from me, or make a break for the AR on the table.

No.

There's a piece, maybe only a small piece, but a piece all the same . . . a small piece of him saying:

*Do it.*

I swing the Glock toward him. "You wanna die, Brady?"

Brady swallows.

"Sometimes."

*No, no, no!*

No, this is not how things go.

Brianna leans over her own legs, forehead pressed to the

industrial carpet. "S-s-sorry, so sorry," she chants, hugging herself.

The library doors open. I spin, aim the gun. I will

KILL

the next

SON OF A BITCH WHO—

"Is that cherry bombs or something? Anybody know what's going . . . oh."

CADENCE FULLER

says this with no regard for the quiet of the library, but she *does* go quiet for once when she meets my eyes. Her shoulders drop. It is almost comical.

"Oh no," she says.

"I told you not to be here!"

"Are you kidding me?" she says. "Are you really doing this, Danny? *This* is what you meant? Come on. Don't be that guy. I don't want to read about this tomorrow! Come on."

"Go home, Cadence!"

Cadence licks her lips. "Can't. I'm involved now."

"Go, god damn it!"

"Danny, I am so freaking scared right now, you have no idea. Please stop scaring me, okay?"

"Cadence—"

"I know how this works! You kill a buncha people then put a bullet in your head. Right? Isn't that it?"

Actually she's wrong. Half-wrong, anyway.

And the pistol. So heavy now. And off schedule. I'll have to go room to room to find everyone on my list . . .

"You're making me think we were never friends," Cadence says.

"I told you not to come today."

"Yeah, but unless you put that stupid gun down, you're gonna die, and that makes me feel like an idiot. Because somehow you think no one gives a shit, and *I* do, Danny. I do."

Brianna is still crying, and it reminds me that my back is to Brady. Tactically a bad idea. I shuffle to the side, where I can keep an eye on everyone, but Brady hasn't moved.

He had a chance to tackle me, and he didn't take it. Some sports hero.

"Yeah, man," Brady says. "I care—"

"Hey, shut up, meathead," Cadence says. "I'm talking to my friend Danny right now, 'kay?"

I laugh. Ha ha, Brady! Meathead Brady, that is great, and I feel so dizzy.

"Danny?" Cadence says. "Let's just go get something to eat, okay? Come on. Don't make me eat lunch by myself for the next four years. You're all I've got, man. Well, Pete, I guess, but he wears those kilts all the time and—"

"You don't love me."

"I don't want to have sex with you, that's entirely different."

"But I love you."

"Prove it." She holds out a hand. "Give me that."

"Will you love me?"

"I *already* love you, dummy. Otherwise I would've run screaming out of this room like an hour ago. Dude, would you look at my hand? I'm shaking like hell. I swear to God, Danny, I'm gonna puke. I hate puking. Don't make me throw up, please."

"If I give it to you, then what?"

"Then we sneak off campus and get some coffee," Cadence says. "Or ice cream, if you want. We could head down to Fifty-Third and Third, go to Jamaican Blue or something. Hey, after this, we can do whatever you want. Just let's go before anyone else comes in here. Okay?"

I look at Brady and Brianna. She's still crying, but totally silent. Brady appears not to have blinked, like, ever.

The problem here is that I have a job to do. The problem here is that if I'm going to get what I want, I can't stop now.

I point the gun at Brady Culliver.

*Okay, Cadence,* I think. *Let me just do this one thing real quick. I just need to*

*DESTROY THIS ASSHOLE*

*real fast. Okay? And then I'll have what I've always wanted.*

# CADENCE

Danny points the gun at the football player and my heart squeezes tight in my chest. I wonder for no particular reason if Dad ever saw someone killed, or if he ever had to kill someone, or if he was just always safe and secure in his submarine. I never asked him and I never really wanted to and now suddenly it's all I can think about before seeing this poor kid's head get blown up.

Except Danny doesn't the pull the trigger.

"I am going to destroy my father," he says, staring at the football player.

He says it calmly, like with a little fake-relaxed smile at the corners of his mouth, his eyes half-closed like he's totally at peace, except he's totally not. He thinks he's fooling me, or maybe himself, but he is anything but serene. Maybe the big pistol in his hand is ruining the image.

I lick my lips and say, "Why do you want to kill your dad?"

"That's not what I said. I said I'm going to destroy him. Slowly. Over years, if possible. It's perfect. Perfection."

"You mean you're not going to kill yourself?"

"Oh, eventually, I'm sure," Danny says with that same fake calm voice. "But not today. I mean, maybe I'm crazy, but I'm not stupid. I won't do well in prison. Honestly, look at me, right? Skinny little faggot. They'll make me snap in there. So sure, someday I'll kill myself. But first? I'll be in the newspaper. I'll be on the news. I'll be all over the web. I'll be famous, at least for a little while. They'll all ask me questions. They'll want interviews. And I'll give them. I'll tell them all about my dad and his little jock-sniffing candy-ass athleaders. And then maybe people will stop talking about how great he is and how great his players are. Maybe they'll finally talk about who those cocksuckers really are when no one's looking.

"Right, Brady? Oh hey, I meant to ask, how *is* my mom's cooking, anyway? You enjoy it so often."

My eyes dart to Brady, then quickly back to Danny. "That's what this is about? You're pissed at the *jocks*? Jesus, Danny."

Something in his eye twitches. His lips stretch apart, tight against his teeth.

"Pissed?" he whispers. He brandishes the pistol, and every opening in my body cinches shut.

"*Pissed?*" he says again, louder. "Look at this weapon, Cadence. *Look! At! It!* Does this look pissed off to you? Does this look like kicking down a door or throwing a plate across the room? Huh? You think I'm *cranky*? You think I'm having an *episode*? 'Tough day at school, sweetie?' Fuck you. And fuck everyone in this—"

"You don't get to talk to me that way."

The shock on Danny's face is about how shocked I am to hear myself say it.

"What?" he says, like he can't believe it.

And I can't believe that I keep going:

"You heard me," I say. "I don't deserve that, Danny. Come on. I mean, if you wanna shoot me I guess that's up to you, but you don't get to cuss me out like that." I take and release a deep breath, and cross my arms. I wish Dad was here. He'd know what to do.

For a second, Danny looks like he might laugh with total disbelief. Then he shakes his head—

And steps closer to the football player, who doesn't shut his eyes.

"Danny," I say.

He doesn't answer.

"Danny, they'll be here soon," I say, trying to sound matter-of-fact. "The cops'll come in here and they'll kill you. Then you won't be able to give those interviews. You've done enough, dude. You got their attention. You'll be on the news. You'll get your chance to talk. You just told me what you wanted, with the news and all that? I'm telling you that you'll get that, even if you stop right now."

"I want *you*. And your family. And this piece of shit wants mine. Well, now, guess what? Nobody gets anything."

"So make him live with it."

". . . What?"

"Make him live with it. Maybe killing him is too good, huh?"

Danny doesn't move. Not for a while.

Then he lowers his arm.

"That's an interesting point," he says.

"Well, I'm sort of smart that way. So? Come on. Let's go. Gimme the gun and let's go."

Danny smiles.

If you could call it that.

"Now you'll just be the pussy who didn't stop me," he tells the football player. "Yeah. I like the sound of that."

Danny picks up the rifle. Now he's got *two* guns, which is not helping my heart rate.

But with a click, the bottom falls out of the pistol. The clip, I guess. Danny hands it to me, sort of like symbolically.

I take the pistol, and it's not nearly as heavy as I thought it would be. But then I've never carried a gun before. I hold it with my fingers, not wrapping them around handle.

"Okay," Danny says. "You win. Let's go."

"What about that gun?"

"Not till we get to the truck."

Shaking all over, I move to stand beside him. "Okay. Thank you."

Danny doesn't answer. We push open the double swinging doors at the same time, like Old West saloon doors, and we walk out of the library together.

# DREA

# DONTE

# BRADY

I turn to one side. Throw up everything I've eaten in the past year. Doesn't amount to much.

*Kid was right. You pussy.*

Brianna is crawling on the floor. Dragging herself by her fingernails toward the door. Gasping for air. I shuffle toward her. Put a hand on her shoulder. Brianna moans. Rolls onto her back.

"I don't wanna die," she whispers.

I try to pick her up. Carry her to safety. Be the hero. But I can't. Got no strength. Instead I grab her wrists. Drag her toward a bookshelf where there's more cover. She feels like a dead animal. Can't make my hands work. Slide to the ground with my back against a shelf instead. And start crying. After a minute, Brianna picks herself up. Sits next to me. Arms around my neck. Says nothing. Not crying anymore.

Two gunshots.

Everything inside me goes soft. Then there's voices. Lots of voices. Like Coach. Except not him. People telling me what to do. Giving orders.

So I follow them.

# CADENCE

"*GUN!*" someone shouts right when we push the doors open.

In front of us are two men in uniforms, one in tan and one in black. The things in their hands are pointed at us, and then somehow I'm pointed at the ceiling.

I try to talk but can't. I lift my head, and there's red splatter across my Kermit the Frog sneakers.

Sad face.

How can I ever get them cle

# DANNY

We walk through the double doors together.

"*GUN!*" someone shouts.

*That's me,* I think. *They're talking about me. I've still got the rifle in my hands. Shitballs, I should have dropped that inside if we were coming out here. Except then that dumbass Brady would have it, and screw that.*

*Ow! God damn it, that shit hurt.*

*Yeah, I should have left it in there or something or tossed it out a window or something or given it to Cadence or something and I wonder where she went or something? I wonder where this went wrong, I wonder if I ever really had a chance or if I really knew what I was doing and ow, hell this hurts, doesn't it? Doesn't it? Yeah. Ow. God it's cold.*

*God damn it's cold in here.*

*I could use a bottle of water or something. I could sure use some water.*

*Why is my back all wet? God this hurts.*

*Oh, shit.*

*Oh, God.*

*I*

# DONTE

DREA

# CADENCE

# DANNY

*53rd & 3rd*

# COACH

By Saturday night, the reporters have all gone and the neighborhood is quiet again. By early the following Friday evening, a week after his only son murdered five people and wounded several more, Coach has summoned either the courage or the apathy to at last enter his son's room. No one but the police have been in it since a week ago. No one else. He's sure neither Monica nor Amy have stepped foot inside. Why would they?

And why is he doing it himself? Why now?

Coach lets himself in as Monica makes her fifth pot of coffee of the day and Amy stares at her phone on the kitchen table, either daring herself to call someone or waiting to see if anyone will call her first. He hopes she'll reach out. Maybe if she does it now, does it soon, she can be someone other than the sister of the killer.

He's already considered moving. Or maybe sending Amy to live with old family friends in another state. Changing her name. She doesn't deserve to have this hell hanging around her neck.

*Even if she's the one who took the phone?* he asks himself.

Yes. Even then. The phone was a joke. That Brady Culliver committed a crime with it is another topic, now that he knows. That Coach didn't take the time to investigate more fully himself . . . that's the worst crime. Amy, Brady, even Danny; they're kids. Young, stupid kids. He's the adult, and he should have done something. Listened, saw, asked, something. Jesus Christ, *something.*

Monica's sister has been bringing groceries, but only late at night, after most people are asleep and the vulture media and rubberneckers have given up filming the house. The three of them have not left except to travel to and from the local police station, to respond to questions they cannot possibly ever truly answer.

He enters Danny's room.

It has a barren look to it, although the cops didn't take everything, not nearly. Many books are still on his shelf, and as far as he can tell, all of his clothes still hang in the closet or are stuffed haphazardly into his dresser. The computer, of course, is long gone. The detectives won't tell him what they've found, if anything.

*Maybe I shouldn't have let him have it in his room*, Coach thinks. *Maybe that's what did this.*

He's sure it's not.

He sits on the edge of his son's bed, a man older by twenty years than he was a week ago. At his feet, a paperback book peeks out from under the bed. Coach picks it up.

*Hamlet.*

He thumbs through the book, the English as foreign to his eyes as a dead Romance language. There is but one line highlighted in the book. Just one. Almost the last page.

*KING CLAUDIUS: Our son shall win.*

Did he? Coach wonders. Based on what little info the police have fed them, did his son win? Did he get what he wanted?

*If Danny was here*, Coach thinks, *he wouldn't be able to*

*conceive just how badly he's damaged us. For the rest of our lives. How much he's hurt other people. Dragged them into a living hell.*

*You don't know what hell is, son. Even if you're in it, not even now, you don't know.*

"Dad?"

Coach Dan Jennings almost screams, sure it is the voice of his son, here to torment him. But no—it's Amy. She stands in the doorway, and clearly will not come in.

He meets her eyes, briefly, but gives no response.

"Mom said to tell you Mr. Page called."

Coach Page, from high school. The man who did for him what Dan's own father wouldn't. Or couldn't. The man to whom he owes everything.

Everything but this, he hopes.

"Coach? What'd he want?"

"He's renting a house near here. Says we can stay there if we want. Do the whole 'leave under the cover of darkness' thing. Have some privacy. If we want. He said he's poking around with some of his old buddies. Might be able to find a job for you. Not right away maybe, but down the road. Maybe a private or a charter school."

"He said all that?"

"That's what Mom says."

"But she sent you to tell me."

"Yeah."

Dan knows then that his marriage is on a timer. Maybe, if

there's a miracle, they'll be able to get help in time. But he's not believing in miracles at the moment.

"Okay. Thanks, Peach."

"Dad?"

"Mmm."

"I was dating Donte. Or, I was going to date him, I mean. We were going to ask you after the season ended if it was okay."

Donte. Donte Walker. One of the five. An entire career, an entire life ahead of him. Gone now because of—because—

He can't reply to Amy.

"I just wanted you to know," Amy says, and her eyes well. "Because he was a good guy. I really liked him."

"Me, too," Coach says, barely.

"Also? Um—I've been thinking. And . . . it's not our fault. It's not. Me, or you, or Mom. . . it's *not*."

Coach covers his face. Amy presses ahead.

"It's *not*. Nobody forced him to do it. You kept the safe locked—"

"He still got in."

"—and you had him on meds—"

"That he'd stopped taking without anyone realizing."

"—and did everything you could. We did not make him do this. It's on him, it's all entirely on him, Daddy."

Coach nods, just to get her to stop.

"I'm glad you can be there," he says. "I really am. I hope you can stay there. But I'm not yet. I'm just not. Please let me be where I need to be for now."

He can hear Amy hesitating, sense her wanting to say something else. Then she moves away down the hall, her bare feet scraping on the carpet. The door to her room closes.

They blame her, Coach thinks. Her friends, her teammates. Now that the story's out, they're somehow exonerated and it's just me and Mon and Amy, the guilty family, the ones who not only raised a killer but made no effort to stop him.

Coach looks up, as if to make sure Amy's gone before rising unsteadily and walking out of Danny's bedroom. He closes the door gently, but stops, with one hand resting against the wood. He's getting another headache. He's had headaches since last Friday morning, and he wonders if they will ever really go away.

*Maybe they shouldn't*, he thinks. *Maybe that's the very least punishment I can receive.* Their lawyer doesn't think there will be charges pressed, but he's warned them about lawsuits. They're coming, that's for sure. They are coming. The house, savings, stocks, college funds. All gone.

For what.

Coach whispers something against the closed door, eyes squeezed tight against a pain that is far deeper and more piercing than the ache in his forehead. He whispers it again, then goes down the hall to his bedroom where he lies down on the bed, one arm resting across his eyes.

He falls asleep with *Hamlet* clutched unknowingly in his hand. The rest is silence.

# BRADY

They ask so many questions. Can't possibly answer them all. Tell them what I can. But it's not much. Not fair either. The cops get to ask everything. I don't get to ask anything.

*Did you know him?* Sure I knew him.

*Were you friends?* Hell no.

*Did he show violent tendencies?* No. Where's my mom?

*We're trying to track her down. Did you . . .*

On and on. They didn't let me go home till after it was already dark. I watched TV alone at the apartment and the news wouldn't say who died.

Not till this morning. By then I already knew.

Donte's dead. Shot. Everyone's making him out to be a hero. That's cool. Looks like he was trying to help some theater kid. Head of the drama club or something. Dead, too.

Everyone wants to talk to me and Brianna. Everyone wants to know about this short chick in the library. I tell 'em the truth. Don't know who she is. Some people think me and Brianna are heroes.

'Cause we didn't get shot?

Can't feel anything. Nothing. Figure I better go to Donte's place. See Ramon, if he's there. See his mom. Talk to her. Sit with her. I dunno.

But I wait for Mom a bit longer. A while. Then wait some more. Don't really eat.

Friday night rolls around. A week later. I know we're not

having a game because we haven't been back to school yet. How can I get out of here unless I play football?

How can I play football without a coach?

Without D?

The hell'm I gonna do?

I never shoulda took that picture of the fat kid. Thought it might be funny is all. But it's not. Not now. I didn't pull any triggers. But it feels like I did.

The world don't know about that yet. Just cops. But sooner or later the world's gonna find out it was me that did it. Won't be a hero then.

Before the sun goes down Friday, I pack up my football gear bag with all my clothes and walk to D's. His mom's home. But not Ramon. Maybe with his dad.

She lets me in. We both cry a lot. I don't care. I'm a puss. That's fine. But me and D's mom, maybe we'll figure something out. My best friend's mom is all I got.

D's mom tells me I'm alive for a reason. Hope she's right.

D, man . . . I fuckin' miss you.

# VIVI

"You're thinking about something," Sam says as we climb out of my car. I've parked down the street from the corner of Fifty-Third and Third. I recognize one or two cars from school parked nearby. One of them is Kelly's green truck, and I'm glad to see it here. We've been texting a lot. Trying to make sense of things that can't ever make sense.

School. We start back Monday. Some kind of rally first hour. I can't help but wonder how *that* will go. I wonder who all will be there, who can get themselves to show up.

"Yeah," I say. "I was thinking that I moved here from this supposedly dangerous part of town to this supposedly rich part of town, and that's where I get shot at."

Sam takes my hand. "We didn't get shot at. Other people did."

"You know what I mean."

"I do. I'm just challenging you to be specific."

"Quit it!"

"No."

He stops me, kisses me briefly, and we keep going. It's as intimate as we've been since a week ago.

We walk down Third Avenue, which is a small little street that's mostly just parking for the line of businesses on either side of it. Bars, touristy gift shops, things like that. I stop short when we come within view of the corner. There's already a handful of people there, and I watch them hanging out for a second. Some people are sitting, some are standing. Some are hugging. A few might be crying. I stand on the sidewalk, watching them. Zach Pearson is there, sitting near a heavier guy beneath a tree at the top of the hill. The heavier guy has a cigarette clamped between his lips, his eyes narrow as if the smoke is getting in them. It looks like he's shuffling cards.

Were any of them in the library that morning? How close did the people here come to being victims?

As close as Brianna Montaro? Brianna, now hailed as a brave survivor, a hero.

"Why did Zach text you, do you think?" I ask Sam as I watch the corner kids from the safety of the shadows cast by a white streetlamp.

"Not sure. It was just something that was happening. Hey, look at that—we're where it's happening now. *We're* the popular kids."

"At long last. Be still my heart."

Sam twists me around, scrutinizing my face. "How are you? Really."

"Good. Fine. I think. Honestly, a little nervous about Monday. Why?"

"You seem different."

"We're all different now."

"No, I know, but this is—" He laughs a little. "Different."

I half step back from him, to better return his scrutiny. "What do you mean? Now I'm worried."

"Don't be." Sam pulls me close again, and we keep walking,

his arm over my shoulder and me hanging on to that hand with my own. "You actually seem more confident. Since everything happened. Or—well, maybe since before then, and I just didn't pick up on it."

"Maybe I am," I say, not sure at all if it's true. My instinct is *No way, uh-uh.* I'm just Vivi from the Dez, still wondering what my old friends are up to tonight.

Except, I also feel like Sam might be right. I feel better than I have in months. Definitely not because of what Danny Jennings did; I didn't sleep for three straight days after it happened. But since then . . . yeah. Maybe it's just that even though I never saw him that day, never had a gun pointed at me or anything, I made it out. I'm alive. I've got Sam, and my dad, and other than my school making national headlines, things are going pretty well.

"Maybe," I say again.

"Well, I like it." Sam kisses me above my ear just as we reach the sidewalk surrounding the grassy area.

There are not even ten people there; just Zach, sitting under a tree with the other guy, then a few others I've seen in classes or in the halls. I don't know any of them except Kelly.

"How's it going?" Sam says to everyone.

They all respond somehow—a nod, a wave, a "Hey."

Together, Sam and I walk onto the grass and sit between Kelly and Zach. The four of us trade subdued hellos.

The smoking kid smiles at me. "You are from school?" he asks Sam and me.

We nod.

"Would either of you care for a cigarette?"

I can't help grinning a little at his formal tone. "No. But thanks."

"What is your name?" the heavy kid asks.

"Vivi. This is Sam. You?"

"I am . . . the Art Man," he says with a wry grin. At least that's what I think he says. It comes out kind of muddled with the cigarette in his mouth, like one word: *Artmin*.

"Nice to meet you," I say.

"You, too."

"You look familiar," I tell him.

He seems to force a smile. Zach shifts around like he's uncomfortable all of a sudden, and Kelly looks away. The Art Man—Artmin—says, "You may have encountered me online in my altogether earlier in the year."

I'm not following, but Sam grimaces. "Oh," he says. "Yeah. Sorry."

Once he says it, I realize: this is the guy who had his picture taken in the locker room at the beginning of the year, and it went all over school online. I never saw it. There had been a rumor that Danny Jennings took it, but now people are saying that wasn't true.

Either way, it was a terrible thing to have happen to him. It reminds me of being stuck in the bathroom with Brianna and the other girls.

"Sorry," I say, too. "I—well, I don't know exactly what it's like, but I still get it."

Artmin nods. "It built, shall we say, character. Want to play cards?"

"I don't know how," I say, glancing at Sam, who shrugs.

"I will teach you," Artmin says. "How about poker? Spite and Malice? Blackjack?"

"Whatever," I say. "You'll have to teach us."

"Very well. We will start with blackjack." He's taking his time with his words, like he wants to make sure he doesn't say anything to upset us. Or maybe himself. "It is pretty easy to pick up. I will be the house. The goal is to get to twenty-one."

I pick up the two cards he deals me. "You can say that again."

# CADENCE

I got out of the hospital Sunday. My first order of business: was be home! Just be home, with Mom and Dad and Johnny, for five full days. Bask in the scents and the aura of everything Ours, everything Mine. I go to my room, bathroom, kitchen, living room, that's it.

But by Friday, a week after it all happened, I'm ready to roll. I need to get out, go someplace, do something. But I don't know what.

Or with who.

One of my best friends killed people. *Killed* them. What am I supposed to *do* with that? Nobody seems to know. So I figure, maybe I should go looking, ask around, see if anyone's got answers.

Dad doesn't want me to leave. Like, ever. I get the feeling Johnny's not super excited by the idea, either, but Mom comes to my rescue and tells them both to relax, I'll be fine. She slips me ten dollars and tells me to be careful, but her face says something like *Oh my God what am I doing letting my shot kid walk around this dangerous city?*

I promise her everything will be okay.

I've gotten dozens of text messages and voice mails from Faith and Liza and Gloria, who had her baby finally, and even Colin. I talked to them a couple times while I recovered, but it's like . . . I don't know, it's like we don't have anything to talk about anymore. I don't like how that feels. Pete hasn't gotten in touch at all. I wonder if he's okay. I mean, he must be, I'd know by now if he wasn't. I hope.

It's early Friday night, and I wander my way to a trolley stop. When the trolley gets close to Jamaican Blue, I ring the bell and get off.

I walk past the Blue, looking in the windows. It hasn't changed, it's still too dark to see inside. No telling who's in there. I know who isn't, and maybe that's enough to know.

He's gone. He's really gone and I guess there really are some things that can't be cured with a sunny disposition—

Stop it.

I'll start seeing a doctor on Monday. Like a therapist person, Dr. Frances. I guess insurance covers it or something. It's fine by me, maybe I do have some things to talk about. Dad wanted to sue the school and the district and the state and Danny's parents and I think maybe God Himself. Mom talked him down and said there's already people giving bunches of money to different charities and stuff, and Johnny says I can probably go to any college in the known universe for free.

I told Johnny that was cool, but I'd just like to survive what's left of my freshman year of high school first. He didn't think that was as funny as I meant it to be. And neither did I.

I mean, I feel *fine*. I was holding a gun, that was stupid, totally my fault, of course the cops were going to take a shot and it got me in the shoulder. But I'm okay now. It hurt, they fixed it, I might have to put my professional tennis career on hold for a while, but that's it, that's all that happened, I'm *fine*.

While I'm standing there debating what to do next, I notice people hanging around on the corner of Fifty-Third and Third. One group is sitting under the tree on the top of the hill, so I walk over.

I start recognizing people from school. And I think they start recognizing me. I'm not sure I like it. But the guy under the tree waves to me, so I walk toward him. I've seen him around, but never met him.

Then I see who else he's sitting with. Kelly, for one. And someone else.

"Zach!"

He turns, and then leaps to his feet. We run toward each other, which feels way overdramatic and kind of like a movie or something, but the truth is I can't help myself. We crash into each other about halfway up the little hill, and Zach hugs me tight, and it hurts my shoulder like crazy but I'm still on some pretty good pain meds so I don't care much. I squeeze him back, one-armed, and there's one really super fast moment where it's, like, sexy? But that moment goes away equally super fast, and suddenly I'm just crying.

And crying.

. . . aaaand crying.

Maybe I don't feel *fine* after all.

Zach holds me and doesn't say anything. There's those regular cries, like at a good movie or when reading a great book, and then there's these snot-bubble cries, where it's like I can't even make a sound because of all the pressure. This is one of those types. It actually hurts, like my ribs are being twisted one at a time till they break.

Zach can't even rest his chin on my head, he's so much taller than me. After I don't know how long, he guides me to the tree at the top of the hill, where we sit down together. I ask him, "What's up, what's going on out here?"

"Just needed a place to hang, be outside."

"Did you call all these people, too?"

"Some. Sam over there. Some of them just sort of showed up. And this is Kelly, we just met tonight."

"We're friends," I say, turning to Kelly, happy to see someone other than—

"What are *you* doing here?"

Kelly's expression reminds me of a snake, like she's about to snap forward and bury her teeth in my face.

I don't understand. "I was just out and about," I say. "Needed to get out of the house—"

"He told you," Kelly says. "He told you he was going to do it."

Everything gets quiet. Everyone on the hill, people I've seen at school, all stop whatever they're doing and look up the hill at me sitting here.

"No," I say. "He didn't. He sent me a text and told me to stay home—"

"And you didn't say anything?" Kelly jumps to her feet, and I step back. "You didn't think maybe that was a clue, you naïve little dumbass?"

I bite down on my lip. I think maybe for the first time in my life, I don't have anything to say.

And I think that suits Kelly just fine. She towers over me, shoulders pulled back like she wants me to stand up and fight her. Zach holds up a hand and says, "Wait a minute," but it's not enough.

"Do you get what he did? *Do* you, Cadence? Look at this."

She yanks a cell phone out and shows me the screen. It's a selfie of her and another girl. I know her from school. We met at the audition, just that once.

"This is Dre. Andrea. She was someone I cared about, *and that motherfucker stole her from me.* Do you get that? She had stuff she was working on, hard stuff, but she was working on it. She had issues but she was handling them, she was making progress, and he fucking stole it all!"

"Slow down," Zach says.

I reach over, not looking, and grab his hand, trying to signal him not to get involved. If Kelly needs to say it, she can say it. If she needs to hit me, she can hit me. Maybe hitting me is the least she can do to feel better.

"I hear Danny had issues, too, fine, I get it. Maybe his mommy and daddy didn't love him, whatever. Lots of mommies and daddies don't. *So the fuck what?* He didn't need to kill people over it! How was that going to change anything, huh? Dre's parents . . . Dre's mom and dad, they were so stupid when it came to her, you have no idea, but now she'll never have the chance to fix it with them, they'll never know what could have happened, because he stole that from them, he stole their chance to make it right someday."

Kelly leans down, putting her furious face right into mine. "Danny Jennings should rot in hell."

Then she pulls back, breathing hard, her lips stretched back off her teeth.

Everyone watches, everyone waits. Without thinking, I stand up, keeping my free hand straight at my side. I look right at Kelly, and say the only thing that I can:

"I know."

Because I do. I do. Danny was a murderer. Whatever else he might've been or could've been someday if he hadn't done this, the bottom line was he did this. He did do it.

"But I didn't know." I scan the entire crowd, feeling like I'm on stand in a courtroom. "I promise. I'm only gonna say it this one time. I didn't know. And I'm sorry I didn't. I would have told someone if I had. I hope you can believe me."

Everything stays quiet. Cars go by. People on the sidewalk pass, giving us curious looks, but not saying anything. Someone blares their horn down the street.

"I believe you," the kid playing cards says from behind me.

I turn. He's got this sort of easy smile on his face, a cigarette still between his lips. He gives a little shrug.

"I hope you will stick around," he says. "Cards are much more fun with a group. And I have . . ."

He glances around with the same smile.

"I have never had this many friends," he says, and looks down.

Vivi gets up from where she was lounging on the grass with Sam. She walks to me and Kelly, standing to one side between us, forming a little triangle.

"Kelly? It's not her fault."

"The rest of the world thinks it is," Kelly says, glaring.

"That's why we can't," Vivi says.

Kelly keeps glaring at me for a minute, then relaxes just a bit.

"Yeah, okay," she says. "I guess that makes sense." She shuts her eyes and shakes her head. "I gotta take a walk."

"Can I come with you?" Vivi asks.

"Sure, yeah. Okay."

The two girls wander off the hill together. I watch them go, and just before they disappear down Third Avenue, I see Kelly cover her face with both hands and Vivi rubbing her back.

I take a breath. My heart's going a million miles an hour. "I should go."

"Don't," Zach says. "Just give it a while. We'll work it out."

He gestures toward the guy sitting beneath the tree. Zach says, "This is—"

"Art Man," the guy fills in, smiling.

"Hi," I say.

A cigarette lighter flares in front of his face. He inhales deeply from a new cigarette, his expression friendly and relaxed. He's got a black Sharpie in one hand. On the grass in front of him is a deck of cards.

"Tattoo?" he asks, brandishing the marker.

"I dunno," I say. "Of what?"

"Whatever you like."

"Um . . . something Ramones? I could use some Joey right now."

"Roll up your sleeve."

I pull one sleeve up past my elbow, hoping he's not too grossed out by the fact that I've been wiping my nose on it. I sit near him, and he takes my arm, lays it in his lap, and begins drawing. It kind of tickles. The tip of the marker is strangely cold. Musical notes and a caricature of Joey Ramone start to take shape on the skin of my forearm. This guy is *good*. He's got something similar on his left arm, which he probably drew himself.

Zach lays a hand on my back, rubs it quickly, then retreats like he's not sure he should have done it.

"I should've come to see you," he says. "I'm sorry I didn't. I just didn't know . . . I mean, I had no idea what to say or do, and I didn't have your number . . ."

"It's okay."

Zach's eyes don't leave mine. "Are you coming back to school?"

"That's the plan."

"A lot of people think you're a hero."

"And a lot of people don't." I've seen stuff online and on TV, even though I didn't mean to. Me, that girl Brianna, and the football player Brady were all being talked about, like we somehow came up with a plan to stop Danny before it got any worse.

I'm not sure the truth matters to anyone, at least not yet. Maybe someday it will. We'll probably be in books and stuff. Another tragedy for everyone to talk about and forget until the next one. That's what Dad said to Mom, when he didn't think I could hear him crying.

"Don't worry about them," Zach says. "I got your back."

"Thank you."

"You should hang out for a while," Zach says. "I think there're more people coming. A lot of us ended up here last week, after we got off campus, trying to meet up with family and stuff. I don't know if it's just tonight, or if maybe we'll keep coming here. But it's someplace to be, anyway."

"On Fifty-Third and Third," I say. "Cool. I like it."

Kelly and Vivi come back just as Art Man finishes his tattoo on my arm. It looks amazing. I can't wait to show Johnny.

Vivi touches my shoulder, briefly, as she walks back over to Sam, who's lying on his back in the grass like he's studying the stars. When she sits beside him, I notice they have some parts of their bodies touching each other at all times.

Kelly sits nearby, forming a sort of circle with me, Zach, and Art Man. She shows me her phone again, but not angry this time.

"That's Dre," she says. "I really miss her."

"Yeah?"

"Yeah. She was stitching herself back together." Kelly clenches her jaw for a second then looks me in the eye. "But I think you would have liked her."

I study the photo and say, "I'm sure I would have. Thanks for showing me."

Kelly nods once, like she's satisfied with something, and puts the phone away. Next thing I know, the Art Man is giving us instructions on how to play a game called Hearts.

We've been playing for about an hour when, out of nowhere, I see a guy wearing a kilt come walking down Fifty-Third Street. I almost scream because it's Danny, it's Danny and he's back—

But it's not. Of course it's not. It's Pete. And when he sees me, he stops. I stand up.

"Be right back," I tell Zach. "Don't go anywhere."

"I'm here all night," Zach says.

Good to know. I head over to Pete through the grass. He watches me coming toward him with a kind of nervous look. But he doesn't move, and when I put my arm around him, he hugs me right back.

"Hey," I say to him.

"Hey."

I feel the tension leaving his body. I step back. "You look different."

"I do?" Pete stares into the distance, like he's considering the idea. "Yeah, I probably do. I *feel* different."

He works his mouth like he's going to spit on the sidewalk, but then doesn't. "You know, my mom was seventeen when she had me. So she's thirty-four now." He takes a big breath. "I feel a *lot* older than that."

"You smell nice."

Pete snorts a laugh. "Uh, thanks?"

"Well, it's better than smelling terrible. You used to stink a bit."

"Shut up . . . are you serious?"

"Yeah. All the smoke."

"Oh, that kind of stink. Yeah. Well, hate to burst your bubble, kiddo, but." He shakes a cigarette out of a pack and lights it. After blowing out his first drag, Pete says, "But you know what?"

"What."

"I haven't gotten high."

"How come? I mean, I'm glad. It explains why your eyes are open. Wow, your *eyes* are open!"

"Yeah. I don't know. I guess I didn't want to miss anything else." He blows out more smoke. "Been having nice long chats with the cops, too. That might've helped. How about you, they bugging you a lot?"

"Yep. They're nice, though. Are they nice to you?"

"It's not the word I'd choose, but it's all right. I don't think they're going to pin anything on me. Which is convenient since I didn't do anything." Pete takes another drag, then says, "I'm really fuckin' glad you're okay."

"Thanks, man. Me, too."

"Who're all those people on the corner?"

"Um—friends. I think. You want to meet them?"

"I'm not getting a lot of good press these days, dude."

I reach up and put a hand on Pete's shoulder. "Did you get him any of the guns?"

"What? No!"

"Ammo?"

"No."

"Did you help plan the whole thing?"

"I had zero idea he was going to do it."

"Then don't worry about it. Come on, come over here."

Pete shoves his hands into his leather jacket's pockets and starts walking toward the corner. I fall into step beside him.

As we go Pete asks, "So . . . *you* didn't know, either, right?"

"No. I don't think anyone did. Just Danny. He sent me a text the night before, but—"

"Yeah, I heard about that on the news. But it was just like, 'Don't go to school,' and that's it?"

"Yep."

"Well, look at it this way. At least you got something. I never did. Maybe I'm not even supposed to be here anymore. Maybe I was on his list. There's a thought that'll keep a person up at night. Not that it has, or anything."

I reach over and squeeze his arm, because there isn't anything I can say to that.

Pete smokes some more. "Did you know any of the kids who . . . ? Besides him, I mean."

"No."

"I hear you're gonna be on TV and stuff. Be all famous."

"Nah. No way."

"Why not?"

"I don't *want* to be famous. And definitely not for this."

"Cool. So what's up with the corner?"

"I'm not sure. My friend Zach said he called a couple people, then a couple more just showed up, and now it's, like, a thing I guess. There's a guy here called Art Man, he's doing marker tattoos, see mine?"

"Whoa. Nice."

"I bet he'll give you one if you ask."

"Sure, why not."

"And you should meet Kelly. If she's in the mood. Oh, and Vivi and Sam. And Zach."

We get to the hill, and I introduce Pete around. Some of the people are a little suspicious, I can tell, but no one says anything rude, which is nice. Pete ends up sitting with me, Kelly, Art Man, and Zach. Art Man deals out hands of poker, which we play for hours while we talk.

We don't talk anymore about what happened, though. We talk about movies and music and books and get into little pretend fights about all of them. I wonder, as I lose like my fiftieth hand of poker—Kelly seems to win all of them—how come I didn't know all these people before. Why it took something so awful to get us all in one place and talking. I don't know. Maybe I wasn't paying enough attention.

But I can't *think* like that, not now, anyway. Too many

maybes will start taking over and I won't be able to *think*. I have a hard enough time with that as it is.

We stay late into the night, and when Zach offers me a ride home, I take him up on it. Before we go, everyone agrees to come back next Friday night and hang out again. That'll be cool. And I got lunch dates with Zach, Kelly, Vivi and Sam, *and* Pete for next week.

And Danny . . . I don't know where Danny is now. I don't know if God is out there and if he really is all about love and stuff, because what Danny did—I don't know how anyone can forgive that. But then, they didn't know him. I don't think *any-one* did. I hope God does, if He's there. I guess I'll have to leave it up to Him. Or Her.

In any case, I think I've got a whole bunch of new friends. And we hung out together on Fifty-Third and Third, so that's sort of cool. I'm *here*, and my family's *here*, and someday soon I'm going to see if Zach will take me out on a real live date with kissing and everything, and Pete's backed off his drug stuff, and . . .

And I'm still a wee little freshman with a long ways to go.

If you ever suspect a threat at your school, call SPEAK UP at (866) SPEAK-UP (866-773-2587). Speak Up is a national toll-free hotline for reporting potential violence at schools. It features English- and Spanish-speaking operators.

SPEAKUP.com